U Girl

ALSO BY MEREDITH QUARTERMAIN

*I, Bartleby**

Matter

Nightmarker

Recipes from the Red Planet

Rupert's Land

Vancouver Walking

* Available from Talonbooks

U Girl

a novel

MEREDITH QUARTERMAIN

talonbooks

Talonbooks
278 East First Avenue, Vancouver, British Columbia, Canada V5T 1A6
www.talonbooks.com

First printing and electronic edition: 2016

Typeset in Albertan
Printed and bound in Canada on 100% post-consumer recycled paper

On the cover: Susan Bee, *Go Forth* (2001), oil on linen
Cover and interior design by Typesmith

Talonbooks acknowledges the financial support of the Canada Council for the Arts, the Government of Canada through the Canada Book Fund, and the Province of British Columbia through the British Columbia Arts Council and the Book Publishing Tax Credit.

LIBRARY AND ARCHIVES CANADA CATALOGUING IN PUBLICATION

Quartermain, Meredith, 1950–, author
    U girl : a novel / Meredith Quartermain.

Issued in print and electronic formats.
ISBN 978-1-77201-040-4 (PAPERBACK). — ISBN 978-1-77201-041-1 (EPUB).
— ISBN 978-1-77201-042-8 (KINDLE). — ISBN 978-1-77201-043-5 (PDF)

I. Title.
PS8583.U335U4 2016   C813'.6   C2016-902342-7
                                              C2016-902343-5

U Girl

Of course Frances Nelson isn't my real name, and we weren't from Cultus Lake, not the one on the map, but we were from *a* cultus lake, somewhere, nowhere. And of course Joe wasn't the name of my boyfriend, but there were always boys who wanted to be boyfriends.

I liked Joe. He was gentle and sexy in bed, unlike fumbling Jim or fat Eddie, or guys I met at the beach or rock concerts. I liked his dark furry arms and shoulders, his kisses and cuddles. I liked hiking together, on trails no one else knew, up Vedder Mountain or Mount Cheam, pitching our tent, cooking our hot dogs, watching the sunset, then next day tracking mountain sheep, watching the rams butting and rutting. I liked fishing with him for chub and trout on Cultus Lake. I liked that we could escape Cultus Lake together for the city and the university, he to get his Bachelor's in Education, me to get a Bachelor of Arts. I liked that he wasn't a drifter like Dad who slept on a foamy in a warehouse. Instead, like Mom, Joe would settle into a steady teaching job. I liked that we were equals in that buddy kind of way that Mom never had, even though she was more than equal.

By going in together we could afford a place with a proper bedroom and a bed, a proper bathroom, stove, refrigerator, and sink, and even a couch and dining table. Not one of those basement places with a toilet and shower curtained off from the furnace, the kitchen a hotplate on a TV table, the beds mattresses on the floor. Joe and I each paid half the rent, half the food. I made meatloaf, tuna casseroles, macaroni and cheese. He made instant coffee, fried eggs, and peanut-butter sandwiches as footsteps clumped overhead, and we peered out our one window at people's ankles going past on the sidewalk.

Joe didn't study much, but he liked being on the hockey team. His phys. ed. teacher was his favourite prof. I laid out my books every night on the rickety Formica table; he listened to Neil Diamond on the headphones or fiddled with the rabbit ears on our landlord's cast-off TV till he got the hockey game. He got Cs and even failed a course at Christmas, but he was going to make that up in summer school. I showed him one of my poems. He said he wished he could write like that. You can, I said. What do you want to write about? He didn't know. He didn't have any favourite writers like I did.

— What about that story of your homesteader grandfather and that man he supposedly murdered?

— You write it, he said.

It was coming up for midterms in the spring. He went back to Cultus Lake on a fishing trip. I stayed in the city and trundled the laundry over to the coin-op. Waiting for the machines, I read an old *Georgia Straight* article called "Why Women Go Gay" by a straight woman who turned her back on male supremacy and decided to like women no matter how hard it was. Then she fell in love with one and never went back to men. I thought of a picture I'd seen in Dad's copy of *The Joy of Sex* – a woman pulling down another woman's underpants, their naked erect nipples, one kissing the other on the cheek. "Women exciting each other are a turn-on for males," the caption read. So I guess a man was supposed to be watching them prepare themselves for him.

Loving a woman, the *Georgia Straight* woman said, was a lot less scary than sex with a man. Well Joe certainly wasn't scary in bed; it was just too bad he wasn't really interested in *Waiting for Godot* or Plato's parable of the cave, so we could talk about what we were learning at UBC. I folded our jeans and underwear, thinking if I loved Joe, I'd just stick with him. But *did* I love him? Did I really want to live with him for the rest of my life? Probably back in Cultus Lake?

Dagmar, my friend from English class, took me to the Japanese gardens at UBC to see the cherry blossoms. Where I come from, I said, a garden is where you grow tomatoes and beans. Then kicked myself for sounding like my father making fun of anything he thought middle class. Dagmar was going on a trip to Japan with her boyfriend, and she explained how Japanese gardens place every rock and tree according to Buddhist principles. Water and stone are yin and yang; high rocks represent heaven; low flat rocks represent earth; middle-sized are humanity. I like islands, I said, wandering across a bridge to the back of the garden's turtle-shaped islet. *No man is an island*, but I still like them; you find buried treasure on them.

From the island we watched a bride in long white tulle standing with her groom on a little bridge, then agreed that marriage was not for us, and even if we did get married it wouldn't be in that *getup* as Dagmar called it. No, not for us, we said, not for a long time, not till we got our degrees, till we got somewhere on our own, though just where we didn't know. What about your boyfriend, I asked, will it be him someday? She didn't answer my question. She lit a cigarette and wondered where the carp were hiding. We wandered along the winding path past the tea house and the miniature moss-covered pagoda.

Dagmar told me all about Virginia Woolf and Vita Sackville-West, and how it didn't even matter that they were married to someone else; they dashed off on wild flings to Paris; they wrote passionate letters about writing and art and books; Vita dressed as a man; they made love in Vita's castle at Sissinghurst. The love of your life, Dagmar said, you had to find that nothing-else-matters passion – like Virginia and Vita, or Daisy Buchanan and Jay Gatsby.

What would it be like dressing up, I wondered, me in a suit and tie, my hair in one of those puffy boy's caps, or even cut short and slicked back, Dagmar in a fur cape and long gloves? I could wear a moustache and smoke cigarillos. Stroll her along the seawall, escort her into Ladies and Escorts, buy her a martini. What would it be like?

We sat on a sunny patch of grass looking across the lake to the turtle island swimming in mirrored water; she showed me her sociology paper, A+ blazing out from the front page, above the title, "Marx's View of Women and Children." How simple and straightforward she made it, her thesis

3

boldly stating the paper would discuss five ways Marx failed to consider women and children. It took her about a day to write it. I had struggled for weeks and finally called mine "Various Considerations on Marx's Theory of Exchange" for which I rightly got a B. What a fresh new thought hers seemed compared to my scattering of barely understood summaries.

I didn't think, though, that I'd ever care about Marxism as much as I cared about writing a novel. Dagmar pulled a notebook from her bag and handed it to me. She'd seen me writing in a little spiral-bound Hilroy, separate from our student notes. She thought I'd like to try something more "exotic." A properly bound book with hard covers of green suede. You're writing a book, she said. All you need to do is fill these pages.

A notebook! She'd given me a notebook! Could we too write passionate letters of poems and art, we too meet in hotels, brilliant, dashing, mysterious? Bound together like identical twins, bound together against the world, writing books, reading each other's work – the two of us unstoppable?

Her poems had already been published in a University of Victoria magazine. You should probably go into journalism, she said. A lot of the best novelists started out as journalists. Like Orwell, for instance. I was going to have to travel too, to Europe, I had to go somewhere besides Cultus Lake and Vancouver. Dagmar went on her own to Europe for months at a time. But then Dagmar's dad owned an art gallery in the ritzy South Granville area.

I had to admit I didn't love Joe in that mad-passion way. The great love of my life would love books a lot more than Joe did, and hockey a lot less. I had to admit I was never going to settle down and have kids with him, and wasn't that the next step once you shacked up? I should never have moved in with him, but if I left now where would I go? We barely afforded together this underground cave with its proper furniture ten miles from campus. Alone, I thought, I'd end up in a frat house on campus full of guys drinking and puking and screwing prostitutes. Or I'd end up on a foamy with the rats in Dad's studio down on Water Street.

Housekeeping Room. According to the paper that was all I could afford. It made me think of men I'd seen hanging out on Water Street near doors to dingy stairs, men holding bottles in paper bags, men in clothes that hadn't been washed for months, men picking up cigarette butts from the sidewalk, men spitting gobs of white phlegm, men who leered as you walked by keeping your eyes straight ahead, men who owned nothing but their welfare cheque, or didn't even have welfare cheques. I'd have to share a bathroom with men like that. My room would smell of sweat and piss, it'd be greasy, cramped, and full of cockroaches, it'd be dark as Dad's grungy toilet, with only a tiny dust-caked window.

But now I'd admitted that I didn't love Joe, I had to go, somehow. I didn't tell him. I wouldn't until I found some place to move my stuff. He came back from the fishing trip with a good catch, and we put some trout in the tiny fridge freezer for later. We carried on driving to campus in our separate cars so he could go to his late-night or early-morning hockey practices.

Driving through the forests of the University Endowment Lands, surrounded by the safe, restful feeling of thick trees reminded me of Mom's cottage at Cultus Lake. But then I thought sometimes on these trips how, in trees like this, you could never really see any distance, only out to the edges of the clearing, and how refreshing it was to look out over an ocean or a city up to a mountain. I thought about Mom and all Dad's girlfriends over the years, the "open marriage" they supposedly had, and I wished he'd get it over with if he was going to leave her, or that she'd kick him out for good. Why, if she was so keen about me studying women's rights at UBC, didn't she enforce some of her own? It wasn't like she went out with other men.

When we got married, she told me (he'd been married twice before), it was understood he needed a strong woman who would support his art. I made a commitment, she said. Tammy Wynette, "Stand by Your Man," crooned through my head, which was not the way Mom thought at all; she was too smart for that. She had a Bachelor of Science. She even talked to me scientifically about Masters and Johnson and how women achieve orgasm. The real orgasm, the full deal — not the vaginal one which was a complete myth. She made sure I was on the pill as soon as doctors could prescribe them in 1969. I was seventeen and getting jobs fruit-picking or cooking in firefighter camps, where I made full use of opportunities to climax. Joe had been better than some, worse than others, and there were always more, these days.

So I was going to leave Joe, but for a while I carried on making hamburger and onions on rice, listening to *As It Happens* on CBC. We dried the dishes, then I memorized Spanish verbs or helped him with Algebra or an essay on Kinesiology. Or he listened to Led Zeppelin or The Mothers of Invention on the headphones.

One night he wanted to know why I was looking at him funny. I said I was just working out an essay idea, but the truth was I was thinking about Nigel, my English prof, and what he'd said on the library tour, months before, at the start of the course. Once you know how this works, Nigel had said in his beautiful English accent, you have the keys to all knowledge. We were standing in Main Library with its granite arches, stone balustrades, and churchy pointed windows. Like Oxford, I thought, and if I opened the card-catalogue drawers, Nigel's England, whose empire stretched around the world, would flow into me and fill the hungry emptiness of my brain with histories of butterflies and skeletons, epics and mythologies, Bacon and Descartes, Napoleon and Nietzsche. Instead of rattling these foreign names in my empty head, I'd know them like old friends and weave beautiful thoughts with them in essays for Nigel.

I'd have the keys to Chaucer, Shakespeare, and Milton. The keys to castles, cathedrals, cloisters, and the quadrangles of Oxford and Cambridge. The keys to laboratories, experiments, discoveries, atoms, molecules, and enzymes. The keys to ideas, motives, schizophrenias, societies, wars, ESP. The keys to Greek, Latin, French, and the language of sepulchres and chasms, bright-haired maenads, lyres and clarions. The keys to all that was never seen and only vaguely heard of in Cultus Lake.

I'd slip through the carved oak doors of Main Library, losing myself in its hidden passages, dark narrow stairs, and confusing maps snaking arrows between blocks of shelves like clues in a treasure hunt or threads in an enormous maze – the maze of all knowledge. Here I'd find gold.

I'd meld together something completely new, completely original, and add its card to the hundreds of drawers in the high-vaulted catalogue room. I pulled their little brass handles and breathed in the scent of aged wooden boxes, the smell of secrets and wisdom.

But classes met in concrete blocks with grid works of identical windows, long hallways of identical doors, and rows of seats bolted to linoleum floors – the very opposite of the library's quirky nooks and crannies. I dreaded entering the massive rectilinear block of Commerce and Psychology, its vacant boxy entrance filled with wind-blown rubbish, its sterile functional stairways, its black-and-white exterior mashing itself into the sky, like teeth of an aggressive car salesman, or a giant barbecue grill. Too bad none of my classes were in the vine-covered stones of Chemistry with its oak desks and leaded windows.

– Yeah, I bet it's for English, Joe said, jolting me out of my daydream again.

I told him it was an essay on natural selection for biology. Survival of the fittest, he mumbled and gave *me* a funny look.

I found a room close to campus. In a house, that had once been grand, with wide veranda, elegant eaves, and carved trim, a house with attic nooks under a dormered roof. Now it was chopped into rental rooms surrounded by concrete parking slabs. Stucco hid its original clapboard and closed its front veranda with aluminum windows, pitted by weather. Aluminum railing ran around the top of the boxed-in veranda but behind it you could still see the wood sashes of the original bay windows, and above that, under the triangle of the roof you could see a fan of carved spindles.

Cracked concrete steps stuck out baldly off the stucco box. I knocked on the water-stained door, the hollow-core, key-in-the-knob kind with three tiny rectangles of glass. Gauze curtains fluttered behind the aluminum windows and the landlady let me straight onto a plastic carpet protector in a room tinted aqua. A brown couch and armchairs – like something you'd buy from a catalogue – looked never used, their arms covered by white lace squares and plastic protectors. A TV stood on an aluminum cart with wheels in carpet-protecting cups.

From her accent I guessed she was from eastern Europe – wiggly lines around green and yellow patches I imagined somewhere near Russia, somewhere near the Black Sea, the place where fairy tales came from, which was somewhere near the Mediterranean, and a long way from the west coast of North America. She dried her hands on her apron, her hair too dark for someone around fifty-five. Her hips and breasts stretched and tightened her flowered shift; I wondered how she could bend to scrub floors or put things in the oven.

She took me back down the concrete steps, round the side of the house, and I followed the tops of her knee-high stockings bobbing in and out from under her hem as we climbed the long wooden flight of outside steps to the second floor. We passed through a door of yellow bubbled glass to a dim hall, where I could just make out six dark panelled doors and a small fridge with a pull-down handle like a forties icebox.

She pushed open a door and waved me onto a sea of green linoleum flowers, my eyes dazed now by the light pouring in the bay window from which I could even see, past the chimneys of the houses across the street, the smoke-coloured bluffs of a mountain. The room was not greasy – a paint-chipped hotplate stood on a spotless cabinet in one corner. The room had a door to the balcony over the boxed-in veranda that was now the landlady's living room. The room was well furnished with a table on metal legs, two kitchen chairs, a single iron cot (the kind I remembered from summer camp), a bookcase, and a chest of drawers, and it was only $55 a month. It was also painted the kind of bright turquoise you see around swimming pools or ads for holidays in Hawaii. The banana-coloured cabinet and dresser, and the pink-and-mauve bookcase, danced across the turquoise like someone's crazy LSD trip.

Could I paint the room, I asked. Yes, but her husband would have to like the colour.

The landlady had painted her eyebrows where hair used to be, and coated her face with cream and powder that did not hide the crease lines stamped vertically above her nose. She stood in her bulging flowered housedress and blotched apron, hand on her hip. I wanted never to be someone like her.

She opened two doors in the hall, one to a toilet, the other to a bath-tub and sink, all rather grey and stained. I pulled down the lever on the battered fridge. Corroded metal racks held a carton of milk, some sliced cheese with curly edges, and a soggy tomato. Someone had scrunched a half-eaten ice cream carton between the thick slabs of ice coating the hanging freezer compartment.

— You rent, you take care of fridge, she said.

When I said I'd take the room, she looked me up and down, and I suddenly thought of the patched jeans and shirt I'd been wearing all week — I supposed I should have worn a skirt. I told her I was a stu-dent but I had a part-time job. She wanted to know if a file clerk made enough money and what kind of grades I got. In the living room on the brown couch in front of the china rose bouquet, she made me write a cheque to her husband.

— You pay beginning each month. You keep clean. No guests overnight. No noise ten p.m.

— You do good in school, she said as I went out. Good grades. I looked back when I was halfway down the street, and she was still watching me from the doorway.

I suppose I stood out to Nigel cuz I'd been out of high school a couple of years. I read the books, I spoke up in class — sometimes I'd be the only one speaking up. Then too, my clothes stood out. Other women wore crisp new bell-bottoms or smart wool skirts and matching sweaters. I wore homemade shirts, hand-me-down jeans, thrift-store cowboy boots, and a purple, red, yellow, and black poncho I'd patched together from strips of old coats. I didn't think it mattered what I wore or looked like, because the best people, the ones who mattered, like Nigel and Dagmar, would see the real me anyway, in the same way that a white person could see the real person beyond the skin colour of a black person. That's what Black Like Me had proved, I thought.

The day of my move Dagmar and I sat in Nigel's class, flipping through Waiting for Godot. Nigel leaned against the front desk, crossed his arms, and gazed at us through his round John Lennon glasses. It was March; April exams coming up. What's this all about, Nigel asked. Who're these characters? Why're they waiting on a road? People fiddled with pens, flipped pages back and forth, or hid behind curtains of hair.

I wanted to say something, Nigel was so cool, it'd be so cool to get to know him, to know books the way he did, so we could have a real conversation, but all I could think of was, we're all on the road like these characters with their weird names. Waiting. Stuck somewhere on a road. We don't know where the road goes, but we know we're on it, and it'll go somewhere. The road of being twenty and full of ideas and thoughts if only you met someone who was interested. The road of things you want to do, and you know you can do them, like I knew I could write a book, if only a door would open to the way to do it. The road of becoming that person that people would look at as *somebody* with a part to play in the real world of real jobs and real people who had money and even houses, people who did things that you read about in newspapers. We were on the road with be-ins and flower power, and one day it would take over and be the real power. Everyone, even the squares with their corporate greed, would turn to love and peace, dancing and singing. Blacks, whites, Chinese, Indians, men, women – all would be equal – no mean bosses; no gouging businessmen.

We would become *who you really are* like Alan Watts said. Who you really are already there. Somewhere on this road that would break over us in a surge of love.

I didn't say any of this, just looked at a page of Estragon and Vladimir – they were so hopeless, their road was never going to go anywhere, what could you say about them, there were a great many people like that on hopeless roads, which was why love and flower power were so important. Like for men I saw near the rundown warehouses on Water Street where Dad had the work space he crashed in, and for people like Dad himself whose road never seemed to arrive anywhere though he kept setting out to run a resort in Princeton, then to the Cultus Lake artists' community, and then to a painting studio in Vancouver. Mom was the one who held everything together with her steady teaching job. I wasn't going to be like Vladimir and Estragon. I wasn't going to go down a road like Dad's. I was going to go down a road that mattered.

I moved my boxes into the room, set up my turntable and speakers, trying not to think about the devastation at my old apartment – the way Joe's eyes widened then focused to hard black dots, the way he dropped his skates in the middle of the table, mouthing you what? – you're moving? – why didn't you say something – we could've talked. The way he just stood there watching me load stuff into my rusty Datsun and then threw himself face down on the bed.

I put my hand on his shoulder to say goodbye. We can still be friends, I said, though I didn't really want to be friends with my Cultus Lake past.

He whipped over and yanked me down on the bed – his face streaked with wet: you think you're too good for me, don't you? You think I'm just a little hick boy from out in the valley and you've got bigger fish to fry – like your English prof.

I pulled away but he clenched his vice-grip on my arms and held me down.

– Don't think I don't know. The way your face goes all shiny around him, and those books he gave you.

(Nigel had given me Northrop Frye's *Bush Garden* and Margaret Atwood's *Edible Woman*.)

– So if you *knew*, I said, being ruthlessly logical, why didn't *you* say something? Anyway, they were just promotion copies. He was going to throw them out.

– Yeah, bullshit. Bull Shit! (He straddled me, pinning my arms.) What's he got, a bigger dick than me?

– He's not my boyfriend.

– Yeah, till tomorrow.

Trying to topple him, I whacked my knees into his butt and twisted sideways. It was nothing to do with him; I was moving into a room by myself.

– He's about old enough to be your dad.

– No he's not; he only just started teaching a couple of years ago.

— Are you dumb, he's already grey.

— Lots of people go grey in their thirties.

Joe collapsed again, his face twisted.

— We were just starting, he choked out. You didn't even give us a chance.

I put my hand on his shoulder. He grabbed it and begged me to stay or at least say he could see me, we would just live in separate places, but he could come over. I went on mechanically telling him I'd left lots of food in the fridge, he'd be all right. He needed to find someone different, someone more interested in the same things as him.

— Please, at least can we study together? he said. I was sitting on the bed. He curled himself around me, wrapping his arms around my waist: I know I haven't studied that hard but ...

— You don't even like studying that much.

— I know, but I know I can learn from you ... It's just so different than high school.

— I think we need to be apart for a while and figure out who we are on our own.

— But you said we could be friends, so let's do that, let's study like friends.

In the end I promised he could phone if he had study questions. I said I'd let him know my number as soon as I got the phone hooked up. I wouldn't tell him where I was living.

— Why are you such a perfectionist? Why does everything have to be exactly like you want it? And not like at least half the way I want it?

I left him sitting on the bed staring at the floor.

In my turquoise room, I unloaded books into my pink-and-mauve shelves, and tried to lose myself in the sun-barred thunderclouds of my favourite Doors song "Riders on the Storm," but it was useless. I switched it all off and lay on the floor in piles of clothes, records, and books, staring up at the ceiling as night filled the room with shadows. Someone tapped on my door, and it turned out to be a man from the room kitty-corner across the hall. His name was Jack, he wore a cigarette pack under his T-shirt sleeve.

— Heard from the landlady you're a student.

— Yeah.

– Wondering if you could use some towels?

– Um.

– Cuz I got extras; my mom got them on sale. I got no use for them.

His slicked-back hair reminded me of high school bad boys with back-pocket combs, but I had only one threadbare towel, so I accepted, suddenly realizing I'd need to buy soap and shampoo and something to eat for dinner. I followed him across the hall to his tiny room at the back of the house, while he opened his dresser and retrieved the folded towels. His hard hat and tool belt hung off his one chair. His shoes and boots stood in a row under his cot. He'd mitered the corners of its sheets and blankets, and tucked them in along the sides. His one small window looked at brown clapboard six feet away on the next-door house. He gave me two towels and a bag of apples, and told me not to worry about it, his kid sister wanted to go to university too.

Probably in construction, I thought, probably catcalls every girl that goes past. I thanked him for the towels. Well at least he wasn't like some of the men I saw sleeping in doorways down on Water Street.

Painting my room was way too much work. Instead, I covered up the turquoise with whatever I could find. I hung my favourite of Dad's watercolours on the wall, a scene near Cultus Lake: firs, birches, and a log house mirrored in the water, near rolling fields, horses, a snake fence, and a garden. I wished he would just paint like this all the time instead of yakking with his friends about Trotsky, Marx, and Gramsci, or setting up free art events, or giving talks on dome building at the Stanley Park squat.

In a shop on Fourth Avenue, I found a poster of sailboats in the Bay of Fundy, and another one of Tiny Tim with his wavy curly hair falling like a bashful girl's over his hook nose and buck teeth. Then I found posters of modern artists I'd heard Dad mention – people like Jack Shadbolt, Jack Wise, and Toni Onley. Dagmar's dad had a Toni Onley show in his gallery, so I chose the poster of his *Polar No. 1* and tacked it to my wall. From the pillow of my cot, I drifted in its curious jumble of smudges and faded lines, its city of half-built tracks and circuitries, leaping from patch to patch of rose or blue, meandering through rims, lips, and frames to a small brown door hidden under a hobbit-house roof.

I gazed at Tiny Tim: where did he shift from male to female, female to male? Did he want to be that way or was it just my imagination? Then I lost myself in the sailing poster – the men leaning over the edge of the hull pulling against the taut vertical wings of the boats that sliced the wind, scooping and moulding its invisible muscle. How exciting it would be to grasp those wings thrusting a sleek hull through tossing water.

My first nights in the turquoise room I opened my door a crack to check and tried not to meet anyone in the hall on trips to the fridge or to the bathroom to wash dishes under the tub tap. I thought they'd be loggers out of work or women like the landlady without a family, stuck waitressing forever, some WWII veteran who'd lost an arm, now living in clouds of smoke and cheap wine, or some failed business type, always trying to sell you something, who'd lost everything investing in mines on the Vancouver Stock Exchange. Whoever they were they certainly weren't going to talk to me about Shakespeare or Plato or operant conditioning or Spanish verbs. They'd think that stuff a lot of hooey, wonder what I was doing here in their world, tell me I should be married and settling down. I could already tell from the fridge they didn't eat healthy food like I tried to. They'd probably think that weird too. I lay awake listening to clumping overhead, clicks and snaps of keys and door locks, muffled TV, The Beatles' mojo beat from across the hall.

One Friday night, I heard noises from Jack's room. Noises like Mom's fights with Dad. The word *bitch*, followed by sobbing. Then more anger and demanding questions that I couldn't make out. The way Dad would accuse Mom of twisting his words, and Mom would cry, Why're you so defensive? Round and round, low voices, high voices, pounding, sawing, wearing at each other. Now Jack's voice. *Get over here. Get over here, right now!* Followed by a thump. Then repeated slaps. Someone was getting hurt. I opened my door a crack, but just at that moment his door also opened and a woman in miniskirt and heels, her backcombed hair all askew, headed into the bathroom.

— Girlfriend's a bit upset, Jack said. She'll be all right, just had a fight with her mother.

— Okay, I said.

— Don't worry; I'm taking good care of her.

— Okay, I said, and closed the door. But the thumps and nattering voices went on well into the night, and made me think about readings we covered in women's studies that said 80 percent of violence against women came from men they knew, and how police thought domestic disputes were none of their business. What would happen if I phoned the police, what would Jack do next time I met him in the hall?

After Jack's room went quiet, I lay awake worrying about my coughing and spluttering Datsun that hummed to life only to hang back as though choking on something. The carburetor, one garage told me, saying they fixed it as best they could without getting a superexpensive part.

Monday morning my Datsun coughed and wouldn't start. Shit, I'd be late for university. I lifted the hood. Engine block, fan, radiator, distributor cap with its four black cables, battery, dipstick – what did I think I could do? The guy across the hall from me clunked down the outside steps, and I bent closer to my grime-covered car innards, twiddling a nut on a blue contraption I thought was the carburetor. I hoped he'd go on his way, leave me to figure it out. Women're equal, so just act equal, I thought.

— Car trouble, he said, leaning against the driver door and resting his elbow and mug of coffee on the roof.

— No, everything's fine, I said, slamming the hood shut.

— Sure didn't sound fine a minute ago.

— Had some problems, but they fixed it.

— Sounds like your carburetor's clogged up.

— No, that's fixed. Anyway I gotta go.

— Name's Dwight.

He continued leaning against my car door, showing a bunch of stained teeth and holding out a hand with grimy nails and tobacco-stained fingers. His face under its mop of frizzy mousy hair was the colour of

15

things found under stones, like someone who'd been locked away in a dungeon. I hesitated.

– They're clean – really.

He held them out, palms up, then turned them over. All washed. He put the hairy back of his hand to his nose.

– You can smell the soap. Here take a whiff.

– That's okay, I said, holding out my hand.

His felt toughened yet limp as though he wasn't used to shaking hands.

– What beautiful long fingers you have (he bent over my hand in the way of a connoisseur, examining it from all angles). I bet you play the piano.

What a line, I thought.

– Hey, I'm a certified auto mechanic, so let me take a look at it.

– Gotta run, I said, grabbing my bookbag and locking up.

– Okay, I'll catch ya later, he said. I'm across the hall. Drop by for a beer.

I left him sitting on the steps, smoking a roll-your-own and drinking his coffee in the morning sun.

In Nigel's class, we continued with *Waiting for Godot*. The play, with its hopeless, goofy characters, stood before us as stupidly as a stone and we looked at it as speechless as rocks. Each thing we read in Nigel's class began as a stone that hid things under its closed surface. Usually Dagmar was the first to crack the code. She'd spot something from the Bible or a Greek myth, and use fancy words like *modernist, Freudian,* and *surrealist,* but Dagmar was away today. Why would Beckett put a tree in his play, Nigel badgered, tossing a piece of chalk from one hand to the other. His hair fell in wavy layers to below his ears. He had the same inscrutable gaze as John Lennon, staring at you coolly from magazines. Have you run across a tree in any other literature, he nudged. We scraped away at the stone of our text, until by the end of the class we caught a glimpse of fantastical shapes, the facets of a marvellous crystal hovering above it. Here you crossed, I thought, from the language you spoke to friends to the language of books. Here you found the language I wanted to write.

I hitched a ride off campus, and a yellow VW bus pulled over that turned out to be Nigel. I hopped in, jolting back in the seat as he shifted gears. Rubber boots, rain slickers, ropes, chart cases, and small double pulleys I later learned were called blocks littered the van. I asked him where he was from in England and he told me a part of London called Hammersmith.

— Why did you come to faraway Vancouver?

He glanced at me, smiling through his John Lennon glasses, like he did in class when he wanted us to do the real work of thinking, and figure it out ourselves.

— Because I wanted to see the world.

He leaned on the horizontal wheel, swinging the van past sea-view mansions with stone walls and picture-book rhodos, and zoomed us down to Spanish Banks and the harbour, and I wondered why he wanted to come to the far edge of North America if he wanted to see the world. At the beach, the tide was out, leaving bare, puddled sand flats for half a mile into the bay, where black-and-red freighters seemed almost grounded on their anchors.

Nigel pulled in for a quick stop at the UBC Sailing Club, and we tromped along the sand-covered planks outside the white barn of the club to a table of sunburnt men with clipboards and a cash box. Sign Out Before You Leave, a sign said. Another mentioned sailing courses starting next week. Men in yellow slickers went out carrying sail bags and rope. A young woman in a denim miniskirt followed them, banging the door shut, and through the window I saw them roll a boat down to the water. The men at the table wrote Nigel's name on their clipboards, and by the time we left I'd joined the club, and signed up for a course.

Sorry I don't have a radio, Nigel said, as we pulled away. He wanted to know what kind of music I liked and was surprised when I mentioned Vivaldi and Beethoven. He thought I'd be more interested in The Beatles, and I admitted to liking them quite a lot. Then he wanted to know which Beethoven and which Vivaldi I liked.

— Um, Beethoven piano concertos, I guess (unable to think of any except the picture on the cover of Mom's album at home), and Vivaldi's Four Seasons.

— What about the Moonlight Sonata, do you like that one?

— I don't know if I've heard that.

— Oh you probably have, it's about the most popular of his piano sonatas, moody and romantic.

I said I'd look out for it, and he said he was rather fond of Sonata No. 27 in E Minor.

— What's that one like?

— Beethoven said it was about Count Moritz trying to decide whether to marry a ballet dancer.

Who was Count Moritz, I asked, and it was like walking into a talking library as he told me all about Count Moritz who was the younger brother of a Moravian prince and close friend of Beethoven's.

— Moravia's in Czechoslovakia now.

— Oh, I said, thinking vaguely of yellow and green and pink patches somewhere east of Germany, and then noticing the chiselled look of Nigel's face, its shadow of beard, unlike the soft-skinned men in my classes with cheeks barely past peach fuzz.

Outside my rooming house he turned off the engine, and we got onto books and how I was reading *Martha Quest* by Doris Lessing. He knew all about the Martha Quest series, the Children of Violence series, he called it. He wanted to know if I'd read *The Golden Notebook*? *Five* was his favourite of hers, the book she got the Somerset Maugham Award for. But had I read her latest, *Briefing for a Descent into Hell*? About a man who thinks he's on a raft in the middle of the Atlantic versus the doctors who are trying to normalize him. No, I said, but it sounded interesting. *The Golden Notebook*, he went on, wasn't really his cup of tea, but people said it was very smart, especially about women because it was the story of one woman broken into four parts, including the personality who writes the novel.

Then I asked him if he knew anything about how to write novels, because I really wanted to write one. And he said he'd think about it.

— What would your novel be about, he wanted to know.

— Sort of like *Martha Quest*, I said, about getting away from home, getting work, about being from outside the city where there's no movies or concerts or art galleries. I could feel myself turning red, so I rummaged among his rope and sailing gear for my bookbag.

Carla, the woman with the other front room next to mine, walked past, waved and scooted by in her leopard-skin overcoat, black platform sandals, and matching handbag. Nigel said he was sure he'd seen her somewhere, did I know where she worked? I pulled the door handle to go, but before I got out, he asked me to join him and a few others on a sailing trip to Passage Island in a couple of weeks — a friend of his had dropped out, gone away on a contract, and there was one space.

I stepped into my turquoise room, my notebook on the table, my shirt over a chair, my basket of fruit just as I'd left it. A room of one's own, Dagmar joked, pestering me to read *Three Guineas*. She read *The Waves*, then lent it to me. What a grand poem it was, she said. I lay on my cot thinking about how *The Waves* circled around through the voices of the characters speaking directly to the reader, how they didn't settle on any particular idea but kept moving and moving, like waves. I drifted in the oddball shapes of the Toni Onley poster, wondering if I could write a novel as fantastic and different as *The Waves*, and wishing I could write poems like Dagmar did about starfish and skyhooks, Humphrey Bogart and begonias, mescalito warriors and lizards, or the power of the river.

Could I write like Doris Lessing had about a young woman getting out in the world, going to psychology lectures on operant conditioning or philosophy classes on the cave parable, then working as a filing clerk, and coming home to Dwight across the hall with his mousy afro — leaving his door ajar, hunching over his table, building a model car or something, grinning as I went past; Jack in the other tiny room at the back, no hot-plate even; and Carla with her paisley bell-bottoms, mini shirtdresses, platform shoes, and huge jewellery?

What sort of names would I call them? I flipped through a list of names at the back of my dictionary, but decided I couldn't just call Jack and Dwight *Wilbur* or *Montgomery*, and Carla was definitely not *Edith* or *Hope*. Why did it change someone if you called them *Maxine*? And what would I call myself in this novel? What did real writers call themselves? I couldn't be a writer in the story anyway. I was a student, a woman. Not a woman like Mom wearing cameo brooches, tailored suits, stockings, garter belts, and pumps, and carrying a briefcase to school every day to teach high school girls how to sew dresses and bake cakes and test pastry recipes and make aprons, and then, after doing that all day, coming home and cooking a meatloaf and a pie for Dad and his sing-song buddies with their wine bottles and ashtrays and guitars all over the place. I wasn't that, and I wasn't a woman like Hedda Thorston, my sociology prof – jowly and stern as an army major, as though she'd stepped out of a Marxist commune and only ever worked for the party.

Who was I going to be? I couldn't just be my real self. I had to be a heroine like Martha Quest, and I couldn't be Martha Quest because she was already a character in somebody else's story. I had to be original – someone who got an interesting job writing stories for magazines – not a dull dull dull insurance-company filing clerk. Her entire day taking files from wheeled carts and fitting them into a rack of dividers as long as a bed: 860798 went between 860700 and 860800 and after 860725 – in a windowless back room, the only lightbulb hidden behind shelves of lined pads, letterhead, pencils, and erasers. 273334 went between 273100 and 273400. Then damn, I'd put 263334 in with the 27-whatevers. I hunched over the racks, my eyes glazing over in the hot dusty air, my body falling forward, drifting off. How long till coffee – oh gawd another half hour till I could sit on the saggy couch near the boiling coffee urn and the window to a wall of another office block, and maybe read *Martha Quest* if the other clerks didn't come in – lumbering Lorna with her glasses sliding down her nose and her sack-like clothes, and Kitty, the executive's daughter who was starting at the bottom and training to be an adjuster – whatever that was – what did they adjust anyway – I thought of Mom talking to Aunt Bee about my cousin not being well adjusted and whether he would be, after they put him in a special school for kids who couldn't read, but what did insurance adjusters adjust – if it said you got the money, didn't they have to give it to you? Or did they try to tell you you weren't covered – yes that probably was their job. That's what Kitty was going to be in her white dress with red frills and matching heels and handbag or her blue shift with white polka dots and matching blue gloves. Or her mix-and-match plaid maxi skirt with gold jacket, or the gold jacket with the gold skirt and black blouse and heels, chattering away about the parties she'd had over the weekend in her Beach Avenue apartment on the twelfth floor – she didn't rent that on $2 an hour – the hors d'oeuvres they'd served for her boyfriend's office cocktail party; martini glasses of Rooster Tails, olives on swizzle sticks. I'd never been to a cocktail party. I doubted whether Lorna had either, unless it was as a waitress.

Lorna lived above a store in the triangle between Broadway, Main, and Kingsway – traffic roaring by on three sides of her. She thought it must be wonderful going to classes and learning things, school was her favourite place to be. How do you do it, Frances, how do you, you know, get enough money *and* go to school; come to dinner, tell me. In her bachelor apartment I stumbled over boxes of her boyfriend's and his motorcycle buddies' empty beer cans. Rumpled sheets and blankets lay heaped on a foamy on the other side of the room. Lorna opened two cans of spaghetti and poured them into a pot, put the shaker of parmesan on the table. She switched on the radio to the Beach Boys. Steve, the boyfriend, came in with a fresh case of beer. We didn't talk about Lorna's dream. We said, pass the parmesan please, and thanks, and did he find anything today, and no, he wasn't really looking. She showed me her African violets. Oh please stay, have some beers with us, Steve's friends are coming over. She walked me down the stairs to the street. Who's paying for all the beer? I asked. I do, he doesn't have any work. You don't have to live with him, I said. Make him move out unless he gets a job! Oh no, I couldn't; we've been together since kindergarten. She took off her glasses, began polishing them with the hem of her skirt, dropped them, sat down on the steps.

I couldn't have friends like Lorna in my novel. Martha Quest's friends were more like Kitty. Burning candles at both ends, partying all night and going to work all day. But then why did Martha have to end up just getting married – to a man she doesn't even know?

To be a Martha Quest heroine too, I would need huge principles like saving blacks from apartheid. Where in a rooming house would I find that?

Something more than being against the Vietnam War and for workers' rights. Maybe I could save women — but people believed women were equal now, we weren't like the blacks in *Martha Quest*. Then why did Mom go on in her unequal world, letting Dad walk all over her? Letting him call her a *universippy lady* when her degree meant so much to her?

In my novel I wasn't going to be like Mom. I could form a women's commune. Carla and I could kick out Jack and Dwight and even the landlord and landlady and the attic people and take over the whole house just for women. Dagmar could be our resident poet. Lorna could get away from her boyfriend and go back to school. We'd walk down the street together and no one'd dare catcall because we'd be so cool they'd want to be like us. We'd really be equal, we wouldn't be the second sex, we wouldn't be the other — we'd be the one and all the others would be ones too. No more heels, skirts, and lipstick marking us as decorations, sex toys, and helpers instead of doctors, lawyers, or construction workers.

In my novel, I thought, I'd be a sensing device like people wave over beaches searching for metal, like a stethoscope searching for a heartbeat, or a radar searching for headlands, rocks, whales, other ships. But I couldn't call myself Radar because he was a *M.A.S.H.* character. Maybe Antenna, but who in the world has a name like that?

All evaporated with a tap on my door.

CHAPTER 2

– Hey, U Girl, c'mon over for a drink.

(Carla's throaty cigarette voice.)

An iron-frame double bed, an armchair, and a chest of drawers almost filled her room. Clothes bulged out of her closet and over the bed frame – mauve and pink patchwork prints, bold black and white stripes, cubist abstracts of turquoise and tangerine. A row of shoes and boots ran along every baseboard and under the bed.

– Like Southern Comfort?

She held up a bottle.

– Well it's all I got anyway. She poured a couple of glasses.

– Unless you have something.

– Naw, I said. I don't.

– Didn't think so.

She held out a pack of Rothman's filter tip. I hesitated. I'd quit a couple of years back, couldn't afford to smoke, didn't want Mom and Dad to know I smoked anyway. It was so bad for you. Gwan, have one, she said. I won't tell. I took it, held it awkwardly between two fingers while I tried to strike a match. She flicked her lighter, and I took a drag with the hot jolt of sticky sweet Southern Comfort. She wanted to know how much I made, filing.

– \$2 an hour! No tips – honey, you gotta get yourself a better job than that!

She told me she got \$2.50 an hour and with tips it worked out to \$4. She told me lots of students worked in bars, and she could probably get me a job.

I thought of the Cecil or the Yale, someplace Dad took me once, a barnish room like the UBC Armouries with its four hundred exam tables, only these tables were round and covered with beige terry cloth and the room was the opposite of quiet. Waiters, flipping coins and bills out of their change belts, whizzed back and forth to a distant door, carrying trays of sloshing beer-glasses or sudsy empties. Men in plaid shirts or hardhats bunched around tables, talking, smoking, tipping their chairs back or staring haggard-eyed into their glasses. Thirty men in red UBC Engineering jackets clustered around a double row, whooping and laughing. Their campus enemies the Aggies, who every other day painted the E on the Engineers' cairn into an A, sprawled around another double row in their grubby barn clothing. Nowhere did I see even a single woman. Dad's taken us through the wrong door, I thought, we should have gone in the Ladies and Escorts door.

No way, Carla said. *She* would never work in a beer hall. *She* was a cocktail waitress at the Biltmore and mainly served highballs. She had her bartender's licence too and when the regular one was off, she worked behind the bar. Now that's really good money! I bet you don't have any food, she said suddenly. Yeah, I have food, I said, thinking of my carefully saved jar of hamburger and mushrooms in the hall fridge.

— Yeah, I bet you eat at the Naam and shop at Lifestream, right?
— Nope, Safeway.

In the armchair, I swung my feet over one arm, shucked my shoes off. On the bed, she lounged back in her hot pink miniskirt, and tapped her Rothman's on an ashtray.

— Ah gwan, I bet you don't eat munchie food.
— Sure I do. (Swaggering with Southern Comfort on an empty stomach.)
— You look so healthy you probably only eat brown rice and alfalfa sprouts. No wonder that peaches and cream of yours is zit free.

She swung off the bed, rummaged in a cupboard, and brought out a huge bag of Cheezies.

— The only other thing I've got's Ritz Crackers.
— I've got peanut butter, I offered.
— Wait wait. I want to show you something.

She pulled out some boxes labelled Coolique and started laying out peace-sign pendants, yellow daisy rings, strings of beads, studded chokers and matching wristbands, earrings for every astrological sign. A little business I run on the side, she said. I get them in the mail and sell them to friends. No pressure, she laughed, running her long frosted nails through piles of bangles and metal ear ornaments. Fake by the way, she waved the nails at me, when she saw me staring at them. She bought trays of these accessories for $200 and if she sold every single item, she'd make $280. You had to buy a minimum of two trays. More than a month's file-clerk pay. And then buy a minimum of one tray every six months. I could try it, she thought (she got a bonus for getting a friend to do it).

– Uh, no thanks.

– Here, try this, she held up a twisted rope of black and gold baubles, That'd look great with your jet-black hair.

Jet – it made me think of Rhett Butler in *Gone with the Wind*. Carla slipped her hands under my hair, flooding me with honey-coconut perfume, and clasped the piece at the back of my neck. Actually I don't wear this stuff, I was going to say, but she'd already attached my Virgo sign, a woman's face swirling in tendrils of hair, to my ears and dragged me over to the dresser mirror.

– That's so you, isn't it?

Her face beamed beside mine in the glass.

– Actually it's not me, I said. I never wear this stuff.

– Honey, you can't just go around in jeans all the time.

– Why not?

– Cuz there's more to life than jeans.

I unclasped the choker and earrings and laid them back in their box. Her bright smile wilted, and I saw beneath the glaze of her face-cream the hint of hollows under her eyes. She was a bit older than me, in her thirties I guessed.

– You're not one of those, are you?

– One of what?

– One of those that gets it on with girls.

– You mean women.

— Women, girls, it's just a way of talkin. Or maybe guys sometimes, girls other times?

— I think women should be allowed to love each other if they want.

— So are you one?

— Anyone can be one, you could switch if you wanted to.

— And you switch, gwan, tell. I'll still be your friend.

— No, I don't switch. I'm not a lesbian.

— But you'd like to try it wouldn't you. That's what girls do these days.

— I might some day.

She blew out a long cloud of smoke, took another drag.

— Frankie, she said, squinting her thick lashes and studying me from across the room. I bet they call a tomboy like you Frankie.

— No.

I scoffed some Cheezies; we were on our second Southern Comfort by then.

— No one's called me that.

— But I think you really are one. You really. Are. A Frankie. I'm going to call you that.

— Okay, just don't call me Fran.

— Oh I'd never call you that.

— I mean *Fran* is like bran is like bland is like clam – grey and soft and clammy. Yuck.

But Carla liked *Fran* as a name. She thought it was light, airy, and homey. We got onto our favourite men's names.

— *Jethro*, I said.

— Yeah like the rock star.

She liked *Miles*, it made her think of being on a cruise in the open ocean; she'd never heard of Miles Davis though. I liked *Dudley* because it sounded English although it also reminded me of my grandmother's big black yellow-eyed, long-haired cat. She liked *Grant* because it sounded solid like granite.

Then we both thought we heard a noise that might be Dwight out in the hall, and we climbed through her window onto the balcony with the Southern Comfort, the Cheezies, the Ritz Crackers, and a blanket, because for sure he'd try to crash our party if he heard us. I went into my room through my balcony door, which was never locked, and got the peanut butter and a knife. She poured us more Southern Comfort.

– Dwight, what a wuss of a name, she said, calling him a creep and a lech and warning me to watch out, because she'd seen he had his eye on me.

– When? Where?

– He was coming down the hill across the street, I could see him from my window, and he stopped kinda behind that pine tree, and I thought what's he lookin at, and it was you in your purple-and-yellow poncho, and he waited by that tree till you'd got into your room, then he moseys along pretending to look at people's tulips till he comes up here.

– He said he was an auto mechanic.

– Drug dealer more like.

– What, like heroin?

– Probably. He's got a kid too, a little girl, don't know what he does with her in there, she's only five, his room's a wreck, paints and brushes and clothes and dirty dishes everywhere, no toys or anything. Her name's Janey, cute little thing.

– I don't mind grass, if that's all he's dealing.

– All I'm saying is watch out, U Girl, there's only one thing he wants.

Leaning against the wall below her bay window, we basked in the late afternoon sun and soaked up heat radiating from the tar of the balcony deck. A guy with shoulder-length red hair waved to us from across the street. We clinked glasses.

– So how's your John Lennon date, she wanted to know.

– Who?

– Guy with the yellow bus, don't pretend you don't know.

– You mean Nigel ... He's my prof.

– Same round goggles as Lennon, same wavy hair, same beak of a nose except it isn't crooked. John Lennon, the professor.

– Nigel Blackwood.

– So does he sing "Imagine" in class? Imagine all those people in books?

— No, of course not.

He said amazing things in class, I told her, like when a guy said *Waiting for Godot* was stupid cuz it didn't mean anything, and Nigel asked if he, the student, meant anything? And if so, what?

She liked the name Nigel Blackwood. It sounded like a distinguished family going back to lords and ladies. But for looks she preferred Paul Newman, now there's a man for you. But she guessed I went in for longer hair. She'd seen Nigel around the Biltmore.

— So is he datin ya or what?

— Just rides home, but we're going sailing in a couple of weeks.

— Well you're not the only one, she said. Just so you know.

She told me he always came into the Biltmore with a short plump redhead who wore weird clothes like pullover sweaters with old-fashioned gathered, waist-banded skirts.

— Well maybe he's changed his mind, maybe he's choosing me now.

— Maybe.

I closed my eyes, slid further down the blanket and soaked in the sun. Did she really think Nigel should just stay with this redhead even if he liked me more? What if I was his great love and he mine, he should still stay with her? People changed their minds. People had open marriages. Love was everything now. Love flowering in the blankets and bongo drums of the be-ins and happenings. Love melting squares and business types. Love building patchwork families in loving communes.

— I love your perfume, I said. It smells like honey and coconut.

She told me what it was, and we got onto scents we liked and didn't like — patchouli, orange spice, English heather, cedar, carnation, lavender, pine, juniper. I told her my favourite was balm of Gilead on the cottonwood trees in spring. Chanel No. 5 was her favourite. She crawled back into her room, brought out a tiny bottle, and dabbed some on my wrists. Chanel No. 5 — the name had its own amazing fragrance of silk, pearls, elbow-length gloves, stone chateaux, the cool gaze of a magazine model with pulled-back hair, a miniature Eiffel Tower on a squarish patch of Europe. Chanel No. 5, I'm wearing Chanel No. 5, I sang out, swirling fairy dust and tossing back more Southern Comfort. I felt myself strolling through Paris in a black trench coat with upturned collar.

Carla sprawled out on the blanket wondering if anyone could see us if she did some tanning; then so what if they did? After days of rain and cloud boxing the city in gloom, all of Vancouver was out to greet the sun. Eagles and gulls circled high in the infinite blue. You could see the snowy peaks again, the bright spinnakers and the brawny freighters in English Bay. You could smell the spices, feel the silks, and imagine strange customs in their destined ports. And you could lounge on balconies like Carla and me, downing Southern Comfort with peanut butter and Ritz Crackers, while CKLG on my transistor radio blasted out "American Pie," Neil Young searching for his "Heart of Gold," and the infinite hit parade of timeless sun.

My phone rang from its home on my floor. I yanked the door open, careened into the doorframe, and knocked the receiver flying, across a sea of linoleum flowers. Hello, I said, falling onto the cot, Eiffel Tower. Turquoise walls spun around me. Frances, is that you, a calm clipped voice asked on the other end. Who was it, I knew that voice. I closed my eyes and tried to focus through the cartwheels of turquoise patches dancing across my eyelids.

It was Nigel. Was I sure I was all right? I sounded three sheets to the wind.

– Three wha- ...?

– Never mind, I found a book by Edith Wharton you'll be interested in, I was going to show you.

– Show me a book – wow, far out – wow – like right now?

Silence on his end. Then, No, I'll catch you out at school.

He hung up and I lay there listening to the drone of the dial tone, then lurched up and tried to put the receiver back on the hook. The bottom fell out of my stomach. Someone knocked on my door. The receiver flew away on its coiled line. Frances, hey Frances. Dwight's voice. My pink-and-mauve bookcase played pogo sticks on the turquoise wall. A voice on the other side of the door came through a tunnel from Eiffel Tower. Okay you don't have to answer, but I know you're there. Footsteps disappeared back down the tunnel to Pink Floyd's shink-a-shink, and I crawled to the receiver over the swirling blotches of my linoleum flowers. I needed air, the room stank of banana peel left from breakfast. Buckets of churning froth hurled themselves around in my stomach. Or maybe buckets of tapeworms. Buckets of slime. I kept swallowing ropes of saliva. Trying not to tip over the buckets of slime. Honey, you don't look so hot. Carla stood over me. I crawled toward the door, stumbled up and ran for the bathroom.

I remember Carla and Dwight hovering around as I puked up gobs of orange and brown, Carla handing me a damp cloth, making me sip some water. Then nothing till I woke at daybreak and found a bucket and a jug of water beside my bed – the bathroom jug for washing hair. Sunlight seeped around the blinds. I drank water and closed my eyes. No more spinning turquoise. Just thirst and a mouth like a mouldy flowerpot. I drank more water and drifted.

The novel idea had taken hold in my brain, like a tune I couldn't get out of my head. My mind tinkered with it whenever it got the chance. Like a math problem or a chess puzzle or a Soma Cube that wouldn't go away till I'd solved it. I'd call my novel *Turquoise Room*. I'd make Dwight and Carla into characters, but I couldn't just write down what we did. It had to be about something deep and important, the way *To the Lighthouse* was really about phallic ideals. How did you get stream of consciousness the way Virginia Woolf did? Thinking the way other people thought. I'd have to find out, act friendly to Dwight and Jack, find out what went through their heads. What would they do once they were in my novel? Did there have to be a mystery to solve or a love affair? Or could it really be as in *To the Lighthouse* – people doing things as ordinary as going on a picnic, yet tangled, like schools of fish all swimming in different directions, in their wishes and longings?

Like fish, my thoughts swirled around, darting here and there among the castle ruins and plastic seaweed in my mental aquarium, till I decided to surface, write some of it down; but as soon as I did, someone drained the tank – my thoughts sank as heavy as broken anchors. I made instant coffee and stirred in Carnation, then dragged up my thoughts on the beach of my notebook the way I dragged my streaming, waterlogged body out of ocean's buoyancy.

I started making characters do things. Started making a fictional world, a country with a border you passed through from the real world. With many crossings out, insertions, and arrows to neighbouring pages, I described the scene of my turquoise room with its hotplate, its pink-and-mauve shelves, its posters, and its sea of linoleum flowers. Then I, the narrator, studying psych notes on how rats can be trained to more actively and continuously press the food pellet bar if the food comes intermittently, rather than at a predictable time, and how this operant conditioning was the same way a wife should plan her husband's favourite meals, so that he would regularly and consistently show up on time for dinner, instead of hanging out with his buddies at the office. Then Carla (I called her C) barging in, I showing her operant conditioning idea, and she saying, *First you have to have a husband*, and then demanding to know whether my mother had done that. She bet she hadn't, and she bet it wouldn't work even if she had. Then she said it sounded like a pretty boring marriage, always planning everything. *What about sex − would she plan sex like that too?* Because in her view men cared more about sex than food.

The Carla of my novel already seemed right at home in my head, and she didn't mind letting me know what she thought. Where had she come from? Who else lived in there?

Dad came round for our trip to the library. I tried the ignition in my rusty Datsun. Too much choke, Dad said, as the car spluttered and coughed, cut the choke. It died. Now you've flooded it, he said. We sat in the car waiting for it to unflood itself. Dwight emerged at the top of the outside stairs and drifted down in his laid-back way, as though he were freewheeling a bike; he had an air about him, a faint smile like he was already buzzed on weed. He strolled along the sidewalk toward us.

− How's the morning after, he drawled, when I'd rolled down the window.

I told him fine. Then he said I should let him look at my car, he was a certified auto mechanic.

– I know, you told me that.

– So, let me look at it, pop the hood.

– We're just going somewhere.

Then Dad wanted to know if he could score some dope, and Dwight said drop by when we got back. He drifted off down the street but of course the car didn't start, and we ended up on the Fourth Avenue bus out to the university.

I wanted Dad to quit calling it the *mooniversity* and the *unileetasy*, and see that anyone could go into the great stone library with its granite balustrade, oak doors, and carved ornaments and crests, anyone could read its treasures, an artist like him could read hundreds of art books there and find out all sorts of things about painting. We walked past the stone pool in front of the library where the Geers threw arts under-grad reps. But he stopped to watch some men in blue coveralls marked *Physical Plant* setting up barricades around a manhole cover. Union guys, he said, they'll be getting good money on a Sunday – time and a half or double even – look at that chump, doesn't even know how to use a crowbar – he's got the pry in backwards.

I steered him inside, past the Circulation Office with its maze of carts and tunnels to the stacks, then up the inside stone steps to the great hall, where we stood in the banks of card-catalogue drawers in the hush of the vault three storeys overhead – a grand space streaming with blue-and-gold haze from its stained glass – and filled with the muffled energy of drawers slipping out of sockets and knocking on noteboards, fingers shuffling cards, pens marking paper, and librarians whispering advice.

Dad said he had to take a leak and I told him where the gent's was. He hadn't shaved for a few days and his jacket was stained. But know-ledge was for everyone, no? Here in the card catalogue all knowledge was possible, here it all began in the white author/title cards, the pink subject cards, and the yellow location cards. The clues to facts you welded in fantastic new ideas.

Waiting for Dad, I stood out of sight of the reference librarian, having recently met one who had turned out not to have magic access to books of keywords that would lead me to scintillating discoveries for my term paper on the ecology of dolphins. One had to be careful with librarians, one didn't want to bother them with obvious questions. I opened a drawer and thumbed through the cards, looking like I was searching for something. Dad came back and I asked him which painter he wanted to look up. He started pulling out drawers randomly. I explained we had to look up painters by name in the author/title cards, or if we wanted books about one, we had to look in the pink subject cards. Who did he want to look up? I pulled out a noteboard from the bank of drawers and held a pen over a page. He opened another drawer, then shook his head.

— All this rigmarole.

He waved his hand at the rows of drawers in front of us with their little brass handles.

— Just give me a name.

— What name?

— Names of painters that you want to see.

He stared around at the aisles and blocks of card drawers.

— I don't know what to do with all this.

— Okay maybe we can just go down to the stacks and browse.

I took him back outside, past the stone pool and around the corner to a door half-sunk below ground level, the whole Fine Arts Library being housed in subterranean layers. We squeezed between grey metal shelves and wound down skinny stairways between three floors stuffed in where normally there'd be two. He did not want to look at Tiepolo, Tintoretto, or Titian. We knocked some books off a shelf, trying to find our way to something more modern; they would not squeeze back in, and we had to zig and zag, stripping off jackets and unbuttoning shirts in the oven-like heat between walls of books, back to a reshelving cart. Letters and numbers on spines held up their indecipherable code; maps on the ends of shelves mentioned only the call numbers. At last I found a book of Bruegel, and we hunched on a couple of mobile stools, flipping through the pages.

— You like Bruegel, I said. You used to have a book on him. Which is your favourite painting?

They're all masters, he said, then shut the book complaining that Bruegel was hundreds of years ago, and what was he supposed to do with it? I opened the book again to the *Wedding Dance* and asked him what he saw in the painting that was specially important. He told me that paintings tell stories and make your eyes move in certain directions. Look at the white and the red in the clothing, he said; see how it makes the viewer's eye follow a circular path around the painting. But my eyes kept coming back to the foreground, where all the dancing men had erections. I didn't mention this. How could I be just a viewer if it all came down to erections? How could I be equal and do everything he did?

I said his watercolours around Cultus Lake were full of fences, cows, crop fields, stones, barns, cabins, and rusting tools, just like all the things going on in Bruegel, and why didn't he paint more of them? That's not the way art works, he said. This whole thing here, he said, sweeping his arm toward the walls of books, this isn't about art — it's about a bunch of stuffed shirts talking about art. How *does* art work, I wanted to say, but this was obviously too big a question, and it wasn't going to make him go back to painting. C'mon let's get outta here, he said, and get back to your boyfriend.

— He's not my boyfriend.

You had to learn a whole language to talk to Prof. Thorston, a stocky, no-makeup, no-nonsense Marxist. I wedged myself into a chair-desk, between a man wearing beads and a woman in angora sweater and pearls, and prepared for the final lecture on commodities, class structure, and exchange value — words that kept sliding around in my head like not-quite-dead fish on the dock. Hedda Thorston came into the room with Dagmar, whose Twiggy-cut wheat thatch fell over one eye as she talked to our prof like they were long friends. They stood just inside the classroom in the din of students opening books, comparing drinking feats, and looking out the window to catch a glimpse of the naked Lady Godiva riding bareback through campus, surrounded by cheering Engineers. I heard the words *patriarchy* and *capital*. Hedda, with her files and pile of handouts, smoothed back straggles of long grey hair and nodded vigorously to whatever Dagmar was saying; then Dagmar scribbled down some notes and took the seat in front of me.

I studied Dagmar's corduroys and tweed jacket, so different from Carla's clunky chokers, bright headbands, and stylish outfits right out of magazines; Carla and her outfits fascinated, they were such an act, such a performance, fun like Halloween or charades, or the powerful and magnificent costumes in a Shakespeare play, but who could do this every day? Why would I spend all my time acting like how I looked was more important than the Vietnam War, unequal pay for women, or writing a novel?

Dagmar never went flashy like Carla. Dagmar's Levi's, her suede or linen jackets, her shirts plain as a man's, free of frills and embroidery, her leather boots, her woven bookbags – yes, oh yes, I'd wear Dagmar's outfits, but then you had to have money to buy that kind of stuff. Anyway, clothes shouldn't matter. Dagmar should like me no matter what I wore. She should like me for who I really was. Or she wasn't a true friend.

Should I put Dagmar in my novel? Make her a painter like Lily Briscoe in *To the Lighthouse*? Instead of writing poems, she could paint portraits and landscapes. Except Dagmar wasn't really like Lily because Dagmar wrote lots of poems whereas Lily struggled doubtfully to paint her portrait of Mrs. Ramsay. Lily was more like me, but I had to stop saying *me*, more like the *I* that was writing the novel, the U Girl – should I make Dagmar U Girl? She could paint her characters like trees at the edge of a lake looking down at themselves in the water. Then stepping into the lake ... then what?

Halfway through the lecture Hedda had covered the board with words like *surplus value, exploitation,* and *production*. Students scribbled notes as she walked comfortably back and forth, talking, explaining, arms folded between her large breasts and round tummy. Her sad and weary eyes gazed at us, as though she'd spent decades in the trenches on the losing side of an endless battle. Marxism offered great hope for feminists, she said. Dagmar raised her hand: Didn't Marx completely ignore work inside the home? Students sat back in their seats while Hedda explained that Engels nevertheless looked closely at unequal treatment of women.

But Marxist thought never really looks at the cost of raising kids, does it, Dagmar went on. Then someone else chipped in that protecting workers makes everyone better off. Yeah, class oppression is much more important, another voice added. But why aren't women at home considered workers, I asked, thinking of the landlady cleaning the bathrooms and waxing the hall floor in my rooming house; thinking of Mom doing all the "not real work" at home while Dad got on with the "real work" of being somebody who knew things, somebody who talked about Marx at protest meetings, somebody people talked about and followed.

Engels understood that private property created oppression of women in the home, Hedda explained, so if you get rid of private property, these problems should be solved. On the other hand, feminist thinkers also have to adapt Marxist thought to the needs of women. How, I wondered. It was as though she'd stopped at the edge of a cliff and told us we needed a bridge to the other side of the ravine, but nothing about how to build one.

I rode home in Dagmar's Fiat Mini with her piles of *Ubysseys* and *Georgia Straights*, where she sometimes had articles. Like a flood of wood and mud freed from a log jam, her words swirled over me. Marx completely ignores the whole underpinning of the system of production, namely reproduction of humans who will operate the system of production. She squealed the tires as we veered past the frat houses decorated by Greek letters, ranch-style clapboard bungalows so unlike the stone pillars I'd seen in pictures of Greece. Letters tacked on to something they didn't belong to.

Dagmar's torrent swirled on as we bumped over tree roots on University Boulevard and through the tunnel of boulevard trees to the golf course and the shining windows of apartment blocks and Safeway. Seize the means of production, seize the means of reproduction; pay women for work inside the home or make men do half of it.

Then, as though Dagmar's torrent had met a granite mountain, it changed course, and she drove me to the Women's Auto Collective, where I could learn to fix my car myself from women who had a LIP grant to teach women about cars. Empower yourself, she beamed at me, cigarette dangling from the corner of her mouth. We turned into a back lane between two streets of houses and pulled up at a wooden shed whose boards were fraying at the bottom edges. The back end of a Valiant stuck out the dark cavern of its mouth, like the shed was swallowing more than it could chew.

A woman in coveralls and ball cap emerged, and Dagmar flung her arms around her: Cleo, darling. They kissed and it wasn't just a peck; they kissed on the lips – French kissing – eyes closed. Dagmar had a boyfriend, Murray, but here she was kissing a woman the way men and women kissed in movies. I felt myself blush. I thought of the *Georgia Straight* article by the woman who made herself love women. Cleo and Dagmar, Virginia and Vita. If I liked Dagmar and wanted her to like me, could I be ...?

The two of them stood gazing into each other's eyes, saying nothing but *Soooooooo* back and forth. I walked around the car, hoping I'd stop blushing if I looked at oil cans, wrenches, filthy rags, and the purple jeans of another woman sticking out from under the jacked-up front end. On a dolly, I guessed, clanking away at something under the car. What if things leaked all over you when you went under cars? What if the jacks collapsed?

Dagmar said, hey come over tonight after you're done here, and Coveralls Cleo said she would. She had lips the colour of dried blood and Cleopatra hair. She had to have this hair, she told me, because after all I'm Cleopatra. Cleo's my road buddy, Dagmar said, France, Germany, Italy. Remember Monaco! Cleo's laughter erupted like a bolt of irrepressible jokiness, as though she'd just won the lottery. Then Dagmar said I needed to fix my car, so Cleo should tell me what the Women's Auto Collective did. You don't need a *man*, Cleo laughed, looking at Dagmar, you need *Liquid Wrench*! She listed off the things I could do with Liquid Wrench: change the oil, flush the radiator, change the spark plugs, change the battery. In the shadowy interior of the shed, a lightbulb on an extension cord hung over the open hood of the Valiant.

– So when can you bring your car around?

I couldn't commit. The truth was I didn't really want to fix my car myself. But I should, I thought, cuz that's how you proved you were equal, you did everything men did. Had Dagmar changed the oil in her car? No, cuz her dad just got all their cars done at a Dunbar place. But it's your car, isn't it, I said. Why wouldn't you do your own maintenance?

Yeah, Cleo smirked, Why wouldn't you do your own maintenance? (Like it was some sort of in joke, something sexual.) We don't need mechanics, do we, Dag, she went on, those guys are useless. She glanced at the legs on the dolly. The two of them stared at each other till Cleo burst out laughing again.

– It's easier than you think, Cleo said to me. It's free too, you could come tomorrow.

Purple Jeans began muttering under the engine, wanted Cleo to hand her a wrench. Cleo handed something from a toolbox on the floor to the greasy hand at the edge of the car, the shed empty but for the tools, some bald tires, oil cans, tire wrenches, and funnels. What did they do if no one brought a car around to learn about?

– You should do it, Dagmar said, taking a joint out of her cigarette box. She toked up and passed it around.

– Why should I do it if you don't?

– Because. It's a rite of passage. Toughens you up. Doesn't it?

She grinned at Cleo, who laughed again and said, oh Dagmar, you're too much. The smeared face of the other woman rolled out from under the Valiant, glared at Dagmar, and spat out, What the hell are you doing here?

– Just bringing you some business.

– Yeah, what happened to the business we had, eh, what happened to Women's House?

– It's still going, isn't it?

– Why would you care, with your silk shirts and trips to Europe?

In the car Dagmar told me not to mind Rosie, she was always gruff like that – proud of her working-class roots. Women's House was a project she and Rosie had started for battered women.

CHAPTER 3

On the sailing trip to Passage Island, Nigel set the boat on a close haul and handed me the tiller. The wind hummed over the sail into my arm like a deep bass choir and billowed my purple-and-yellow poncho. We plunged through the choppy harbour, dashing under ruddy hulls of freighters waiting to load grain from elevators or sulphur from a mountain of yellow with its blue octopus of conveyor belts. *Waiting in the roads*, Nigel called it, as though the sea could have dotted lines like highways, the sea had roads only sailors could see. We crossed the open water toward rugged north-shore peaks, wind and sun rushing through me, the world full of majesty and freedom like I felt on the summit of a mountain hike.

Out in the harbour, we stopped and played around for a while. Nigel showed me and a grad student named Hal all about things I was picking up at the sailing club: sheets, cleats and winches, jibing and tacking, commenting on how well I kept the sails from luffing, whether it was a close haul or a broad reach. While Hal lounged with his feet up in the cockpit, I, proud that I could crew with Nigel, bustled about the boat, keeping watch and following Nigel's directions to set the jib on one side and the main on the other, wing-on-wing before the wind.

The island itself was oddly disappointing, just a chunk of rock sticking up out of the sea that made the rickety steps and thin cottages clinging to it look like pesky insects on the back of a hippo. We tied up to one of the private docks and while we were eating lunch, Hal, whose black hair, rosy cheeks, and roundish body reminded me of those painted wooden egg-dolls that were made in Finland or Russia, told me about his thesis on Hermann

Hesse, and I thought of his thesis in Main Library, with its own card in the catalogue, and Hal crossing over to the world of knowing things, Hal meaning something for the whole world. That's what I wanted, I thought, to mean something to the whole world, the way you did when you wrote a book and it was in the library forever, even long after you died. To mean something, the way Nigel did and Hal would too once he got his Ph.D.

I absolutely had to read *Steppenwolf*, Hal told me, it was about a man who thought he was half wolf and half spirit, who finds a book addressed to him personally by name. It has a magic theatre in it too, he said, that shows how the mind works.

I could be that, I thought, I could be half-wild from outside the city, half magic-book. I felt my eyes turn gold and strange as the coyotes' at Cultus Lake, a coyote humming with lore, humming with people and ideas, humming with university ... universe ... city.

On the way back from the island, the wind dropped, and Nigel showed me how to hoist the spinnaker by folding it into a bucket with its corners stuck out and then attaching a pole to hold the sail away from the boat. He stood behind me, I felt his chest and arms guiding mine as I hoisted the sail along the forestay. My stomach lurched. Could he ...? Could we ...?

The spinnaker puffed its billowing blue-and-white sack of wind over the bow and tugged us along in our gently rocking cradle.

Next time I saw Nigel was after the exam for his course. He stuffed the pile of papers into his briefcase and said, why didn't I come back to his office, he had the book he kept meaning to give me, all about novel writing. We ambled back, talking of plans for the summer. He was hoping to buy a boat and maybe he'd take me sailing again. I wasn't going anywhere, just working at my job at the insurance company, which he said sounded deathly dull.

In his office, he handed me the book wrapped in a Safeway bag. He'd found it in a book bin on Tenth Avenue for ten cents. *The Writing of Fiction* by Edith Wharton. For your quest novel, he said. She tells you how it's done.

— Not a quest novel, I said. A novel like *Martha Quest.*

— Doesn't matter, he said. Your characters have to be looking for something, otherwise there's no story.

I gazed again at his shelves of D.H. Lawrence books, the subject of his thesis.

— Did Lawrence think that when he wrote *Sons and Lovers?* Because he seems to be writing a book about the Oedipal complex.

Nigel said of course Lawrence's characters were on quests. Love is a quest and Paul Morel is in love with Miriam and then Clara, but his love for his mother gets in the way. The conflict between his quests makes the story.

— What if you don't want to write a love story?

Then Nigel said I could write a story of vengeance or rebellion or betrayal or rivalry or ambition, things that strongly motivated people.

— But then you are just writing the same old stories that have already been told in all the Safeway magazines. What if you want to write a story about someone figuring something out?

— A mystery story. The quest is to solve the mystery.

I flipped open *The Writing of Fiction* by Edith Wharton and browsed through the pages: the novel of psychology was born in France, but the novel of manners was born in England. I flipped some more: point of view and time are the central difficulties. U Girl's quest, what could it be? What if she's nuts about photography, and she takes pictures of Carla in her room next door, then when she blows up the photograph she sees that behind Carla's smiling face is a cupboard door bulging with clothes and from the sleeve of one of Carla's kimonos jut several fingers? Like the muzzle of the gun peering from the shrubbery in the movie *Blow-Up.*

U Girl waits till Carla has gone to work, then sneaks in through Carla's window and finds a body stuffed in the closet. Man or woman, she can't tell, only the fingers are visible, no nail polish. Through the cloth, she feels a rubbery arm, then a rubbery leg. She sneaks back to her room to call the police, but the phone line's dead, none of the other roomers has a phone. She runs out, heading to the landlady, meets Dwight in the hall. He asks her if she's all right, she looks pale, she almost faints but blurts out everything. Dwight says, Don't phone the police, your fingerprints are all over the room, they'd just throw you in jail, you'll fail all your courses. He gives her a beer to calm her down. Tells her to get locks for all her windows and doors, he'll help her install them. He's nowhere around when she gets back from the hardware store. She looks through Carla's window, but the body's gone. Her phone line works. She puts locks on all her windows and the balcony door. Carla makes fun of her, asks her if she thinks she's a thief. I'm gonna sneak over and lezzie-rape you! There's a report in the paper of a young construction worker gone missing ...

— What's so interesting about that page, Nigel asked, you've been reading it for about ten minutes.

Then he said how would I like to go for a walk, and get the cobwebs out, as he put it. He'd always wanted to see Wreck Beach. What were all the nudists doing down there on this chilly April day?

Past the Japanese gardens we followed a gully through moss-coated maples and Douglas fir down the shore bluffs west of campus. Salmonberry clawed at our clothes, and sword fern sprayed our legs with wet. Water seeping from the bluffs spattered mud on our pants.

— Wish I had my wellies on, Nigel muttered.

— What are wellies?

— Rubber boots to you colonials.

— Why are they called *wellies*?

— Because Wellington invented them.

Okay who was Wellington? Something to do with a battle, maybe something to do with Napoleon, but I didn't ask, didn't want him thinking me an ignoramus.

The beach spilled out below us as we descended the trail, waves continually rushing in like someone pulling sheets out of a washtub and plunging them in again. Waves starting as glimmers in the haze of Vancouver Island, then crinkling the sea as though it were tinfoil that had been scrunched and unfolded, then finally brandishing foamy crests, till they fell on the sand and spilled their cargo of kelp and tide wrack.

We headed along the deserted beach past one or two naked die-hards sheltering behind logs, and stopped to look up at the cliffs above, the mat of roots resting on top of the sand like icing on a sliced cake, the rug of soil under all the buildings of UBC. Chunks of the mat had broken off and slid with their islands of plants down the crumbling cliffs. People had tried to stop this with stout-rooting bushes and berms of boulders against the waves.

– One day it's all going to slide into the sea, Nigel said. Office towers, classroom blocks, heads, deans, chancellors, the whole bloody lot, into the sea.

And I thought of us in our classroom, talking about *Waiting for Godot*, hanging out in midair as the sand fell away beneath us, then slowly tipping down the sliding crumbling slope till we slid into the waves. But I didn't want to think about the university that way; I wanted to think about it being there forever on top of the cliffs, full of its knowledge and wisdom, full of its curiosity, full of people finding out new ways to do things, people putting their minds together to find the best new ideas, people being the best they could be. And it would be there for at least a hundred years, so why would Nigel just think sarcastically of it falling apart? Or was that the way people like Nigel, who'd really seen the world, always talked about things they cared about – like they didn't matter?

We wandered along the beach, and he picked up a long stem of bladder kelp, waving it at me like a sword, *Come, for the third, Laertes: you but dally.* I grabbed one too and we whacked away at each other, slathering our jeans with kelpy sand till we fell onto a log, huffing and puffing.

– The thing is, he said, looking out the long finger of the breakwater, sloshed by waves on the sea side, calm on the land side, maybe you are writing a love story like all other love stories, or an adventure, or a mystery, but you'll tell it in a completely new way because no one from these mountains has ever written a novel. They're all wild. They're all new. No one owns them. I mean, look at you, I bet you're as nimble as a mountain goat up on those bluffs. I bet your blood runs with forests and wolves. I bet you've got roots into these mountains right back to George Vancouver himself.

There it was again, Steppenwolf: my half-wild being; I was a kind of mountain wolf or tree wolf. Maybe that was what intrigued Nigel about me – a kind of wolfishness or treeishness or mountainishness – an impenetrable, unspeakable wildness that he'd never find in London.

I did not feel very wolfish a few days later hunching over file-sorting racks and trundling bins of sorted files out to the floor-to-ceiling shelves. I prayed I hadn't got a lot of high ones, but no – each one made me climb the ladder, shift the bulging folders on the shelf, stuff in the returned file, climb down, move the ladder, pull another file, climb up – until I longed to be back in the sort room, where at least I could rest every now and then. If only Kitty or Lorna would help, but Kitty was off on some special assignment, and who knew where Lorna was? The files were so thick that some of them were stored in special folders with accordion ends. At times I thought I simply couldn't lift another one over my head, and I cursed the rows of adjusters spread out below me on either side of the file bay who blithely ordered these folders but never had to put them back. How long did I survey them from my ladder top? I don't know. I hoped none of them would look up. They talked on phones with long coily rubber cords or bent over open folders making notes on yellow pads. They had cups of coffee, and some even had colourful desk ornaments or a photograph and sat in padded swivel chairs. Twenty minutes went by; I managed to file nine folders. I had at least thirty more.

A woman told me the office manager wanted to see me in his office. Not, as I thought, to tell me to work more efficiently, but to put me at a typewriter desk with a swivel chair and a file full of addresses and phone numbers. I didn't remember saying I could type. I'd failed it twice in high school. On good days I could do twenty-five words a minute. Numbers were out of the question. Type each address onto an index card, he said. I rolled a card into the Underwood. Keys jammed or didn't strike the platen. Each key needed a sledge hammer to make it work. Number, pause, check the list, number, pause, look at keyboard, number, pause. Women nearby looked over from files on their desks. I back-spaced and stuck white correcting tape under the ribbon carriage. It didn't line up with the letter it was supposed to be erasing. I scrolled up the card and tried to erase it with a rubber disc, brushing off the crumbs with its green bristles, then yanked the smeared card out and started again.

At the end of the afternoon, I had cards with red letters typed over in black, cards with white patches of correcting tape, cards where the address didn't line up with the printed lines, cards with extra commas and periods. I stacked them up and fled the office.

Near the bus stop, Lorna grabbed me and pulled me into a door alcove for a seldom-used exit – only the day before I'd seen a bag lady sitting here smoking a cigarette beside her rusty cart of hoardings. Lorna'd called in sick and didn't want Kitty to see her. She'd taken the whole day off and read a book at the library, and now she wanted me to go to the library and show her more books to read.

– They have all these drawers of cards so you can look things up, but how do you know what to look up?

It turned out that the book she'd read was *Charlotte Sometimes* about a new girl at a boarding school who wakes up in the bed of a girl in board-ing school back in 1918. Every night they switch and Charlotte keeps up a double life, until she gets trapped and can't return to the present. Lorna wanted to know what a *prefect* was, but I didn't know.

The public library was so small compared to UBC. We wandered around the shelves, picking up books facing out and looking for a place to sit away from a red-faced man snoring in front of a newspaper. Almost no seats available. You have to have a reason to look things up, I told her, like an essay to write on a topic. Or maybe a book you've heard about that you want to read.

– So you have to go to school to know.

– No, anyone can use the library.

She couldn't think of any titles. She wanted to read what I was reading in school. We looked for *Waiting for Godot* and *Hamlet* but there were no copies on the shelves. *Martha Quest* was out too. In the end she picked *Stranger in a Strange Land*. I told her how to get the UBC application forms. We walked to Granville Street together and took our separate buses.

At the rooming house, though, I felt I was carrying bag-lady cart-loads of Lorna and her book dreams up the wooden steps – my legs barely lifting her soft, spreading bulk. How could she find her way to university, with her mom a waitress and dad a part-time janitor, far away in Prince George?

When I got into my room, I found a folded piece of paper slipped under my door. *If you're going to drink my beer*, it said, *you could at least share it with me. Your pal across the hall.*

What beer? I hadn't touched his beer. I opened my door and glared at Dwight's, which was shut for a change. I knocked. No answer.

Carla, in snakeskin tights and gold miniskirt, came in with a brown paper bag. She trolled around my room, saying how much she liked turquoise, and that I had the best room, like a real home with even a little kitchen nook.

— Wow, you sure read a lot of books.

She stopped at my bookshelf and read out titles: *Contemporary Psychology: Readings from Scientific American*, and Keeton, *Biological Science*, saying how important they sounded and how she tried to improve her reading sometimes by buying *Psychology Today*, and maybe one day if she got the time she'd get her high school diploma. And what good taste in art I had too, though she liked Dad's picture of trees and fields reflected in Cultus Lake better than Toni Onley's piece. That reminded her of a big bin of paper scraps she'd seen in a box factory where she used to work.

— Look what I brought you.

She opened the bag.

— Rice Krispies squares! One of the other girls brought a huge batch!

I thought of all the times, as a child, I'd pestered Mom to buy big bright-coloured boxes with their free toys inside. All the *nos*; we eat oatmeal. All the looks that said, why are you asking when I've told you a hundred times; why make me say it again? I bit into the buttery, sugary, snapping compressed puffs. How horrified Mom would be. And Mom was right, wasn't she? Science was right — Sugar Pops were bad for people.

Carla waved her cube of marshmallowy Krispies at Onley's kaleidoscope of lines, planes, cock-eyed pyramids, half-formed walls and tunnels. She could see it was art with a capital A, but how did you know it wasn't just doodles? Before I could come up with an answer, she said, You know what I've always wanted to do? Go to the opera! Like, really get dolled up with furs and gown and go to the Queen E. Theatre. Wouldn't that be great?

– Did you borrow one of Dwight's beers, I asked.

– Why would I borrow ... Is he accusing me of stealing his beer?!

I showed her the note.

– That creep, he's only after one thing. Why doesn't he pick on someone his own age? I'm gonna take his beer and put it behind the bathtub, and when he comes looking, I'll tell him to back off and leave you alone, or I won't tell him where it is.

– He'll just think I took it all.

– I'll leave *him* a note. If he knocks on your door, don't answer.

– All right, I said, but I don't think it'll work.

I closed my door, flopped down on the cot, and drifted off in Dad's Cultus Lake picture, wondering who Carla would be under the glassy murk of my novel. Through the looking glass, through the laking glass, I would find what Edith Wharton called the story's *magic casements*, its *vistas on infinity*. Dwight would be a lonely, tortured Heathcliff and Carla, the lost daughter of a Russian princess. Here the trail petered out, and the friendly satanic neighbours in *Rosemary's Baby* took over. Carla and Dwight belong to some kind of cult. They're luring U Girl into it, pretending not to like each other so U Girl won't be suspicious. Carla gives her drinks and cigarettes and takes her to the movies. When she gets back to her room, someone's turned the books in her bookcase upside down and written weird messages in her journal like *Lily dances lapwings* or *Take six banana steps to Arcana* or *The hangman waits under the underwood*. Carla says she knows someone who'll teach U Girl how to make these into poems. He sees people late at night in a beautiful room lined with Turkish rugs and silk cushions where you learn special exercises ...

I heard the outside door slam, Dwight's Yale lock snap, the fridge open and shut, then banging on my door.

– I know you're in there.

He rattled the doorknob.

– One beer is fine, okay, you're a starving student, but six beers isn't.

Maybe Carla forgot to write that note. I heard her platforms clunk across the floor, door click open.

— What's your problem?

— Oh of course it was you, I shoulda seen that from an alky.

— Fuck you, asshole. Whaddaya want?

— I think you know.

— Leave her alone, okay?

— Where's my beer?

— What beer?

— The ones you took.

— I don't even drink beer, why would I take yours?

— Hell you don't, you probably drink shoe polish.

— Fuck you, go shoot up in your dreamhole. Or better still, shoot yourself *up* your dream hole.

Carla's door slammed.

— Didja tell her all about your trips to detox?

The door banged back.

— More like you down in detox. Didja tell her what you did to Carrie?

— Didn't do anything to Carrie.

— That's why she left, eh, cuz you didn't do anything to her. Finally get someone nice in here and you fucking couldn't keep your hands off her.

— Ah shut your gob. Carrie was all over me, anyway it's none of your business.

— At least Carrie was your own age.

— So where's the beer?

— Leave her alone.

— Who alone?

— Fer Chrissakes, you want your beer or not?

— I guess she's over nineteen ... Okay so what am I s'posed to do, ask your permission to speak to her?

— Quit following her. Keep your hands to yourself and your dick in your pants.

I heard the clink of bottles going back into the fridge. Minutes later Carla burst in through the balcony door and we sprawled on my cot

48

smoking and saying to each other *I wouldn't drink your beer if it was the last drop in hell.*

Dwight put Pink Floyd on and cranked up "Money" full blast.

– I can look out for myself, I told Carla.

– He bugs you, you call me.

– No need. I can handle Dwight, I've had lots of boyfriends.

– Hon, there's plenty you don't know. Hey, you're just a babe.

Once I'd completed the sailing course and crewed with Nigel, I was keen to try out my new skills with a dinghy from the club; but then there were so many reddened men at the club who shouted jokes, heaved around boats, and told first-years, Don't forget to say *Ready about* when you're tacking. I needed a buddy, I thought. Someone to do things with. I missed the way Joe and I hiked and fished together. I didn't phone him, cuz I didn't want him clinging, but I hoped he was all right, hoped he'd found his way.

Maybe Dagmar could join the sailing club, we'd take out boats together; we'd be our own sailing team, like the men in the poster on my wall. We wouldn't make fun of each other; we'd become brilliant sailors, and we'd race against the men and win.

Dagmar said she wasn't crazy about joining the club, but sure, she'd come out with me. She said she'd sailed lots of dinghies on Okanagan Lake as a kid.

On a sunny day with a good breeze, we rolled our boat down to the water and floated it off, got the sail up, pushed off with the paddle. I belted on my life jacket and said she should put hers on too. I can swim, she said. Trust me; I spent half my life in Okanagan Lake. She stowed her jacket under a seat. So who's going to be skipper, I said. Does there have to be one, she laughed. It's only a dinghy, not a fifty-foot yacht. We were sitting in the stern of the boat, which was now drifting ashore. You always have a skipper, they told us in the course. Someone has to take charge.

– Well I guess it's you then.

– Okay, where are we going?

— You're the skipper.

— I know I said that, but I need to learn, you will tell me if I'm doing something stupid, won't you?

— Well that depends on whether I think it's pedagogically sounder for you to be told or to work it out for yourself.

She was grinning, her brown eyes full of fun. *Pedagogically* – what was that, I thought.

— We better figure out where the wind is, I said.

— *Who has seen the wind*, Dagmar quipped.

— Very funny.

The boat was now sliding sideways into the beach. A guy on a Laser gliding along beside us asked if *you girls* needed help.

— No, we're fine, I said. Then to Dagmar, I think we better row out.

But we couldn't really do that with the sail up. So we paddled, one on each side for a bit past the end of the pier, I hoping no more breezy-looking guys pulled alongside. I dropped the centreboard and set the boat on a close haul, searching for the hum of the sail tight against the wind. We picked up speed. The wind ruffled Dagmar's hair. And I silently celebrated my buddy, my twin – this ally against the world.

You're quite the pro, she said, lounging across the gunwale. Did you learn all this from Nigel? What's he like anyway?

— Whaddaya mean, what's he like? You know him as well as I do.

— Not as a date I don't.

— It wasn't a date, I was just filling in for someone who cancelled on a group sail.

— I'd call that a date, she said, except that *date* is so fifties high school. I mean who *dates* anymore, you just hang out, do your thing, go find someone to bed when you want to. *Date* – reminds me of hanging around by the phone waiting.

The boat was well out in the bay, far from shore. We began to heel over, and Dagmar wanted to hike out off the gunwale, but I didn't want her falling in, so I opened the sail to a broader reach and veered the boat more toward shore. You're going back in already, she said. No, I said, just not going too far out. She wanted to get both sails up. Okay, I said, but

50

there might be too much wind. She hoisted the tiny jib sail and cleated it. This course worked for a time; then the jib began rippling. I thought the main was stealing wind from the jib; she thought we should head off on a new tack back into the bay. I pushed over the tiller and we came to a halt, the boom swinging back and forth, the wind pushing us toward shore.

A guy in a dinghy whizzed past us, waving, the bay full of boats from the club, mostly guys, or guys at the tiller with a girlfriend tanning on the bow, some of the guys racing sleek Lasers that had almost no cockpit and that skimmed over the surface like water-skis with sails.

Push the tiller over more, Dagmar said, or we'll be grounded. I can't, I said, it's already over as far as it'll go. Oh, was all she said.

Eventually, with the help of an oar, we got back on tack again, zooming out into the bay.

– I call going for walks a little more than teacher-student, she went on.

– What walk?

– Down to Wreck Beach, I saw you and Nigel after the exam.

She grinned. I tried to laugh it off, that he was just giving me a book, and it was nothing, but it wasn't nothing, and we both knew it. She said lots of people date their professors, and why not anyway? Then, what'd you get on the exam?

She'd got an A, of course; I got an A-. I screwed up the Yeats question, whereas Dagmar had predicted it and prepared. Meaning she glanced through a book of Yeats poems – no, didn't write out an essay on it ahead, just looked through his *Collected Poems*. Something I'd never even thought of doing.

I tacked back into the bay, and we rocked on an easy sail parallel to the shore. Dagmar lay back against the life jacket and closed her eyes, muttering something about all the wind and sun making her sleepy. I kept my hand on the tiller. Could she really be my double, my twin? And what if it was more, what if you passed through the mirror from just friends to ...?

Two guys in a dinghy heading out to the bay yelled *howdy girls* wanting to know if we'd go for drinks after. No thanks, I said. And we're not girls either, I felt like adding but didn't. Dagmar woke up.

– Turn the boat around, turn the boat around, she said. Let's chase them. Let's really make this thing sail like the men do.

She wanted the sails as tight to the wind as they'd go for the best speed. The guys were about three dinghy-lengths ahead, but they were heavier, she said, so we could catch up. Our boat started to heel. Great, she said. Keep it going. We were gaining on the men. Then, Keep it heeling, don't slack off. She slid her bum onto the gunwale, locked her feet under a seat and leaned out. We were one dinghy-length from the men. I need a trapeze, she yelled over the wind and water, but this'll have to do. Okay, I said, but if you're going to do that, at least put on a life jacket. Let's catch up to them first, she said. For one glorious long moment we held it, the wind in the leaning sail, her counterbalance, the boat zooming forward toward the men, the tiller humming in my hand. Then, whoops! and we were over, the boat scooping up water, the sail flat on the surface, me in the chilly sea yelling, hang onto the boat, hang onto the boat, Dagmar, don't let go, are you okay? And luckily being rescued by several more men in various dinghies and Lasers.

– I should never have let you do it without a life jacket, I said, through chattering teeth in the car on the way to her place.

– Crap, she said. You've got to think like a man, take risks.

Nigel told me to meet him at the Safeway on Fourth and Vine, and he'd show me a sailboat he was hoping to buy. The sun low in the sky, I stood in the lot watching a grey-haired lady in purple hat and gloves yank her cart from the stuffed row under the red S of the sprawling store. Then a mom and two kids, one in the kiddy seat, the other turning over potted plants. A man came out with a bag of charcoal briquettes and slammed his cart into the row. Cars jolted into slots, cars got stuck waiting for other cars to back out. Nigel's yellow van pulled into the far corner, and I zigzagged toward it, around open doors, raised trunks and heaping carts of Safeway bags.

He had his head down on the steering wheel when I got there, but said he was fine, nothing wrong. His briefcase on the floor bulged with folders labelled things like Majors, Honours. What had he been doing? Curriculum committee meeting. I thought back to grad-party committee in high school – I was the secretary – two boys, president and vice president, argued the whole time about whether we should rent the Jehovah's Witness hall or the United Baptists'. Nigel's committee probably wasn't like that, I thought.

He manoeuvred the van past the clog around the beach, then suddenly launched into how it was so different over here from England. You didn't get a degree by picking up courses in psychology, botany, and English like packages of cereal at the supermarket; you read literature and its social context. You went to lectures all year; at the end of the year, you wrote exams on the whole lot. No one taught you how to write essays. You figured it out by talking to your friends and seeing what other people did with their tutor. And if you didn't figure it out, the university told you to leave.

I pictured Nigel's professors and tutors passing on rituals from ancient Greeks in churchlike halls, something grand and beautiful unlike the concrete blocks of beige UBC classrooms with their perfunctory buzzers.

– But wouldn't your tutor help you?

– You wouldn't dare ask, he retorted. If you got it wrong, you learned.

– I wouldn't last five minutes in your university.

– Of course you would, you're not stupid, you'd figure it out.

– Not if I couldn't ask the prof for help.

– You'd ask your friends. You're a smart woman, Frances, you haven't had much education but you're smart, you know how to pay attention, figure things out.

We drove past Kitsilano Beach with its neatly spaced logs for sunbathers. Then headed past the concrete flying saucer of the Vancouver Museum with its movies of outer space.

At the marina, a brisk breeze rattled rigging against metal masts. Like elves, tapping and pattering empty tins and pails. On the floating dock, we passed sailors off-loading to wheelbarrows, hosing decks, and snugging in boats for the night, till Nigel leapt onto a black hull called *Windsong* and began unlocking the cabin. I asked if he was planning another trip to Passage Island or maybe across the strait to Vancouver Island.

– Not particularly, he said, jumping back onto the dock and walking slowly along studying the sleek hull, checking the fenders and lines.

– Or maybe I am, he went on, I'm planning the trip of life; and this will be my home.

– I like the name *Windsong*, I said (glad it wasn't called something like *Babe Ahoy*, or *Pyjama Girl*). He thought the name sounded too California, he might change it, but he didn't know what to.

– What about *Hamlet*, I said.

– My home is my castle is my hamlet, ship as village, hmm. But we can't have a ship that doesn't know which direction to go, can we?

– No, I suppose not.

I told him I liked the varnished wood and brass fittings on the deck. Teak, he said, then showed me the laminated spruce mast and the 15-horsepower outboard motor. We stepped down into a cabin you could barely stand up in. He showed me the bar fridge, the gas ring, the lockers under the galley seats, and the spinnaker and genny sails stowed under the sleeping platform, a triangular space big enough for two, tucked beneath the foredeck.

– Where will you take a bath?

– No baths, he said. The marina has showers.

He would move out of his rooms at the end of the month, move all his books to his office, no more landlords, no more rent. I sat across from him at the galley table. Our knees touched underneath.

– But where will you sail, you're not just going to live at the dock all summer?!

– Well since you ask, he said, pulling a chart off the ledge above the table, I'm thinking about a trip about three days up the coast to Desolation Sound. Far away from drunken motorboats and noisy marinas.

On the chart, we studied blue-edged sandy blodges of islands, headlands, and peninsulas woodgrained with contour lines. Water, dotted with depth soundings and danger markers, cut the land into channels and ragged tangled fjords. Tenedos Bay nestled in the crook of a craggy peninsula. That was where you ended up, he said. He'd heard the water was warm and green as Hawaii and you could catch giant crabs. I thought

Tenedos sounded like something in a Greek myth, and he told me all about Tenedos Island where the Greeks hid their ships from the Trojans while they built their horse and prepared to storm Troy.

– You see what I mean, Frances, he said. You know things, you just don't know you know them.

But that was the problem, wasn't it? I didn't know what I knew, which came to the same thing. I said Desolation Sound reminded me of a TV movie about a prospector, lost in the bush, who stakes a vein of gold, then gets killed with his pick-hammer by a mountain man.

Nigel thought it was a place for an epic about George Vancouver and his ship *The Discovery* sailing into the wild unknown for the first time, sending out dories of men and officers to mark and measure it. Rowboats of men with plumb lines, telescopes, and sextants, he said, surrounded by unimaginable mountains of tangled forest. Men drenched in rain, rowing for days away from the ship. Men starving, men ambushed by Indians, men stranded with *The Discovery* aground on a rock.

Darkness swallowed up the mountains and apartment blocks, turning the water to an oily black. Night birds swooped around the masts. Boaters on the dock packed up and went home, leaving us in the solitary bubble of *Windsong*'s cabin light. Nigel said he was thinking of going to the Biltmore, which was the closest thing to a proper pub he'd found since he'd come to Vancouver, so did I want to come? A steamy, lamplit room full of Dickensian top hats and watch-chained waistcoats, I thought, served by big-boned women in boobsy peasant blouses.

It wasn't like that of course. We took one of the booths away from the tables of jeans, tie-dyed T-shirts, bell bottoms, and greasers, and suddenly I remembered this was where Carla worked. Nigel ordered a bottle of Toby and fish and chips. I ordered beer and the cheapest thing I could find – a grilled cheese sandwich. Draft or imported, the waitress asked, and since I didn't know what draft was I said I'd try a Toby. On the far side of the room, Carla wove through tables, drinks tray on her shoulder, her black minidress hoiking up her fishnet thighs. She waved and blew me a kiss. I told Nigel she lived next door and he said she was usually here when he came. Then he smiled at me with puzzled amusement, like the Friendly Giant looking at the tiny chairs he arranged for his audience.

— You've never been to a pub have you?

— Sure I have, I said. I've been to the Cecil downtown, it's more of a beer hall I guess.

I asked him whether his girlfriend liked the boat he was buying.

— Girlfriend?

— Yeah, Carla says, you come in here all the time with your girlfriend.

— I don't know if she's much of a girlfriend, he said. She's gone up to Prince Rupert to write a book.

I asked him if he'd sail up to Rupert, but he said *Windsong* wasn't a blue-water boat, and anyway Sandy (that was her name) wasn't the least bit interested in sailing. He had no idea when or if she'd be back and suggested we change the topic.

Carla came by and leaned over our table so we could see right down the scoop of her minidress. Big black hoop earrings swung under her chestnut curls. She made a fuss about calling me Frankie and telling Nigel that she was going to get me a job, a real job, at the Biltmore. Catch ya later, she said, with her amazing frosted lips, and, winking a big eyelashed eye, went back to the tables on her side and started joking with some guys in Mao caps and beads. Nigel wondered how I could imagine working at the Biltmore. Why not, I said. Lots of students do. This is the last place you belong, he said, and I said where did I belong?

— Roaming the fields on horseback rounding up cattle or guiding bear hunters into the mountains!

He said he could tell I wasn't from the city. But I want to be from the city, I told him, I don't want to be from Cultus Lake. People drown there, *cultus* even means *worthless* in Chinook. He told me the city was just tinsel and glitter, just a tiny cluster of flashlights, the real stuff was darkness.

— What's an office block to the immense endlessness of night, he went on. What's a supermarket or a rock concert or all those UBC heads and departments? All those silly exam papers with their tiny answers?

He reached across the table and ran his hand through my black hair.

– That's what you've got, he said, that darkness. That's what your novel's about. The darkness of the mountains George Vancouver could never fathom from his cozy English countryside.

Darkness, what did he mean? I thought of night sky swallowing us up in *Windsong*'s light bubble, disappearing the mountains and the city. Cars, trucks, buses stopped buzzing along roads. People stopped working, stopped talking, stopped trying to pass exams. They fell through a porous barrier like bacteria osmoting through walls of cells. People osmoted to the night world, the dream world, and the night went on and on forever outside the bubbles of days; it was what we couldn't even think of beyond the constellations of stars. How grand to be part of that mystery. Yes, to actually *be* darkness. But what on earth did it have to do with Carla, Dwight, and Jack, and the story of my *Turquoise Room*?

I kept mulling this over as Nigel drove me home in the unreal gleam of street lights and passing cars, their passengers smudged out in blackened windows and darkened deserted streets. Darkness pressed the city into silence, like a thick black layer of cotton batten. How could darkness speak?

CHAPTER 4

My toils at the insurance company continued full time during the summer break from UBC. In the morning we prayed for mail so we could escape the file-sorter rack, the trundling of files to shelves, the climbing and stuffing them with aching arms, the climbing down, the getting of more files, the climbing up. Kitty, in her new yellow polka-dot dress and matching yellow heels, led the way to a windowless fluorescent-lit meeting room packed with storage boxes and fake woodgrain table. She untied the mail bag and spilled the contents, instructing Lorna and I — with our metal openers ready to stab the envelopes and slit their sides — not to start till she'd decided where the piles would go. It was like Kitty the sugar bowl of a yellow daisy tea set instructing a closet of dark furs (Lorna) and an attic hobbit (me). We then began stabbing and slitting — stamping everything with R'cved Jn 20 72 or whatever the date was, and piling cheques in one place and the other things in other places, which could only be determined by the sugar bowl as they came up, for the sugar bowl was the only connection that the hobbit had to the networks of In baskets and Out baskets on the three floors above us.

I'd open a handwritten report on policy number 6773542. Where does this go? With a flash of her stubby strawberry-frosted nails, Kitty would pick it up. Oh that goes to Mrs. Sparks up in Marine. Or I think that goes to Claims or maybe it goes to Inspections, I'll look after it, and she'd start another pile. Or it might go to Personnel or Residential or Pam — she's an exec secretary, the one who works next to Alice, my dad's secretary. How do you know, I'd ask, certain there must be some logic as to which documents went where, which I could learn and follow and therefore be better at my job. Oh don't worry, her cheerful scarlet lips assured me, we don't get many of those. Maybe the sugar bowl herself didn't know how the floors above, with their corridors, dividers, desks, and secretaries, fitted together – their reasons for being departments of a system feeding into other departments, which, instead of locking in neat stacks of Lego blocks, floated around in my head under words like *Personal*, *Commercial*, *Life* and the forbidden territory of men in sleek dark suits – the execs who slipped in and out of the building invisibly, by different stairs and elevators than we were privy to. How would we get to wear suits and work on those floors if we didn't know how the whole thing fit together?

Of course we did not stab and slit any faster than we had to, and we each took one bathroom break – not together because that was against the rules.

I want to take her out for lunch on her birthday, Kitty said when Lorna was out. It's in a couple of weeks. We'll get some of the girls from Accounting. Then she leaned toward me so I could see the little clumps of mascara sticking to her eyelashes, and lowering her voice, she whispered, She's so quiet all the time, never goes shopping or to parties, sometimes I wonder if there's something wrong with her, so fat and everything, she seems to get bigger all the time, there must be something wrong with her, like cancer maybe or mental problems.

– Maybe she just thinks shopping and parties are a waste of time.

Kitty's eyes widened as though I'd date-stamped her new dress.

I know you've been talking about me, Lorna said, heaving herself into her chair and surveying the sugar bowl and the hobbit from her odd closet of dark. I don't mind. We spun out mail as long as we could, then Kitty took the cheques to the cashier and all the other papers to wherever she went in the floating maze above our heads, while Lorna and I went back to the sorting rack and the trolleys and the shelves. The hours crawled by. Twice my eyes glazed over and I dozed off on the sorting racks. Stay awake, a numb part of my brain told the bags of grey wool in the rest of it as I trundled files out to shelves. I moved as slowly as possible, the room a blur of beiges, greys, and dim outlines of adjusters on phones, typing and talking barely reaching me through the blanket over my head. All the way home, clinging to the sweaty pole in a bus full of other hot tired damp people, I felt perspiration, as Mom would call it, soaking into my blouse and skirt and clamping my hair to my face, my eyes irresistibly turning upward into my eye sockets where even that normally red cave had turned to ash. I unlocked my door and threw myself onto my cot, unable to move. Even the turquoise had turned to smoky haze where my woolly brain drifted around the fragments of a word: *perspir-* ... *persp-* ... *pers-* ... like a dripping tap.

Out on the sea of linoleum flowers lay another folded piece of paper no doubt slid under my door by Dwight. Eventually I roused myself and grabbed it. *I see you like dropping your tampon wrappers on the bathroom floor. Why don't you think about picking them up? D.*

I was guilty of dropping bits of cellophane on the bathroom floor, but why would he care? The landlady swept them up in her weekly cleanings.

Love your characters, Dagmar said. You have to love them if you want your readers to. Well Dwight could go screw himself, I thought. I ripped up the note and crammed it in the wastebasket.

Dagmar was writing poems in her cabin on Hornby Island for the summer, sending me letters about swimming off the dock under a full moon with Taj Lambert, the hard-edge painter, and Maddox Tate, the playwright, feasts of halibut and clams, hookahs, Carlos Castaneda, and the Zen of unthinking. *This fall you've got to take Hawks's Modern Novel course,* she wrote. *You have to read novels if you want to write them. Hawks is hideously old school. He makes you read all the required books before the course starts and throws you out if you don't pass a test in the first week. But he is the best. Be my buddy in Hawks's course; we'll ace it.*

Another letter included her poem about the island:

> *Saturnina sailors*
> *in the Salish Sea*
> *1791.*
> *Ruffles, lace, quills, and paper*
> *to Malahat, Cowichan*
> *clastic rock*
> *and red-twigged buckthorn.*

Saturnina, Dagmar explained, was the Spanish ship whose Captain had named the island Isla de Lerena before George Vancouver got here. *We might all have been Spanish!* Then she told me Cleo, whose father was an editor at the *Province*, was coming to stay for a week. Cleo gave a champagne and body-painting party, and no one can get the purple out of their hair. Cleo won the Sunday magazine fiction contest last year, the youngest person ever to do it.

Damn Cleo, I thought.

Carla's cigarette voice buzzed through my door wanting me to watch *Edge of Night* on her tiny TV. She tuned in to the electric organ theme and splashy white letters plastered on city skyscrapers. Before I knew it, she'd poured me a Southern Comfort and told me Laurie Ann's mother died saving her from being run down by a car, her father Mike Karr married Nancy, a newspaper reporter, so Laurie Ann would have a mom. Mike, a lawyer, and Bill, the police chief, were best friends, but Nancy's sister Cookie was mixed up with a real psycho type, son of a rich family that hated Mike and Bill. Cookie's husband was mixed up with some loan sharks. Nicole Travis was accused of murder but Adam Drake, a lawyer in Mike's firm, got her off the charge, then hired her as his secretary and went to work for Jake Berman. Nicole wanted Adam to propose but instead Jake proposed.

The first Tide commercial came on.

– Still playing with fire, I see. (Carla topped up our drinks.) Don't pretend you don't know. I saw he picked you up. Hard to miss that yellow bus.

– He's breaking up; she went to Prince Rupert.

– Okay, she took a drag and blew out a long cloud of smoke. So ...

– So, he's sailing up to Desolation Sound.

– And you're going to go!

– He hasn't asked me, but if he does, I want to. He's taking his friend James.

– One chick and two guys. Good for you.

We went back to Nicole Travis and Jake's proposal. Would Nicole dump Adam, the man who saved her from prison and maybe even the electric chair? Would she run away to New York with Jake?

On the next commercial Carla started in on how, if I was going to work at the Biltmore, I'd have to jazz up. No pants at the Biltmore. Here, try this on, she said, and I squeezed a black miniskirt over my too-big hips.

– Have to buy you one, Carla said. We really aren't the same size.

– Oh no, I can't – I have to save money.

– We'll get a cheap one you can wear different tops with. Anyway you'll be earning more money so you'll be able to afford it. Trust me.

I said I doubted I'd be any good at waitressing, most likely get all the orders mixed up, forget which table they went to. Naw, it's easy, she said. You just remember the number of the table, and most people order the same thing.

– Your girlfriend's a sharp dresser even if she does wear pants.

– Who?

– The one with the Twiggy cut, nice boots, cords, silk shirts.

– Dagmar.

– Cool name too.

The electric organ crooned. Jake left his law firm and set up in New York. Adam begged Nicole not to follow Jake. She ran away anyway. Would Adam follow her to New York and finally convince her to marry him? We'd have to tune in tomorrow.

– She's a lezzie, eh?

– Who?

– Your pal Dagmar.

– No, I said, avoiding this uncertain Dagmar territory.

– Sure she is, you can tell, the way she cuts her hair and always wears pants.

– Well she has a boyfriend, Murray.

– She's one of those AC/DC types.

– Whatever that is.

– Swings both ways. Don't get me wrong, I don't mind what people do, long as it's not in my bed.

A framed picture of a man in army uniform stood on Carla's dresser – maybe nineteen – his wide, large eyes under a floppy beret gazing into the distance behind the photographer as though he could see the war itself and the wrong it would right. Carla never knew her dad. Her mom and dad never married, there wasn't time before he was blown up in the Battle of Dieppe. She remembered her mom checking the paper, then taking her to "parties" of people dressed in black and telling her to eat as much as she could, her mom slipping things into her bag. They'd have tarts and sandwiches and cakes for days after. Her mom had other boyfriends – oh sure, yeah. The last one, a longshoreman, started out really nice – he took her to restaurants and the PNE – they were going to buy a house – a real house – then he started asking her to sleep with one of his work buddies. They could make some extra money that way. She said no, he dumped her. After that she worked in the Woodward's ladies shoe department. Until she collapsed of a heart attack, in the middle of getting a different size shoe for a customer. She died a few days later.

– So how do they do it?

– Do what?

– Two girls, how do they get it on?

– I don't know.

– With fingers, do you think? Or tongues.

– Why don't you become one and find out!

I got up to go. She begged me to stay for the next show, promising not to tease me any more about lezzies, promising the next time her manager needed someone, I'd get the job, wanting to know what I had to do that was so important.

– Actually I'm writing something.

– Like a story ... like for a magazine?

– Sort of.

– You should send it to *True Story*. Mom and I always used to read that.

– It's a bit longer than that.

– Who's the heroine? What's she like? Is her husband mean?

– I don't think you'd like it.

– Yes I would. Let me read it. I'd love to read it.

– Well it's not really written yet.

– So is it going to be a book? I'm reading *The Secret Woman*.

– Yeah, it's going to be a novel.

– So ...

— So ... it doesn't really have a heroine.

— Honey, it's *gotta* have a heroine. *The Secret Woman*'s about Anna, her aunt leaves her an antique business, but it doesn't work out, but the aunt's nurse gets her a job as a governess. She falls in love with a ship's captain she meets at the castle. That's where her governess job is, but he's still married to a crazy woman from a Pacific island and they all end up on this island.

Carla wanted me to hurry up and write it so she could read it. She would even go out so the TV was off. I said it didn't bother me but she said she was going to go anyway, over to the Biltmore, see if it was busy and she could pick up a late shift, grab a bite in the kitchen. I got a couple of drumsticks and potatoes out of the fridge and threw them in a pot on my hotplate. Her platform heels clumped down the outside stairs.

In front of my plate I propped up Edith Wharton and opened it to my favourite passage about *magic casements of fiction* to *vistas on infinity*. Windows in the dark mansion of my brain, I thought. Everyone telling stories, sending them out like the arc lights on their tipping and revolving kettledrums that car dealers used to announce a new model, beaming fat bars of light into the night sky — everyone's bolts of lightdust criss-crossing, weaving in and out of each other on and on forever. They made conflicts and epiphanies like in Katherine Mansfield's "The Doll's House" and James Joyce's "Boarding House" — people like dolls living in stories — big strapping women like Mrs. Mooney who cut up morality with her butcher's cleaver. Doll children like Kezia who wanted to share their toys with the kids in dreaded mismatched rags. Unhinge the front of the rooming house, I thought, four characters in their rooms — let their stories beam out into the night sky on light waves to infinity.

But, Edith Wharton warned on another page, beware of autobiography! The novelist of autobiography is trapped in his own story. Casement turned to cryogenic capsule, freezing novelist like a snowman in a paperweight in her own little world. And yet *Martha Quest* was really just the story of Doris Lessing leaving home, wasn't it? What was this story I had to find that was not autobiography?

In my novel, Carla worked in a drab office of phone cubicles calling people all day trying to sell them vacuum cleaners. But she wanted to get into fashion design. She sews her own clothes, making up patterns just from seeing magazine pictures. Her boss takes her dancing, and his dates are fun but after a while he just wants a quick screw in a motel and then home to his wife. After ten months she's saved $65, but the vocational school doesn't have fashion-design courses. Why don't you train as a cook or a hairdresser, they ask. Or you could apprentice in a tailor's shop. Or work as a garment seamstress. The counsellor's wearing an orange A-line with brown sandals and green baubles. Carla's wearing a zebra-stripe jumpsuit and matching headband. Carla asks people she telephone-solicits if they know anything about fashion design and where you go to learn. Go to Paris or New York, a man says. Meet me after work, I'll tell you more. She doesn't sell any vacuum cleaners that day. Her boss says she's not with it in bed, she's not turning him on enough. He pushes her mouth over his cock.

Dwight, in my novel, was a hippie who worked part-time at a shoe store, and hung out at be-ins and happenings, playing his guitar. He loves to walk along the beach with Cynthia, a yoga teacher, simple and free, wearing something long and flowing down to her ankles, something wispy and light he can see through to her breasts. He writes songs for her and everyone loves them, including Ricky, a guitarist from Country Joe and the Fish who promises to show the songs to Country Joe. Next time Dwight sees the band they have a new guitarist. What happened to Ricky? He's starting his own band, doing warm-up at Rohan's. Rohan's bouncer won't let him back stage. A waitress brushes past his thigh while Dwight drinks two glasses of beer waiting for Ricky and his band. Then Ricky comes on in a white suit strobed to purple flashes and sings Dwight's song. Who the hell are you, Ricky asks Dwight.

I lugged my greasy dishes into the bathroom and squirted detergent on them under the bathtub tap.

Out in the hall, I found Dwight leaning against his doorframe.

– You really should let me look at your car; I could probably fix it in half an hour.

I hadn't driven my car in weeks. A thick layer of rotting tree blossoms blanketed its windshield.

– It's kind of obvious you're not driving it.

On Dwight's dresser stood a painting of crumbling mountains and burnt-out skeletons of skyscrapers.

– Yes, I painted that, he said following my gaze. He pointed at a chair.

– Sit down, I won't bite. I'll even leave the door open so you can make a quick escape.

Toolboxes and workboots, dirty clothes, food-caked plates, forks, and cardboard cartons of books completely covered the floor, the only free surface being the striped mattress on the iron cot, half-covered by a tired grey sheet. Piles of books stood on the dresser – Jack Kerouac, Allen Ginsberg, Charles Bukowski. Robert Creeley's For Love lay open on the striped mattress. On the tiny table between us lay a half-finished picture in icy blues and blacks of a woman staring at the moon while sitting in a boat drifting on a swirling river.

– I'm no longer blaming you for the missing beer, he announced, opening one and handing it to me. His eyes bulged from pasty cheeks under his frizz of mousy hair.

– It was Carla.

– That was weeks ago, I said. How come you're just telling me now?

– How come this is the first time you've deigned to talk to me, he smirked.

– How come you write me weird little notes about tampon wrappers?

– How come you don't clean up after yourself; the landlady's not your mother!

I asked him where he was from. His eyes gleamed. You're avoiding my question.

– How come you leave the toilet seat up?

– You're avoiding my question.

– Okay, I should pick them up but you're not my mother either.

Dwight swirled his beer in and out of his pale cheeks, fixing me with a pop-eyed stare, then swallowed, and told me he was from Sardis, which was about six miles from Cultus Lake.

– Like your licence-plate holder says Chilliwack Motors, eh, so I knew.

We'd even bussed to the same Chilliwack high school, and had the same English teacher, Mr. Stopworth, who'd made the same joke about women and spots in the "out out damn spot" scene, though Dwight'd gone to Chilliwack High ten years before me. Yeah, he smirked and added with a shrug, as though trying out for a lark an outlandish coat or the costume of Lady Macbeth, I'm from the ancient Persian city of Sardis. He leaned toward me, resting his elbows in some possibly wet paint and his chin on his hands. And I thought, yeah Sardis had a funny name like it wasn't from around here, but then most names were like that.

I said, so?!

– So, it's in the Book of Revelation. (Trying-out-for-a-lark shrug.)

– Not your Sardis.

– Nope, that's for sure, my Sardis is miles of hop fields and an instant-milk factory.

He held out a tin of Player's. I said I'd quit, and he said, You can quit again tomorrow. He tamped orangey-brown shreds into the V of a cigarette paper, rolled it, folded the paper under, licked the edge. Leaning against a cardboard box on the floor was a painting of a broken-off pine tree on a rocky crag; one stub of a branch held a few green needles above its burnt bark. It reminded me of Jack smashing things at his girlfriend. Dwight shared a wall with Jack, but said he hadn't heard anything.

Making a big show about *Did I mind the door being closed so we weren't both busted?* he kicked it shut and pulled a leather pouch from some hiding place in his closet. On the moon-staring woman's painting he tipped out a chunk of hash, carved off a piece, and rolled it with some weed into a joint. Down near the leg of his cot, another version of the icy-blue face stared from a hole in a brick wall clawed and tangled with roots.

– My ex, he said, waving the joint at the face. I toked, and we talked in little rasps, holding in dope.

– Okay, I said. Ever frame these, show them around?

– Naw, just do it for fun.

Somewhere on the floor he uncovered a portable record player and slid the *Dark Side of the Moon* out of its black cover. He thought of maybe setting up with the Stanley Park painters sometime, he said, but that would mean getting easels and packing all his shit and being organized. He was more of a spontaneous kind of guy.

– But you go to work, I said.

My eyes drifted back to his flames burning up skyscrapers and skulls, windows in the skeletal towers like frantic raging eyes. He said he set his own hours at the garage, pretty much went in when he wanted, quit when he wanted. Pink Floyd belted out the climbing bass, clinking coins and cash-register dings of "Money." *Spontaneous* linked to *combustion* linked to getting busted, linked to pigs on horses at the Maple Tree smoke-in, linked to fire linked to spontaneous generation, microbes in test tubes of broth, Bunsen burners ...

– But if you plan to go to work, you're not spontaneous ...

He tipped his chair back balancing himself on the back legs and fixed me with a crooked-toothed grin, Whoa ... that's heavy. Which was swirled away in the spacey organ chords and dreamy sax of "Us and Them" and its trailing echoes of *me me me* and *you you you*.

– But if you plan to be spontaneous ...

My thought wafted on a chorus of *Ahhhhhs* to golden clouds of Pink Floyd heaven.

– What?! Dwight's eyes widened and bulged above his stained teeth.

– If you plan to be spontaneous, it's not spontaneous.

He closed his eyes in the music's echo game with *blue*, then popped them open as if surprised to see me.

– But if you go to work when you want to it *is* spontaneous, isn't it?

I mulled this over. *Spontaneous* was getting mixed up with *cutaneous* and its horrible sidekick, *cute*, or even worse, *cuticles*. I zinged back to my train of thought.

– But if you plan to do work it isn't.

– Why not?

– Because plans are the opposite of spontaneous.

Echoes of *down* and *out* slalomed down the white slope of this thought leaving interlocking zigzags in its pristine powder.

– But where does the plan come from?

Dwight leaned across the table, resting his chin on his hand, elbow in a grungy saucer, and stared at me bug-eyed.

– It comes from ... (I didn't want to say that stupid word that everyone says vaguely in high school, but what other word was there?) Society.

– Society says we have to work, I called after him as he went out to the fridge and brought back two more beers.

– Society ... (He cracked the beers.) Like those boobsy ditzes in their little diamond tiaras on the back pages of the paper.

I didn't read the paper.

"Brain Damage" crooned of daisy chains and heads containing aliens. The song's lunatic laughter spilled from the leer of Dwight's stained crooked teeth, his hands clawing the air above his head, bat-arms mocking a madman in the attic, or the blood-dripping nails of a corpse rising from a tomb.

– Anyway, I said, noticing that night had darkened Dwight's tiny window, you can't plan to be spontaneous.

– Or, I added, miscellaneous or simultaneous.

He flipped the needle back to "Us and Them," lit a large red, drip-laden candle and turned off the overhead bulb. Beer swirled around my tongue, golden, sparkling, carrying me off on a rushing creek I'd never tasted before.

– But you can't not be spontaneous, he said.

Candlelight puffed out bags under his eyes and smudged his face with two-day growth. The song flung us against the walls of a giant spinning PNE teacup, till I finally asked him why not, and he said because the plan to be spontaneous is spontaneous. And I said but how do you know you're being spontaneous, because if you know you're being spontaneous then you're not being spontaneous, it's like planning not to plan, and he said knowing what you know in that moment when you know you're being spontaneous is spontaneous, and it's just as spontaneous when you know that you're planning not to plan.

I broke off stalagmites of wax around the candle-flame and melted them down into a lake of molten wax, and then he did it too, pressing

69

channels in the soft edges to release new runoffs of blobs, drips, and tears down the slopes of its mountain.

— So why did you paint her face bricked off by a wall like that?

He gave me a sharp look as though I'd poked him with a stick.

— Because she's going to die.

— Oh ... I'm sorry.

He mashed another V in the candle, letting down a trickle of wax.

— She's got breast cancer.

— Lots of people get cured from that nowadays.

— She's not going to be.

— How long has she got?

— I dunno. She's lost all her hair. Can't eat much. She lies around, cries a lot.

We said nothing for a while, the album went on in its dreamland.

— I had to get out, he said. I couldn't stand it anymore.

— So she's your wife?

— Yeah ... I guess so ...

— Carla says you have a little girl.

— Yeah — she's five — stays with her grandmother a lot.

The needle bumped and scratched against the centre of the album. I thought of Dwight's wife wandering around shadowy rooms of her apartment, lying down, not sleeping, sitting in a kitchen chair, not drinking a cup of tea, holding onto a doorframe, not reading her magazine.

I thought of my grandfather, who died far away in Winnipeg when I was ten. I remembered being six and watching him washing his green-and-white '56 Chev — wiping off the whitewalls and polishing the chrome — me standing in the garage looking at his pinkish saggy face and his pinkish hairless head, him in his plaid shirt and suspenders looking at me, saying nothing, then carrying on sponging off the car. Maybe he was still mad at me because I told him in front of the whole dinner table, Aunt Bee and Uncle Ted and my four cousins, that I (like Dad) didn't believe in God, and he couldn't make me. The whole table stopped, forks halfway to mouths. I'm not going to, he said in his whispery voice like a hollow ghost talking.

Gramma said he'd been gassed in the trenches in World War I, and that's why he had lung disease and almost no voice. Dad called him the old man. All the old man cared about, Dad said, was his car and his TV and his church on Sunday. The old man believed in God and life in the hereafter; Dad believed in the here and now. The old man believed in suits and ties; Dad believed in nudism and tie-dyes. The old man believed in Diefenbaker; Dad believed in Tommy Douglas. What did the old man know about art or being creative? Nothing. The old man hadn't paid for Dad to go to art school. The old man had made Dad into a carpenter, and now Dad was screwed up, he said, and would never make it as an artist.

Then the old man died. He wasn't Grampa, he was just the old man in a far away place, who was still wearing plaid shirts and suspenders and washing his '56 Chev, even though I knew I could never see him again. People would put him in a box and bury it in the ground. Dad didn't cry and neither did I when he died. Now *old man* was hip lingo for a guy you shacked up with.

But maybe there was something wrong with you if you didn't cry when your own grandfather died; and what if it was a friend talking to me one day and then never again the next? What if it was Mom? Or Dad?

I stood up.

– Thanks for dropping by, Dwight said.

– Thanks for the beer, I said, and headed back to my room.

It was late, but I couldn't sleep. I got out the green notebook that Dagmar had given me, brushed the soft suede cover across my cheek, opened it to the smell of clean new pages. Here I wrote scenes and ideas about Dwight, Carla, and Jack – D, C, and J – what they said to each other and U Girl. What they fought about. How they tried to live their lives according to plans that didn't quite work. What would happen next? I plunged into the blank future of my novel. As I typed up pages on the library typewriters, a long train of story stretched out behind me. Where was it going, behind its comet engine blazing into the dark?

The notebook made me think of Dagmar in her cabin on Hornby Island. Was she too writing in the middle of the night, beside her wood stove, in a pool of light from a Coleman lamp? Was she writing me a letter or writing a poem to send me? She was always so quick and brilliant when we talked, so full of ideas and books I'd never heard of — I was tongue-tied — but writing a letter, I could take my time, rewrite.

I would tell her about writing at night when everyone was asleep, like walking through fresh new snow, just you making footprints, no one else around. Everyone was dreaming; everyone had given up trying to be something, trying to make their way and instead let themselves be flooded with dreams. But you, writing at night, walked around in this dreamtime.

Tiptoe through the tulips, Tiny Tim whispered in a high falsetto, gazing at me from my turquoise wall, with his bushy-eyebrowed, hair-over-the eye, her-him look. Tiptoe, tiptoe. Things like this would happen, and I would think, did that happen to me or did that happen to U Girl? I became another I in my novel, a glowing novel I in a glowing novel country. I passed through a frontier. I became not I — I and not I at the same time. I had to get outside my story, Edith Wharton said. I had to not go back through the border.

I could tell Dagmar this in my letter ... Did she too become another person in her poems? I thought of Dagmar reading my letter, Dagmar all to myself imagining me in my turquoise room, Dagmar imagining worlds behind my words, just as I imagined her hikes up Mount Geoffrey, or her reading to islanders beside the loom of her friend, the silk weaver. *Worlds* and *words* — only one letter different.

Next morning I found the pen and the journal tangled in my sheets. I rushed off to work.

CHAPTER 5

One night, lying awake in the dark, after even Carla had got home from the Biltmore and gone to bed, I heard thumps and shouts from Jack's room. *This is what you get, bitch.* Then slaps. Maybe it was just the way they did sex. I thought vaguely of sadism — it was some Freudian thing wasn't it? Some sex game. But Dad's *Joy of Sex* said nothing about people getting off on hurting each other. Or getting off on being hurt. Why would they need *that* to get turned on? People with whips and spikes and claws. Rattling around in my head with the Marquis de Sade and some other guy in a bathtub in a lunatic asylum.

From Jack's room, a crack and the shattering of glass or china. *Now look what you've done. Stupid little hussy. Stupid cunt.* Her voice, *Don't, Jack. Don't, please, please, please. I'll clean it up.* Followed by, *No, Jack. No,* and a series of crashes. I leapt out of bed and, leaving my light off, stuck my head into the hall. The diamonds and squares of linoleum glared in a sleep haze under the dim light. The grubby little fridge kept its blank face shut. Dwight's door and Carla's were darkly locked. Wood cracked. Jack's girlfriend hit a wall or chair. He was beating her up. I should stop him. But how?

He yanked open his door.

— What do you want?

He stood there in jeans, no shirt — belt dangling from his hand. I kept my T-shirt, underpants, and bare legs behind my door.

— Is she all right, I asked.

— Mind your own business.

He slammed the door.

Silence. I gathered my blankets around me and huddled on the cot in the dark. Should I phone the police? But maybe they'd stopped. Would the police do anything, or would they just say, as we'd learned in women's studies, it was a *domestic quarrel*? Bickering erupted again from Jack's room. Then smacks and yelps. I curled up on the bed and wrapped the pillow around my ears, but that didn't stop me from hearing Jack yell, *well get out then, stupid little slut.* Bodies crashed and scuffled in the hall. Something banged into my door, making it crack and jolt against the lock. I threw on some pants and a sweater and opened it. Jack's girl-friend slumped onto my floor – eyeshadow and mascara smeared down her cheek, her patchwork go dress (one of those mini-length smocks so popular then) ripped off her shoulder. Her torn underpants fell down as I helped gather up her purse and her sandals scattered around the hall and took her into my room.

I offered her some safety pins. Her hands shook so hard, she couldn't pick them up. She told me her name was Cheyenne, and let me pin her torn dress together. She didn't want an ambulance or the police. She was all right. She was sorry for disturbing me. No, she didn't want a coffee or water. She wasn't sure about a cab. Jack was okay, really. He didn't mean any harm. It was her fault. What was her fault, I asked. She took out a compact, applied some lipstick, and wiped a Kleenex over streaks of mascara. It was nothing really, she said, just ... she didn't do things very well. She wiped another tear off her swollen face, was again sorry to disturb me. Maybe she should take a cab, but don't call yet, call in a minute. In a few minutes. She started backcombing her hair on top of her head, smoothing long locks away from her bangs and over the backcombed tangle.

– No one should treat you the way he did, I said.

She remained silent, pulling hair across her face. I thought about waking Carla; Carla would talk her language, would *honey* her and *girl* her and *baby* her into going home.

– What do you want to do?

– I don't know.

– You must take a cab; you must stay away from him.

She studied her hair, looked toward Jack's room, then at last let me call a cab. We sat silently waiting for it. I got up every few minutes to check. I told her women had rights, and she deserved better.

– I'll be okay, she said. He's not really that bad.

The cab pulled up and she went down the outside steps clinging on to the rail. From my window, I saw her go up to the yellow car and start talking to the driver. In the glare of a street lamp, her bare shoulder poked through the safety-pinned dress. I went back to bed but the whole stupid scene kept reeling around in my thoughts. The cab drove off. Then footsteps came up the outside stairs, and she went back into Jack's room.

Next morning, a sudden flash of light jolted me from my balcony door. I leapt up clutching blankets and sheets around my T-shirt and bare legs.

– Don't mind me, Carla said, sneaking in without going through the hall.

I fell back on the bed, heart pounding, eyes too bleary to open.

– Hey, open your eyes – look what I brought you.

A cinnamon sticky bun right under my nose. It was already past lunch time. Didn't hear a thing last night, Carla said. They must've been gettin it on.

She winked. Then flopped down next to me on the pile of blankets in her turquoise-and-orange mini jumpsuit and black patent leather sandals – big plastic turquoise baubles on her wrist, neck and ears. Harry, her boss, wanted to try me out at the Biltmore, this afternoon!

– But he hasn't even interviewed me.

– He knows you're smart – a U girl; long as you look good, he's happy. Anyways two a' the girls are sick, he's desperate.

She knew the perfect place on Fourth to get me a black skirt and maybe some fishnet hose. I refused; my $10 budget for the week already gone.

– It'll cost pennies; it's a secondhand place – anyways you're earning more money, you can afford it.

– I haven't even got the job.

She dragged me off to the store. I could use another skirt for my filing job, I thought, instead of wearing the same old beige A-line. What about this, I said, holding up a shirt like one of Dagmar's, a plain cotton with army-uniform shoulder straps, and a pair of black jeans like I'd seen her wear.

— Nope, ya gotta show off more.

— But I love these.

— So get them anyway; you'll get the money back on your first paycheque.

She found me a tight black skirt with a slit up the back, but nothing in the tops fit. I didn't get the shirt and jeans.

Back at my room, Carla lent me a low-slung tank top; Mom's old T-strap sandals completed my outfit. Then, oh, I didn't realize you didn't shave.

— So?

— So — you shave your legs.

— Yeah.

— So why not your pits?

— I get rashes.

— Honey, in a top like this, you can't have hair.

She said my razor was dull, I'd be fine if I used her electric one, and why not try some Right Guard as well, handing me the spray can. (Mom always got the no-scent kind, squeezing on her underarms small squirts of Yardley for Men. One more thing I didn't need to buy.)

I pressed the button on Carla's aerosol, filling the room with a cloud of tart cologne, and spreading an icy shrivelling blast onto my "pits." I thought longingly about the shirt and pants back at the store — the way I wanted to look, like Dagmar in trousers and shirts and jackets, not dolling myself up for men, the way Carla did, and now here I was dolling myself up — because it was Carla, and it mattered to her, and I supposed I wouldn't get the job if I didn't.

She dashed over to her room through the hall, getting things so she could do my hair.

— You can't have it down when you're serving. I waited, in the black skirt and top, trying not to think about taking orders from tables full of Geers and Aggies, who might throw me into the pond in front of the library. Carla will be training me, I thought, it couldn't be that hard, thousands and millions of women do it.

A whistle sounded from the door. Dwight leaned against the frame, one blackened tooth snagged across another in his pasty face. The fridge slammed, and Jack too stuck his head in, beer can in hand. Oh nice, yeah, he said. And sorry about last night. Yeah, she's fine, everything's fine. I'm takin good care of her.

— What's the occasion, if I might ask, Dwight drawled.

— She's getting a job at the Biltmore, now out — both of you!

Carla breezed in with hairspray and bobby pins and slammed the door. I felt jittery and unreal in this horrible charade of womanhood, the exact opposite of the smiling bronzed men leaning out from their hull in my sailing poster. Humming away to herself, Carla piled my hair this way and that, then combed it out again, and backcombed the top, smoothing another layer over that, just as Jack's girlfriend had done with hers. She pinned that in place and began twisting the rest into a French roll, murmuring what beautiful hair, how smooth and easy, how hers with its kinks and waves always sprang out of her clips.

I fled to thoughts of my novel. Where will Carla go in my story, I wondered, as she fiddled and patted and stroked my hair into place, anchoring it with bobby pins. Would the real Carla do telephone solic-iting and get mixed up with her fat, comb-over boss? Would she do that thing to him I'd seen in Dad's *Joy of Sex* — suck his penis? Would she do it to keep her job? Or get into fashion design?

— What're you thinking about, hon, Carla said, adding another bobby pin.

— Nothing really.

— Oh yeah? You were miles away, you didn't even notice me snipping.

In the mirror propped on my table, her turquoise-frosted nails dashed around my ears, tucking in strands of hair.

— I bet, she said, you were thinking about your book!

She picked up the hairspray and told me to close my eyes. After-ward, it felt like shellac Dad sprayed on paper lanterns, my head like a lightbulb inside a crisp tissue balloon.

— What's your book got if it doesn't have a heroine?

— A bunch of people living in a house and their friends outside the house.

Carla snugged and smoothed.

— I'm trying to figure out whether the things they really do should be in the novel or whether they should all turn into completely different characters.

— You mean it's about real people?

— Yes and no … I don't know.

— You're writing about us all in this house, aren't you? About me and Dwight and Jack and your lezzie friend and Professor Lennon! Aren't you?!

— Yeah, sort of.

— Well make my name Tiffany, like Tiffany Whitney on *Edge of Night*, that's my favourite name and make me meet a somebody like Professor Lennon, but not him, someone like him.

The phone rang. It was "Professor Lennon" a.k.a. Nigel wanting to pick me up in half an hour so we could go out on the boat.

— Hey let's get out of here, hon, Carla tossed across the room, we'll be late.

— I didn't know we had a date, I said to Nigel.

— Oh for God sake, tell him tomorrow!

Carla threw her hair things in a bag and stomped over to her room.

— I'd love to go, I said to Nigel, but I'm going for a job …

— Great, he said. I'll pick you up in half an hour.

He hung up.

— So you're going sailing. Harry'll kill me!

Carla, in black heels and matching bag, headed toward the outside door. When I said I was still going to the Biltmore, she threw her arms around me, dragging me toward the steps. Then tapped her fingers on the banister while I stuck a note on my door for Nigel.

— I thought you wanted him to whisk you away in my novel.

— Don't go hookin me up with any two-timer.

At the Biltmore, we headed through the mostly empty tables to an office down a hall past the washrooms – grey walls, like you find in school basements, and no windows, a fluorescent ceiling fixture glaring down on Harry's desk and its clutter of papers. Weird, he looked almost as I had imagined Carla's boss in my novel, waist bulging over his pants, thick eyebrows and fat lips, thin strands of hair combed over his baldness. In a bright smooth voice, like something you'd hear on TV, she introduced me as the smart girl she'd been telling him about. Stand over against the door, he barked, waggling the fat cigar between his lips. Let's get a look at you. He puffed a big cloud of smoke into the room.

– The top's nice, turn sideways let's see what ya got under it. Where'dja get the sandals – they look like something my mother wore in the forties.

– I think she's going to be really good, Carla said in her TV voice.

– Well you're training her so it's up to you.

He took my name, address, SIN, and phone number.

After a few orders, I figured it wasn't that hard. I could really use the money too, if I was going to take days off to go sailing. In three shifts with good tips I could make more than I made in a week of filing.

– Don't write down every word, Carla said. It's taking too long, we're getting busy.

– I'll forget something.

– Use codes like G+T, BLT, or Wh+Ck. And smile more, ya gotta sell more drinks. You look like you're writing a test in school. Gotta sell.

– So how do you sell?

– Tell them what we've got on tap.

She rattled off a string of names I scribbled on the back of my pad.

– Ask the men if they'd like a martini, a Bloody Mary, or a scotch; women like Pink Ladies or spritzers. Have fun. Smile right into their eyes, especially the men.

I convinced a man to order a rum and Coke for himself and a Tequila Sunrise for his wife/girlfriend. Pleased with myself, I took it to the bartender, and rushed off to a table of Geers in their red jackets to see if they wanted another jug. I hoped none of them would recognize me on campus, especially near the library pool.

They'd gotten louder with the first round, bound together in a red clump by a joshing, goofy energy full of belligerence yet faintly sheepish, as though ashamed of the very inability of such belligerence to amount to anything, which made them badger and kibitz all the harder. All except one had hair carved straight across their foreheads and necks and sliced in a curve around their ears. Only one they called Longhair sported a curly red beard and blond hair to his shoulders.

Every few minutes the jokester in the group would make a crack, causing a round-faced man eating a double side of fries to erupt into another volley of giggles and snorts and suckings of air through his nose, which led to even more volleys of hysterical giggles. Or the challenger would stand up and boom out over the table that he bet no one could down a whole glass of beer or eat a whole hamburger without breathing. Another one bet that Professor Harding would fail 50 percent of the class. And someone else said 90 percent. All except Genius, a dark fellow with glasses, who said he'd only passed by a fluke. They seethed and swirled around each other like rushing water crashing and tumbling through rapids, as certain as a river of where they were going.

I had to make Carla and Dwight as certain as this in my novel, I thought, make them dash across the page as sure as Bracken Creek rushing down Mount Cheam, as certain as Lawrence painting Miriam's ideals and Clara's passions, and I too, in my novel, must forge ahead across the page, like stampeding buffalo.

— Hey, Beehive's back, one of them yelled.

I stood beside Longhair, since men with long hair were generally groovy and hip, likely to smoke weed and read books, whereas shorthairs were more likely to be hardnosed and bullying, probably going into business to become squares in suits. Longhairs went to rock concerts and played guitars or flutes; shorthairs went to football games and drove souped-up cars. I grinned like a toothpaste ad.

— Bet she doesn't.

— Bet she does.

— How much?

— A jug.

Did they want another pitcher of Carlsberg?

— Okay who says she doesn't?

Challenger wrote down names.

— Doesn't what, I asked.

– Doesn't go to UBC.

– Yes, I'm a student there.

– You owe me, Challenger bellowed, sparking a round of giggles.

– One pitcher. You gonna drink it all without breathing, Genius commented. More giggles.

– Bet she's in nursing.

– Nope, bet she's in home ec.

– Don't tell.

I stood pencil poised above the pad.

– No, she's too good lookin for home ec.

– Teaching, she's gonna teach grade one.

– All wrong, I said.

– Aw, not arts.

– She's in arts.

– I'm hoping to go into science, I said. I'm taking math, which wasn't exactly true, just something I'd thought about. Carla waved from across the room, then a minute later beckoned me over.

– Longhair's gotta question.

– Ask it, Longhair.

– He's too chicken.

Giggles of nervous laughter ricocheted around the table.

– What?

Longhair pointed at the menu in front of him on the table, asking what it said, and I bent over to read it, close enough to smell oil and sweat on his red windbreaker.

– Cheeseburger, I said, looking up in time to see three pairs of eyes across the table staring down my top. I straightened up.

– She doesn't.

Giggles, elbowing and boasts of *you lose* broke out. Carla signalled urgently.

– So what'll it be guys?

– She's mad.

– No, she's not.

– You're not mad, are you, Beehive?

I pasted on my smile.

Carla hauled me off, saying she had to talk to me. One of your customers complained, she said, but don't worry, I told him it was your first day. It was the rum and Coke and Tequila Sunrise – too slow, she said. Apologize, she said. Be friendly, offer them a free side of fries.

– But the bartender's slow, I said.

– Ya gotta know how to handle him. Watch.

She pushed through the crowd of men around the bar, Excuse me, honey. Just sliding by. Hey where'd you get those fabulous biceps?

Some with straight mouths placed their orders, and slapped down bills, barely moving their lips. Others lounged with one elbow on the bar, leaning there as though they owned it, waving their hands, gabbing away. I could see Dagmar doing that, Dagmar in black jeans, white shirt, and linen jacket leaning against the bar, cool as cool, with a scotch on the rocks, gabbing away to friends about all the things writers know about like Pablo Neruda's lovers or the relationship between Cavafy and E.M. Forster. But Dagmar was far away on Hornby Island; her last letter had been about Rilke's *Notebooks of Malte Laurids Brigg*, a novel made of entries in a journal, which I simply *must* read. And think about for my green notebook. *Brigg is from a noble family in Denmark, but he's now poor, wandering around Paris.*

Carla jiggled through the crowd. The men parted, smiled. She cozied up to Dan, called him handsome, and asked him for a date. He flashed her a smile and filled the order.

I took the drinks over to the complaining couple, who oddly looked as though they might have just come from church, he in a pale-blue Dacron jacket and beige polyester pants, and she in a pleated mauve dress with blue gloves and purse and one of those hats, in a peach colour, from the thirties or forties with netting over the eyes, which might well have been the case, since they were both older than my grandmother. No, they did not want french fries, he said. They didn't eat junk like that. Why would they want french fries when they wanted drinks?

– Oh Ward, why not – what does it matter now?

– Because we don't eat that stuff.

His thin grey hair had the same sliced-off trim as the shorthairs at the Geers' table.

— Just bring us the bill, he said, and find another line of work because you're sure no good at this.

— In a few days I'll probably get the hang of it, I said, stretching the corners of my mouth as wide as possible into my cheeks, and watching the sunburnt faces of Nigel and a friend as they picked out a table in my section. They must've been out on *Windsong*.

Like night burglars stepping through my window, those mountainish, treeish sea-wolf eyes crept under the helmet of my swooped-up hair. Was I Cultus Wolf, or Beehive, Failed Waitress, or Novelist?

— Suit yourself, Dacron Greyhair muttered as though he could read my thoughts, but you won't get my business.

Just treat him like any other customer, Carla whispered, rolling her eyes, when I pointed out Nigel.

It turned out that the friend was the "James" I'd heard so much about but never met. James had gone to university with Nigel, he told me. They'd acted in the same drama club and sailed together out of some place called Shoreham near Brighton. James had a Ph.D. in classics. James had crewed on a cutter from London to Gibraltar and skippered a yacht from Vancouver to Hawaii. He'd gone for a month with no land and days with twenty-foot waves crashing over him. James thought Desolation Sound would be a lark.

— I'm a dab hand at yarding sails, I said, hauling anchor, stowing canvas, sheeting, cleating.

— I expect you'll have seen my sister Sandy in here with this chap, James commented.

— Not lately, Nigel muttered.

— Oh yeah, you're having some sort of tiff, aren't you.

Let Nigel make his own choices, I thought, beginning to not like James very much. Nigel ordered them beers and mentioned that the nosey bloke across my hall was here too.

Sure enough, Dwight, in a paisley shirt, had selected a table near the exit to the washrooms. He sat there alone, slouching back in his chair, picking something out of his fingernail, then resting his elbows on the table and flipping through a book. Like a student in a new classroom, I thought, knowing he could be taking someone's regular seat. He stakes out a place, sets out his books, and doesn't make eye contact.

— So your square friends are talkin about me, Dwight drawled, when I got to his table.

— You didn't have to come here.

He was reading *For Love* by Robert Creeley.

— It's a free country.

He wondered if he should get a Guinness or a Heineken like my square friends, or just order a Moosehead. He'd fixed my car and driven it around to test it out. Oh thanks, I said. How much do I owe you? Just for the parts, he said. Labour's free. This with a crooked-toothed grin and pasty, baggy-eyed look like it was supposed to mean something.

— Don't look like that, Dwight said, when I came back with the Moosehead.

— Like what?!

— Like you're drilling holes right through a person.

— Got any more smart suggestions?

— Ya gotta smile and welcome customers if you're gonna make it as a waitress.

— I am smiling.

I showed all my teeth.

— More like dissecting your victim in a lab. Anyways, I saw my ex today.

— So.

— So she wanted me to go get her pills, she couldn't get out of bed. Then she wanted me to paint another picture of her.

— So, are you going to?

— I might as well move back in, if I do that.

— Maybe she'll get better.

— What is it with you — don't you get it? She has cancer.

— Sorry. I just thought ... maybe it's not for sure. Sorry.

— I think you have an irate customer.

Blue Dacron Jacket waved furiously.

— You don't learn, do you?!

– Oh Ward, don't be so mean.

– Sorry.

I handed him the bill.

– He's not really mean, just doesn't know how to talk to people, she said from under her black netting.

– That's okay, I said.

Carla whispered she was taking a break; I'd be all right, she could tell I was a natural even if Mr. Blue Dacron didn't know a good waitress when he saw one. I smelled a whiff of something. Dwight called her an alky. He said, what was a smart, university girl like me doing hanging out with an alky? She headed off down the hall past the washrooms, washrooms with blue lights, she told me, so addicts couldn't see their veins to shoot up. Dan the bartender followed close behind her, cigarette behind the ear, untying his bartender's apron and swinging it over his shoulder. Harry the boss lit another cigar and took over the bar. All around the room smoky haze wafted in layers and shafts from the light fixtures.

Blue Dacron Jacket left. Another couple took their table – he with freckled face, beefy arms, a frayed T-shirt over a beer gut – she in a dark stretchy tent-like dress – her prim glasses and shoulder-length hair oddly familiar – along with something steadfast and enduring, like a mountain. Oh my, I didn't recognize you, she said when I discovered it was my filing companion Lorna. Of course I remembered, they only lived a few blocks away. He ordered a Molson's; he'd got his welfare cheque. She didn't want anything. You could have a Perrier, I suggested (trying out my new vocabulary). It's water with a bit of fizz. From France.

Looking white, she lurched out of her seat, and headed for the ladies. I brought Steve his Molson's and followed her into the can. She wiped her mouth with a wet paper towel, and we stood in the blue light, our faces like raccoons with shadowed eyes.

She'd been to the doctor that morning; he said she was pregnant. (How glad I was Mom had got me on the pill, how glad I'd stayed on them, not like Dagmar who didn't bother with them, said it was simple enough to get an abortion, she'd had at least two. Maybe when you lived in Dunbar you knew the right people and you could do that. Not me. Not Lorna.) Lorna said she'd asked her doctor for the pill, and he wouldn't prescribe them; he said she'd be fine with the foam. That was outrageous, I said.

She was about a month gone. To get an abortion she would have to ask the same doctor to refer her to the hospital committee; or she could try another doctor, a clinic. More weeks would go by waiting for committee approval, *if* they approved. Her boyfriend didn't know. For sure if he knew, he'd want her to keep it, and then where would they be, him not getting work, and her on a file-clerk's wage. She heaved out big sobs, certain she'd lose her job.

If she didn't get an abortion, she'd be trapped on welfare, she'd never get to UBC. But he'd kill her if he found out. He already thought they should get married.

– You can do it, I said. You have the right to *choose.*

– But this committee decides if my health is in danger. *They* decide.

Her shoulders slumped; a mountain ground down by glaciers. It would be okay, I said. They passed almost everyone because mental health counted for health and obviously she'd be really unhappy if she was forced into this and it wouldn't be any good for a child either.

I put my arms around her and hugged her, but it was she, the mountain, who enfolded me. I'd stepped into her closet of furs.

I'm not really here, I thought, emerging from the can and looking out over the tables and drinkers: James drawing something on a napkin, pointing there and there, dividing the air with a palm; Nigel leaning back in his booth, reflecting bar-lights in his spectacles; the Geers shining, jostling, beaming at one another, listening to Glasses, the Genius; Dwight flashing his grubby teeth at me; Carla straightening her skirt, emerging from somewhere with Dan the bartender. It isn't me doing this, I thought, I'm not really here, I'm not really a cocktail waitress or even a filing clerk. I'm a tatter of smoke wafting in a dream.

CHAPTER 6

Dagmar showed up at my room one afternoon, out of the blue from her island, in town to read with a poet from San Francisco. You wouldn't happen to have some hash I could score, she yelled across to Dwight hunched over a painting and filling the hall with his incessant Pink Floyd. Of course he did. I see you're into Creeley and Ginsberg, she said, when they'd traded baggies and cash. Come along to the reading.

It was in Brock Hall among the caved-in couches of a student lounge. Al Boyd, Dagmar's mod poetry prof, stuck a microphone on a stand and directed a student with folding chairs – a woman in beads and Bombay cotton I remembered from Nigel's class. A cigarette burned on an ashtray balanced on one of the chairs, another dangled from the corner of his mouth. Surveying the setup, he reached into his jacket and pulled out a pack of Player's, started to put one in his mouth, realized there was one already there, took the lit cigarette out of his mouth, stubbed it on the ashtray, and lit up a new one.

A woman with heavily mascaraed eyes and hennaed hair sat behind a row of books on a folding table. Several men stood around another table where a jolly plump woman in halter top and miniskirt sold cans of beer from a box she kept under the table and under her jacket. The men stood with folded arms, occupying space like large animals in a pasture I probably wanted to avoid. I was glad it was Dagmar who was reading with them, but there was no sign of her.

Al Boyd fiddled with a tape recorder, then called one of the beer men over to the mike, who said *test test test, one-two-three-four,* and *Mary had a little lamb* among whines and screeches. *Feedback,* one of the men said.

They stood in a circle swigging beer. One pinched a cigarette between thumb and finger, took a drag, and blew a cloud of smoke out his nose. Another kept his thumb in his pocket and held his eyelids barely open above a bushy black beard. He was a cat down in Texas, one of them said. Blackbeard shifted from foot to foot, looked at the mike. A man came in with a bag of books. Hey man, how's it goin? When's this show happenin?

Dwight, smelling like acrylic paint and engine grime, grabbed the chair next to me and said he felt like he was back in Chilliwack High. He asked me how to take notes and whether there'd be a test. I asked him if he'd cleaned up his room lately, and was Ginsberg his favourite poet? Bukowski's better, he said, wanting to know whether that football huddle was the guys who were reading tonight and when my lady-poet friend was going to show up. He'd never heard a lady-poet read. Quit callin her lady-poet, I said. He ambled over to the beer woman, then looked at the books. A man in a Stetson came in, told his girlfriend to grab some seats while he said hello.

Dagmar strode up to Boyd, who carried on unrolling wire to the tape recorder as she talked. She waved to me in the back row, took some pamphlets out of her bag, and held one out to Boyd. He pointed at the book table and went back to his wiring. Maybe he wasn't the friendly prof she always talked about, hip and open, into dope, the Rolling Stones, and Bob Dylan. Maybe he just wanted to be hip by hanging out with young people. But how could you be friends with someone completely bald except for a thin ponytail off the back of his head?

Landscapes. That was the title of Dagmar's pamphlet. A friend on Hornby printed them. She signed one under the title, *For my faithful friend Frances*, then took me over to Boyd and introduced me, saying I was a novelist. So that was how you did it! You just walked up to people and said you were a novelist. You made up a story. You acted like it was true. But what happened to the real you?

Boyd put a limp hand in mine. He seemed to know that I wasn't really a novelist, and if no one thought you were one, you weren't one were you? He called to Dave to test again and rewound the tape to see if it had recorded. People drifted in. Someone hauled a lamp over close to the mike, but the cord wasn't long enough so the mike and recording equipment had to be moved.

You've gotta get to know people Dagmar said, dragging me over to the circle of men. What was she going to do, make me tell *them* I was a novelist too? But if I was going to be equal I had to act equal. We squeezed between Blackbeard and Hey Man. They went on talking about the San Francisco scene and City Lights bookstore. They'd published Ginsberg and others I'd never heard of – Rexroth, O'Hara, Duncan. They swigged beer, dragged on cigarettes, wondered whether they should go to the Cecil or the Yale after the reading, till someone said weren't all the pubs closed on Sunday up here?

Hi, I'm Dagmar Lindegaard. She held out her hand to Blackbeard. John, he said, switching his beer to his left hand and touching hers for a moment, then going on with where they would drink afterwards, someone was staying with Dave so why not Dave's house. Has anyone read Cavafy? Dagmar looked around the group, made herself taller, poking her head above John's shoulder. So clean and classical, she went on, so droll. She held up the *Selected Poems* with its stern face of Cavafy printed in gold on the blue cover. We need a bootlegger, Hey Man said, maybe Allen'll give us what's left over. Cavafy, Bookbag said, Didn't he die in ... like ... 1933? No one said anything.

Okay now we can start, Ross's here. A short pudgy man with a mane of thick golden hair strolled up to the circle, and threw his arms around Smoke Nose, hey Ken, long time no see. Dave returned from mike-testing and stood with the others around the mass of hands clasping broad backs of Ken and Ross. Then Ross launched into a joke.

— I bet none of you've been to a bullfight and then gone by yourself into a restaurant afterwards and ordered dinner.

— Why's that, Ross.

— Cuz if you had, you wouldn't want to hear about a guy I know who did that.

— Is this the one where the guy eats bullshit?

— Okay I won't tell ... Why's everyone looking at me like I just farted or something ... Okay he went into a restaurant, it was after the bullfight, and he was hungry from getting all revved up watching the fight, he ordered their special, and they brought him a plate with two huge balls on it.

– Ha ha, very funny, Ross.

– Wait, there's more, the next day he went to another bullfight and after that he was hungry again so he went to the same restaurant and ordered the daily special, and they brought him a plate with two humungous balls on it.

– And I bet, Hey Man smirked, that he did the same thing the next day too.

– How did you know, Ross asked. Seriously, how did you know? ... Cuz that's exactly what he did, and again they brought out a plate with balls on it, but they were tiny, so the guy said, what happened to your daily special, and the waiter said, the toreador doesn't always triumph.

– Ha ... uh ha ... uh ha, Bookbag surveyed the room, waving to someone at the book table. John of the black beard shifted from foot to foot, folded his arms, unfolded them. Ken took another drag, blew smoke out of his nose, said nothing.

Boyd said we were ready to start. The circle broke up and meandered over to seats. Squinting at some notes in his hand, Boyd patted his jacket here and there till he found his glasses. John was an anchor man in the Vancouver scene, he said, he hardly needed introduction after his book *Intrical*, which the *Georgia Straight* called "a truly original voice," Vancouver's voice of the decade. Which decade, Ross shouted. More recent than yours, Blackbeard said, ambling up to the mike. The circle of friends laughed.

Anchor man. How did you get to be that? I pictured a Popeye John hurling a boat hook off a freighter.

John placed a bundle of papers and his beer on a chair, and flipped back and forth through his book – he'd been thinking about reading his mirror poem, but now he wasn't sure, maybe he'd try his masturbation poem. The audience sniggered. He began reading in a high-pitched monotone, floating out the words on a perfectly flat plane ten feet above our heads, as though he were a priest intoning mass. Each line ended on the same sighing note with words like *opening the faucet / soap on my*

rocks / bone for bathtub / for you / this waterway / cunt fingers. Someone
in the circle wolf-whistled at the end. Others clapped. Dagmar rolled
her eyes. Gawd, why didn't they get someone like Bukowski, Dwight
muttered. John rummaged through his bundle of papers, started reading something called "Thursday Night," dropped the page, picked it up,
shoved it into the others, decided not to read the poem, then incanted
one about squashed animal guts on the highway, *writing for you with
blood-ink.* Dagmar studied the pile of pages in her lap, moved a book
mark to a different page of her pamphlet. Her turn after the next reader.

John ambled back to his seat, swigging beer. Boyd, threading the air
with cigarette smoke, talked about how Ken had specially asked for Ross
to read tonight and how we decided it was a pretty good idea. Ken rested
his arms across the backs of neighbouring empty chairs and smiled like
one of those giant ancient god statues in the *National Geographic* known
for abundance and generosity.

Ross strode up to the mike and stared out at the audience. He
unclasped a leather case around his crisp typed pages. Gold-and-blue
marbled paper (like I'd seen in old, hard-bound library books) flashed
out from the leather covers. He said he'd start with a poem that was
coming out in *Underdog.* He thought it would be out by December or
maybe early in the new year and it was really funny because when he first
sent it in the editor rejected it, so all you beginning poets out there, take
note a rejection isn't the end. He'd sent it back to the editor with five
other poems in a whole series on Ladies and Escorts. Weird, that sign
that they have on all the bars, Ladies and Escorts, because he didn't feel
like an escort, that was more like ... like ... someone like Prince Philip,
oh my gawd, do you feel like Prince Philip when you take your old lady
to a bar? He started to read the poem. Then, oh, the other thing I was
thinking about when I wrote this was William Carlos Williams, you know
the poem about the plums in the refrigerator where he writes it out like
a list. This piece is written like that. He read a poem called "Lady No.
8," stopping at length between each of its six words: *why / doesn't / she /
go / to / hell.* He looked over at Ken, basking in his spread-eagled pose,
but Ken was watching the beer woman untie and retie her halter top.

So to be equal, I thought, I too will have to say I'd improved on novelists like D.H. Lawrence and John Fowles, I too will have to tell jokes about serving balls, and read stories of some *you* I either hate or want to fuck. I hoped that maybe novel writers didn't have to do these readings, that you could just publish your book, let other people read it and talk about it. You could stay hidden behind its pages, let the book be the only way they knew you.

Dagmar thumbed through her pages and placed a different one on top. She got out a pen, crossed out a word, and wrote something between the lines while Ross talked about Rod McKuen, how he'd met up with Jacques Brel in France and started translating his songs — he was just a guy like you or me working on the railroad or ranching or logging till he went to France. Then Ross too went to France, hung out with Rod on the beach with some cool French chicks, so he wrote a poem for Rod McKuen — *Lonesome Cities* was such a great book. *Sitting on the beach* — at each pause, he stared out at the audience — *with Rod McKuen / in France / watching a chick / with a red bikini / take off her bra / in the blue afternoon / I think / of bananas / of peeling bananas / and putting them / into her mouth ...* He smiled at Ken again, but this time Ken bent down to brush something off his boot ...

And now we have a new voice here tonight, Boyd announced as the clapping subsided, This might even be her first poetry reading.

Did he have to say that, Dagmar muttered. She handed me her insta-matic camera. A friend at the *Georgia Straight* wanted a picture. Take lots, she said.

Dagmar grabbed the mike stand, turned a knob, tried to pull the mike to the right height. I silently begged the mike to slide into place. It wouldn't budge. People shuffled in their seats till Boyd fixed it. She gazed out at the audience. I liked that she didn't smile, just looked hard at them, looked hard right into them, and said she'd be reading some poems about the coast.

I leaned this way and that snapping pictures, trying to get a shot without the mike blocking her face. I should go up to the front, I thought, crouch down, shoot from below, like you see in poster shots of rock stars, but I was too chicken.

One of her poems involved trees and Artemis. In the middle of it, Ross and John and Hey Man slid back their chairs and went outside to yak on the terrace. I hoped she hadn't noticed, hoped she'd had her eyes on her poems, but how could she not notice the sudden row of empty chairs? Ignore them, I thought, my cheeks hot with shame.

She read a poem about words in the "Parthenon forest." Then one about riding a killer whale like Pegasus. Her pages shook a little in her hand, her poems full of sand, kelp, woodstoves, moss, axes, fishnets, dock pilings, ferry crossings. She finished with the "Saturnina Sailors" poem:

> *Saturnina sailors*
> *in the Salish Sea*
> *1791.*
> *Canal de Nuestra*
> *Señora Del Rosaria, they called it*
> *passage to Hudson's Bay.*
> *Carrasco and Narváez.*
> *Ruffles, lace, quills, and paper*
> *to Malahat, Cowichan*
> *clastic rock*
> *and red-twigged buckthorn.*

She stopped suddenly. No one clapped till Boyd brought his hands together in a single smack, which sparked a smattering of pats across the half-empty chairs, except for Dwight and me – *we* clapped as hard as we could. Ken, the beneficent ancient god, left his hands on the chair backs.

The men crowded back into the room as Ken got to the mike. It was good to be back in Vancouver, back in Can-ada (he sprawled out the *a-a-a* in *Can*), he hadn't read here since '69 with Gary Snyder. After the border, he thought he'd spotted a couple of our men on horseback – you folks still have those, don't you? The redcoats with the dinner-plate hats. Mounted on their chestnut steeds? I thought so. He chuckled. Then read a poem about underwear: *men wore it to keep things out of the way / women wore it to put things in the way / the president wore it / the pope wore it / Mao Zedong wore it / wild Indians wore it / even Lady Macbeth had a girdle.* Now it was Ross's turn to spread his arms across the backs of chairs, basking in Ken's gaze beaming out over the audience, basking in Ken's smooth shifts from poem to poem with little stories about taking acid or launching his tenth book. Poems about freeways and Nebraska, poems about the salt lake of Utah, poems about lightbulbs and candles and skyscrapers.

After the reading, Dwight told Dagmar he loved the Pegasus whale poem, and did she have some other ones about that. I told her I thought her poems were way more interesting than John's and Ross's – full of neat language like the Spanish and then the Indian names – and that I loved that it was about here. She looked at me like I was a goof and watched Ross rushing up to Ken with a copy of Ken's book, *San Francisco Nights.* Five or six others bought books and followed Ross over to where Ken was standing by the mike. Boyd found a pen for him, and the beneficent god poured sunshine on his throng of admirers. Ross patted Ken on the back and hugged him. The other admirers waited. Ken nodded and smiled, began turning his attention to a young man with long hair and glasses. Then Ross shook Ken's hand. Then Ken looked over at Glasses, until at last Ross left the crowd.

John and Ross bought another beer, eyeing their piles of books on the book table and the crowd around Ken. They talked to each other but they kept their eyes on the books. A big smile suddenly spread across John's face when a woman in braids held out a book. He signed it and handed it back to her. Ross sat back on the beer table, the woman was packing up. He nudged the frayed edge of carpet with his foot, looked at the crowd around Ken, prodded the carpet again. John shook hands with his book buyer, seemed even to hold her hand for a bit longer, but she dropped her gaze to the floor and quickly left.

Dagmar shoved pages into her shoulder bag, and we sat in the rows of empty chairs. She should just get out of here, she said, looking over at her stack of pamphlets beside the thinner piles of books on the book table. Dwight wanted us all to go back and have a beer at "our place." You mean *my room,* I said. Dagmar supposed she'd have to stay for a few minutes longer, in case anyone wanted a copy of *Landscapes.* No one would of course, she went on. That's obvious. I'd like one, Dwight said. Should I buy it from her or buy it from you? Dagmar told him he'd better get it at the table. Do I get a signature too, he held out the pamphlet a moment later. What beautiful hands you have, he said, as she scrawled her name with a black-and-gold fountain pen she always carried for her notebook.

— What charming flattery you have.

She capped the pen, and Dwight assured her it was not flattery, that she had a writer's hands, and she should be proud of her poems, they made a refreshing change from road guts and sex. Dagmar ignored him and gazed across the chairs at Ken and his fans and Boyd packing up the mike and tape recorder. Winding electric cord around his arm, Boyd thought it'd been pretty good for her first time, but she should slow down a bit and look up at the audience. Smile.

— Especially smile at the audience walking out, Dagmar scoffed.

— Drop by my office and listen to it on tape. You might be surprised.

— Or if you need something stronger, Dwight gave his crooked-toothed grin, I've got some pretty good hash.

Back in my room, Dwight rolled fat joints while Dagmar paced around, fuming about the reading — how *narcissistic* it was, how *provincial*, how completely *banal*. Words I'd heard but never used — how grand it was, I thought to hurl them out like whirling splattering mudballs coating everything in their path with disgusting brown goo.

— I mean, who the fuck cares about someone's cum on his fingers? Or the roadkill in his underwear? Or his boring, facile love letters to his girlfriend?

I filed *facile* with *banal* and *narcissistic* under top insults. She yanked open the door to the balcony, saying she had to get away from Tiny Tim, couldn't I find something better than that dufus to cover up these ghastly turquoise walls, but came back a moment later, wanting to know when the fuck Canada was going to grow up, get some real writers? She toked up, then spluttered out, *these guys* (waving her hand in the direction of Brock Hall), *these guys* … should wake up to the world out there, read the real poets: Cavafy, Lorca, Neruda — go somewhere besides their own navel.

Dwight's eyes bulged wider, he lounged back on the rumpled covers of my cot, his gaze following Dagmar snooping at dirty pots on my hotplate, then roaming over to poke into my bookcase. I had one of my two chairs, Dagmar refusing to sit down in the other. So why'd you read with them then, Dwight handed her a roach-clip.

Allen had got her into it, she'd never realized what a men's scene it was, but it was, it was a goddamned boys' club, and no wonder Plath and Woolf committed suicide! She swooped out on the balcony with the roach, then back saying it was dead.

– Men like Neruda I can take, but men whose big idol is Ken Sperling can go fuck themselves.

– So what're you going to do, quit writing?

Dwight lolled across my pillow in his paint-smelling, grease-smelling clothes, taking up the whole cot; his eyes glinted.

– I don't know, but I'll tell you something – *these guys* (she waved her hand again toward Brock Hall), I give them five years, no one'll give a shit about these guys. In ten years, they'll be flushed away in the toilet of stupidity, their books pulped up and spewed out like sewage.

A knock sounded and Carla stuck her head in the door, drink and Rothman's in hand.

– Couldn't help hearing the party.

– Have some weed, Dwight passed her a joint.

Carla waved it away, didn't smoke that stuff. Tired of snooping around my walls, Dagmar flopped down in the other chair across from me at the table.

– It's a hell of a lot better than getting hooked on that, Dwight pointed at Carla's drink.

– Least you don't get arrested for it, Carla leaned against my pink-and-mauve bookcase, the horizontal stripes of green, maroon, and tangerine on her pants mesmerizing my eyes. Or maybe it was the fantastic object of the pants themselves: each leg made of four separate panels sewn in stiff seams so that they floated around her thighs and calves in squared columns of throbbing, strobing colour. A maroon jacket with pointy lapels, tangerine platform sandals sporting chrome buckles, and a matching studded choker completed her outfit.

Dagmar flipped open my notebook; I snatched it out of reach, so she flipped open Edith Wharton's book on writing fiction.

– Is that your novel? Carla asked.

– Well anyway, Dwight continued, you can't fix the whole poetry world tonight, so why not relax?

– Whaddaya mean fix the poetry world? Carla dragged on her Rothman's.

– *At every stage the novelist must rely on the illuminating incident*, Dagmar read out.

– I like your outfit, Carla said to Dagmar (black linen pants and an olive-brown silk shirt).

– Thanks.

– The name's Carla.

– Oh yeah, I'm Dagmar.

She slouched back in the chair, skimming pages of Edith Wharton. *Magic casements of fiction – vistas on infinity –* you're not seriously following this crap are you?

– Not really, I said.

– Frankie's writing a novel, Carla announced to Dwight.

– Is that a fact?

By now he was lying flat out on my cot like he'd moved in. He gazed up at the ceiling.

– I bet it's about a university girl with a crush on her professor.

– No, it's about a bunch of people living in a house. It's about us. I bet you're in it too, she said, meaning Dagmar, then, looking Dagmar up and down, said she had just the thing for her outfit, and clomped off to her room for some Coolique chokers, bangles, daisy rings, and peace-sign pendants.

– I was just doing a jewellery party at Cathy's house – you know, Frankie, Cathy from the Biltmore.

– Hasn't she ever heard of Virginia Woolf, Dagmar grumbled at the Wharton book.

– Try this, honey. Carla placed several ropes of geometric wooden beads over Dagmar's head; their earthy woody tones quite perfect against the olive-brown linen.

– What's this for?

– They're so you – perfect with that taupe shirt – take a look – Frankie, where's your mirror?

– Oh for Pete's sake, I never wear this nonsense.

Dagmar snatched the beads and pulled them over her head, breaking one of the strands and scattering blocks, cones, spheres, and pyramids under the cot, the bookshelves, and the dish cupboard.

– All right, I'll take the *nonsense* away, Carla stubbed out her Rothman's, no reason to be rude about it. She downed her drink, and we began crawling around my sea of linoleum flowers searching for beads and putting them into one of my cereal bowls. She said it was just a suggestion, and why're people so mean? I said I was sure we could fix it. Dagmar said she was sorry, but Carla should find out about people before throwing beads around their necks.

Dwight got off the bed, ambled over to Dagmar, and stood behind her chair. She had to unwind, he said, massaging her shoulders. He told her he really liked her poem about the whale, he could really see a killer whale bursting out of the waves and flying through the air like a winged horse, flying over the logging trucks and the B.C. Ferries going to Victoria and then under the water through the wrecks of Spanish galleons. He wanted to know what her next poem was going to be about, but she said it was bad luck to talk about things before you wrote them.

I put on Ravi Shankar. Carla and I sat on my cot. She didn't hardly sell anything at Cathy's, she said, and she'd have to buy a new cord to replace the broken one. She was late on her payments too. Her mauve-frosted nails dipped into the bowl of building-block beads, trying to stuff the frayed end of the string through a cube. I dug out a darning needle and showed her how Mom taught me to fold the yarn over the needle and then put the eye over the fold. As we threaded beads onto the cord, Shankar's sitar rippled over us in fans, waves, and cascading shimmers like curtains of northern lights pulled along on the undertow of a drumbeat, that Dwight pounded out on Dagmar's shoulders, up and down her back till she gave up the Wharton book and rested her head on her arms sprawled across the table.

My thoughts macraméed themselves into Shankar's strings, thinking of novels and plots I'd thread like Celtic knots. *The Craft of Novels* by Melvin Dodge said the key was making characters have compelling desires, like making Carla fall in love with Dwight. Not a hokey *Chatelaine* romance, I thought. Instead a novel about real people and real love. But if Carla fell in love with Dwight, what would happen to Dwight's wife? Would she have to die? In which case I would be making her die, I would be murdering someone for the sake of a story. Saying things made them happen; saying it could make Dwight's real wife really die. Only the most horrible and crass of authors would do this.

I could say that novel-Dwight didn't have a wife, but then he wouldn't be Dwight and the story wouldn't be the story. I was trapped in the glass paperweight of my life, like Edith Wharton said. I had to escape. Rewrite it, make it into a different story, and me into someone like Dagmar who'd been to Europe, read lots of books, and knew all about plot and character.

— Just can't keep your hands to yourself can ya, Carla scowled at Dwight, massaging Dagmar on the other side of the room.

— Jealous, are ya, he said, grinning dreamily and pulling his fingers over Dagmar's ribs as though combing the tangled muscles away from her spine. When was the last time you got it on?

I was pretty sure I knew the answer to this question as I'd seen Carla and Dan take quite a few breaks together at the Biltmore.

Carla and Dan, the Biltmore Lounge bartender. They'd disappear together for twenty minutes, half an hour. Usually when it wasn't busy and the boss wasn't around, and Maggie would do the bar though she didn't have her licence. Where did they go? A broom closet? A stall in the can? No time to rent a room upstairs in the hotel. Standing up, crashing into mops and cleaning carts, or mashed into the door of a stall while a guy took a shit next door. Dan thrusting into her, hands on her breasts, her skirt hoiked up. Wham bam back to work. Did he ever take her to the movies or the beach or somewhere they could do it in a bed? Not that I could see.

Carla said Dan lived in a co-op house with some draft-dodger buddies, a complete pigsty, she said. She went once and never wanted to go back. She said they might move in together but then Dan didn't want kids, and she really wanted kids, she wanted a man who'd be a real daddy, she wanted kids *now*, honey, cuz time's runnin out. And then Dan said he wanted her to quit drinkin, even though he drinks like a fish and what am I s'posed to do when he drinks?

– One track mind, ain'tcha, Carla said in Dwight's direction. All you bastards. One-track mind. Wham bam. Thank you, ma'am. Not even thank you. Just getcher rocks off. Never means anything more than that, never means anything real, anything except you and yr rocks. Well you can fuck the hell off the whole fuckin lot of you.

Carla got up, spilling the beads over my cot, and stumbled back to her room, tears streaking mascara down her cheeks.

Around then Nigel phoned, and I told him about the reading. He sounded tense, as though someone was waiting outside the call box at the top of the dock, either wanting to make a call or just hanging around listening. No one, he said, just moths attracted to the light. They kept flying into his face and he kept brushing them away. No, there weren't lots of other people on their boats – all the Sunday sailors had gone home. He thought he might come over to my place, then heard Dwight and Carla talking and said he wouldn't. I pictured him, under the street light that shone all night on the call box. He would leave its bright safety for the empty hulls on their little network of floating jetties, he would wander alone into the shadows on the wharf, untie the small shell of his boat, and drift away from land and university, from the sturdiness of walls, roofs, sidewalks, and streets.

But now *maybe* he wanted *me* as companion against that darkness. I said I'd go down to the boat if he liked. He was silent so long, I asked him if he was still there. Yeah still here, he said, then told me that his friend James couldn't go on the Desolation Sound trip, and did I still want to, and of course I said yes. So why don't you come down, he said, and bring a sleeping bag, see what it's like sleeping on a boat? Sure, I said and hung up. Then wondered did the sleeping bag mean separate bunks, or did he want something more? Was this the moment when we'd become lovers, when our bodies would melt together, his London university wouldn't matter, we'd be equals, we'd talk about everything, even our ideas would make love?

Dagmar was so wasted she didn't want to go all the way over to her parents' house in Dunbar, but rather to crash in my room. She wanted me to stay, she slung her arm around me and we reeled across the room, falling in a tangled heap onto my cot, her hugging me, saying what a good friend I was, how could I leave now, it was our only chance to visit before she went back to Hornby Island? You can stay, I said. Stay in my room. We lay tangled and sprawled sideways on the cot, her arm around my waist, her head curled into my shoulder, already almost asleep. Stay, stay, I thought, yes, stay with Dagmar, but if I cancelled on Nigel I could forget the sailing trip. You can stay, I said. We can visit when I get back from work tomorrow. But she was heading back to Hornby the next morning with a special order of silk for her weaver friend. If only I could stay, I said. But there's no way to telephone Nigel, and we have to plan the sailing trip.

I unrolled my sleeping bag beside Nigel's rumpled sheets and blankets on the platform in the bow of the boat. It was a mummy bag I'd bought in high school, after working for a month picking strawberries, earning just enough to order it from Sears' catalogue. I unzipped it all the way, then went back to the little cabin to sit at the galley table under the open hatch.

The thudding low growl of a tug engine pulling a barge droned past us heading out of False Creek to the open water of Georgia Strait. A black paperback we'd both read, *The French Lieutenant's Woman*, lay on the table between us, along with our beers.

— So you're sure you want to do this, he said. Crewing can be hard work, and I'm not the greatest guy to live with.

His short stubby fingers flipped the pages of the book, turned it over, turned it back. Wide capable hands. Dwight's line about piano playing came into my head.

– Of course I want to go, more than anything in the world.

– What about your jobs?

– I'll quit or get time off without pay.

Nigel doodled our beer caps and the opener around the table and lined them up next to the book.

– So you're not going to crumple in a fit of tears if I bark orders.

I thought of the magic of doing things together, discovering a new island, a new beach, catching a fish, finding a harbour – the we-ness of being the only ones there that always made you closer. We would be lovers, everything we did would make love.

– Crew members should be barked at, I said. I'm sure I can handle it.

– Good, it's settled, he grinned, and proposed a toast to Desolation Sound. We clinked bottles.

He picked up the black-covered book again, its tiny oval of a Victorian woman dwarfed by the giant names of the author and his title.

– So which ending is it going to be, he said. His round spectacles reflected light from a tiny brass lamp bolted to a window frame. I didn't know what he meant.

– *The French Lieutenant's Woman* – which ending do you choose – A: Charles marries the shallow but wealthy Ernestina and forgets about Sarah; B: Charles breaks off his engagement to Ernestina, gets no inheritance but settles down with the disgraced Sarah, who lovingly bears his child? Or C: Charles breaks off his engagement but Sarah no longer loves him and hides his child because she's in love with Mr. Fowles or her maid and all along has been stringing Charles a line?

– I don't want to choose any of them because I don't like any of them.

– But you have to choose; in life you have to choose.

When, I thought, *did* you really choose in life? School for twelve years, then one choice: job or university for four years. Then job. You could go for years without choosing anything significantly different.

– In life, I said, I don't have to choose some hokey formula romance.

– Ah, so romance is just hokey, is it?

– Why is this the only story we tell, it's always about whether the girl gets married. Why can't the girl do something different for a change?

– Sarah could choose just to live the Bohemian life with her artist friends.

– And her secret lover, Mr. Fowles!

He sprawled his arms along the tops of the cushions behind him, and asked who my secret lovers were?

– That frizzy-headed bloke across the hall, he grinned. Or Dagmar, yes I bet there's some secrets there. I bet you and Dagmar are full of secrets. But you're a woman in charge of her fate. A woman who can throw herself at someone, saying it's fate, then walk away.

– All lies, I said, laughing. Then made him tell me about how he'd started sailing so I could listen to him adding r's onto the ends of words ending in *a*, or leaving r's off of words ending in *r*, listen to him saying *bloke* or *tomahtoes* or *mate* or *petrol* or *spanner in the works*. He told me he'd started sailing when he sailed boats in Hyde Park and I thought he meant real boats in a very large lake, but he meant toy boats in a pond. At university he sailed with James, but Nigel had been more interested in rowing.

– Meaning *sculls*, not *dories* like you have over here.

His father didn't have a boat; his father was the manager of a book-shop. A man like Dagmar's father, I thought, picturing a suit jacket, a full chest and waistline – a comfortable, no-nonsense man who owned cars, a house – who worked steadily all his life at the same thing, had accomplished things, a man interested in buying and selling, not painting pictures or teaching children.

His mother had knitted the tea cozy on the pot on his *cooker*, brown and yellow stripes with a pompom like a ski toque. Tea was a meal you ate. Tea could only be made with boiling water *after* you warmed the pot with boiling water. And you put the milk into the mug before you poured the tea.

His mother was a Woolworths clerk. I thought of maroon sweater sets mismatched with black and tan plaid skirts, bulging around the top. Glasses on a chain resting on a full bosom held in check by what

Mom called foundation garments. His parents took holidays in Spain, that place in the *National Geographic* of pale-green water spreading out before white houses clinging to cliffs. Black lace fans and red flounced skirts. Bulls charging through narrow streets. Men waving red capes to the toreador song in *Carmen.*

We crawled onto the platform in the bow next to rope and sail bags, the bow pointing our heads together, leaving our bodies and legs apart. Was this it for the night, or ...?

I pushed closer, feeling in the dark for his sturdy arms and thick, sailor's fingers. I tried a kiss, then more and more, tasting the London, the English, the sculpted strangeness of him, the sheer excitement of his rough cheeks, his supple mouth, his long wavy hair. I tore off my sleeping bag and crawled under his blankets to the rippling muscle of his thighs and buttocks. I pulled off his underwear and tossed my T-shirt, put his hands on my breasts, nudged into his bush, his hard cock, and we tumbled against each other in a thick darkness that smelled of engine gas, dusty vinyl cushions, and the foam mattress – pushing, thrusting, gasping, knees and elbows.

Of course, I thought afterwards, lying in his arms, we're not instantly the great lovers I'd imagined. We needed time to let go of shyness, learn each other's ways, time as friends sailing a boat, time in that we-ness of an adventure together. Soon that time would begin, and each day of it would bring us closer, we'd talk more deeply, caress each other more fully. Till we went on together for our whole lives.

Later I woke in the cool night air, to find his blankets and sheets empty. I stood on the platform and poked my head through the hatch; his hunched shape sat on the edge of the cabin above the galley. Small erratic things like bats flitted through the masts. Across the water stood the dark hulks of West End apartment blocks dotted with occasional lighted windows. He was fine he said, just couldn't sleep. He often couldn't sleep.

A lone siren, probably an ambulance on its way to a hospital, sounded from downtown. He didn't want to talk about not sleeping. It's things you wouldn't know about anyway, Frances, like boat payments and moorage fees. He wouldn't tell me what these were. We sat in silence for a while.

He wondered whether he should haul the boat out and clean the weed off the bottom before making the trip. That would be expensive, he didn't know whether he really needed to do it. I offered to help, but he said I already had two jobs, anything more was way beyond crewing duty.

I crawled over to the cabin roof behind him, and worked my fingers into the rigid muscles of his neck and shoulders. He grabbed my hands. You're so alive, he said, so free. I told him he was free too, everyone was free now, everything was changing to a world where people were free to dance and paint and sail boats, and free to love whoever they wanted, a world that really cared about people, not just businessmen and proper clothes. I felt myself becoming again his tree and mountain woman; I'd wrap him in dark wild power, free him to his own free and wild self.

He'd be free, he muttered, when he got tenure, and people like Henderson (the head of the English department) quit saying they needed Milton and Shakespeare specialists, not a D.H. Lawrence expert. I told him he'd forget all that once we sailed out of the harbour. After that we sat for a long time holding hands and listening to the faint cries of birds high in the night sky who seemed to already see the coming dawn.

CHAPTER 7

In the morning, filing at the insurance company, I fell asleep over the sorting rack, and woke up with my face pressing into metal tags and manila folders. Lorna was shaking me, asking me if I was all right. No, the manager did not see me. Lorna stood in the shadowy supply room next to the racks. The majesty of her ample body always amazed me, filling the room with her massive presence. She whispered to me what should she say to the abortion committee. How did you convince them that having a baby was bad for your health? What happened if they said no? I told her mental health counted. But how did they define mental health – it wasn't as though she was in Riverview Asylum. We heard footsteps, and she trundled out with a load of sorted files.

On my coffee break, I phoned Dagmar in my room. When are you coming down next, I said. When are you coming up to Hornby, she countered. You could work on your novel. But how would I pay for school? We joshed back and forth, and she told me she'd had a pretty good time with Dwight after I left. I kept her on the phone as long as I could. How could she sleep with him of all people? What about her boyfriend Murray? And she said we had a right to shop around, and anyway, love and sex weren't the same thing, not till you found the great love, the love of your life.

After my call, I went to the mail-opening room with Kitty and Lorna, who kept dropping her envelope knife and slowly tilting her great shoulders to the floor to pick it up. Kitty was excited that today was the day we were going out to lunch with the accounting girls. When I shut my eyes the red and white stripes on her new culottes and matching jacket zizzed across the inside of my eyelids. Lorna wore a green A-line that reminded me of the evergreen woods around Cultus Lake.

Candy Cane, Douglas Fir, and Dormouse. At lunch we joined a cashier and two accounting clerks in a diner in the basement of another office block. I got the cheapest sandwich, a Reuben's, a thick bulge of pink meat slices toothpicked with a dill pickle in bread that compressed to paste. A clerk with growing-out dyed hair pounced on Kitty's engagement ring – diamond – 18 karat gold – next June – honeymoon in Hawaii. Was it a passion cut? Where had he proposed? Was she going to work afterwards? Lorna stirred a fry around in some ketchup. Kitty thought she would work for a while, until she had babies. No one should work once she had babies, Kitty thought. Day care – that was what they did in China – they had baby farms; rows and rows of babies in little cubicles. Lorna pushed her chair out, lumbered off to the bathroom. Someone else said they didn't know why women were so keen on working, she'd rather stay home with her kids any day, but they needed the money. But she wouldn't want the jobs the men have; why would you want to work late and spend your days being mean, bossing people around?

The topic changed to dieting. Lorna coasted back to her chair – a freighter coming in to dock – and took a bite of her hamburger. Kitty wanted to know if you really had to eat a half a grapefruit with every meal. An argument erupted over whether potatoes were or weren't allowed, and whether you were allowed ice cream since you could have butter and meat and cheese. I just take Ayds, someone said. They really work. No breakfast. No lunch. Eat all the dinner I want. One of the clerks had a brother on the macrobiotic diet. Nothing but brown rice and vegetables. The worst thing was his chewing – every bite chomped twenty-seven times – like sitting across from a cow with a cud. The cashier, who didn't look particularly slender, said they should quit these fads and go on the *Vogue* Super Diet – it was simple – there were four stages – you only ate certain vegetables in each stage – no bread of any kind – no potatoes, rice, or pasta but you got lots of meat, eggs, cheese, and butter – she was in the induction stage – the pounds just flew off. Lorna pulled the meat out of her hamburger, leaving bite-shaped bun halves on her plate, but snuck a few more fries. Induction – what's that, someone asked. Lorna said she'd read in an article on Vietnam that *induct* was when you got someone to join. But Kitty thought *induction* was a medical procedure.

She ordered a piece of carrot cake, someone lit a candle, and we all sang "Happy Birthday," making Lorna take off her glasses and dab her eyes with Kleenex. *A Birthday Toast*, said a bright-red card featuring a pinkish wine glass, empty except for a maraschino cherry and a fluffy white, big-eared mouse smiling and beaming its black eyes under big curly eyelashes. The gift was a bath set of pink hand soap, pink bath-oil bubbles, and pink bath crystals.

How, in my vertical form of sleep, I got from the bus to my room, I don't know. It was one of those afternoons, so blazing hot everything looked like an overexposed photograph. A cool breath washed over me in my north-facing room, flooding me with the sense of safety and security where my dormouse could curl up and drift in her teapot home. Yet all was not quite as usual. The bed was pushed out from the wall and all the sheets and blankets were untucked. Dagmar had left her cigarettes and lighter behind. A folded paper stuck to my sandal – another note from Dwight: *You're right, she's not a lezzie. Drop by for a beer after work. I want to ask you something. D.*

Dagmar and Dwight in my bed! I thought they must have gone to his room but of course they stayed in mine. And now if I slept in the same sheets it would be like surrounding myself with his greyish skin which, like the colour of the sheets on his bed, reminded me of slugs you find in lettuce, or larvae of underground insects. I heard his door open and shut, his voice talking to someone in his room. It was safe to go to the fridge for a glass of milk, but seconds later he was introducing me to a small girl perched on his cot on the rumpled slug-coloured sheets. Janey did not want to tell me where they'd been that day (the aquarium), or that she was five, or what kind of ice cream daddy got for her that had left brown splatters around her mouth and down the front of her pink shirt. She looked down at her pink-thonged feet and even when Dwight picked her up and stood her in front of me, she pulled her tangled blonde hair over her eyes and wriggled around so she was facing the heap of greasy mechanic's clothes and the rubble of boxes that covered the floor. Janey did not want to show me her stuffed toy, a grey whale, with matted fuzz, a droopy eye, and a missing fin, or tell me its name was Skana just like the real one at the aquarium. She did not want to listen to real whales singing to Paul Horn's flute, but Dwight left the album on anyway and gave her pencils and paper and the album cover to draw on. Janey's mother Shirley was at the hospital. We talked, over the jars of brushes and stacks of dirty dishes on his table. How long in the hospital, he didn't know. He would take Janey to his mother in Sardis (Shirley's mother was dead – a boating accident when Shirley was sixteen – Shirley never liked her stepmother), and Janey would stay there for a few days – she liked her gramma and Shirley liked her too.

I waved the note. He wanted Dagmar's address on Hornby Island, he might go visit her there. Janey on the dingy cot moved her pencil here and there leaving a series of winding, aimless trails. Dwight looked at me, widened his eyes, smirked, and suggested I was highly mistaken if I thought a woman like Dagmar was out of his league, they'd really hit it off.

Carla came in, dumped her shopping bags in her room, and made a fuss about saying hello to Janey and ignoring Dwight. Such a pretty face, and such a shame to see chocolate spots on it, and on her pretty pink shirt too. Honey, why don't you come with me and we'll get you cleaned up. She took Janey off to the bathroom to sponge off her face and shirt. Dwight rolled his eyes, said he guessed he should have thought of it, said Shirley was always criticizing him for forgetting to do things about Janey – she'd tell him to take Janey to the library – then afterwards complain he didn't get the Dr. Seuss books. Or tell him to take her to the park, then afterwards say he should have taken her to the petting zoo instead of lying around suntanning. Or why didn't he teach her to swim?

– I'm too lazy as far as she's concerned.

But how could he say anything back when she (meaning Shirley) was like that (meaning cancer)?

He rolled his eyes again. A new painting of burnt-out towers and streets exploding in flames stood among cans of Creamo and coffee cups on his dresser. Across the hall Carla gave Janey a hand mirror so she could watch Carla braid her hair into pigtails, and when they were finished with her hair, Carla was going to show her something really special that would make her the prettiest girl in Vancouver. She chattered away as she braided, surrounding Janey with that special talk some people have for children, full of high-pitched exclamations, exuberance, and excitement – a kind of make-believe talk, as though you'd suddenly stepped into a story world, a fairy tale even, a magic world where children were really small monarchs or gods with extraordinary powers, whereas adult talk took for granted a spade meant a spade; it took for granted that *I* and *you* both think of the same spade in the same grave or potato patch; and it took for granted that the *you* I see is the same as the *you* you really are, and the *I* you see is really the *I* I am.

Whatever kind of talk Carla's was, Janey remained completely silent. Even when the special thing that would make Janey the prettiest girl in Vancouver turned out to be painting her finger and toe nails, Janey must have merely nodded her head to select the vial labelled Frosted Cherry, for we heard not a peep from her – just Carla: wave your hands, honey. There you go, princess! Go show your daddy and auntie Frankie. She held out her hands to Dwight, down low as though she might not pass inspection, then quickly returned to her post on the cot and her silent wandering pencil lines. I told Dwight the only address I had for Dagmar was General Delivery, Hornby Island.

A small dark bug with a rounded back crawled under one of his open books. I took some brushes out of a jar, carefully lifted the book, and popped the jar over the bug.

– Move right in, why don't you!

– You've got bugs – I want to know what that is.

– Probably a ladybug.

For a moment we both held the jar. I told him I wanted to take it out to UBC to the biology department in case it was a cockroach. *He* had seen plenty of cockroaches and it certainly wasn't one; it was a ladybug or a garden beetle – his mother had them in her window box. Nor was *he* the sort of person who would live with cockroaches.

– How come you're so familiar with them, then?

He looked at me as though I'd just told him I was the King of Siam, then slid a piece of cardboard under the jar, opened the window, and let the bug go. After he left with Janey, Carla got out a can of Raid and sprayed back and forth along the bottom of his door and then for good measure along the bottoms of her door and mine; any bug that walked under Dwight's door would have to cross at least two defence-lines of Raid to get under ours. But of course bugs did not have to go under doors.

Carla dragged me into her room to watch *Edge of Night*, and we lounged on Carla's double bed, eating BBQ potato chips and drinking Pepsi. She loved Ann Flood, the actress who played Nancy – loved her hair and the way she walked, the way she was always so poised and good mannered. Had I seen the article on her in the paper about all the shows she'd been in and about her four kids and her husband who was the head of ABC Sports? She rummaged for the paper but couldn't find it. I said maybe I could look it up in the library.

We lay on the bed watching the show, balancing one bare leg on the knee of the other – Carla's toenails making bright dots of cherry – mine looking like worn bits of goat horn. Carla said it would be so cool to be Laurie Ann, Tiffany Whitney, or Phoebe the nurse, and about ten years ago she even tried. She went down to Hollywood, she had pictures, she knew how to present herself, you gotta go in like gangbusters, like you're the hottest thing on the block, she learned *that* when she was twelve; her mom got her a role on a Sugar Jets commercial. She had to say *My mom's the best*, and eat some Sugar Jets and milk. By the time they'd done four different takes she'd eaten a whole bowl. She didn't mind saying it over and over, because her mom *was* the best mom. Too bad they didn't use the shots because she'd've got more money every time they ran the commercial. It was only the one time, she said, after that she was too old.

Down in the States she waited for parts, waitressing at clubs where scouts and directors went. She met Dan – he'd had bit parts in *General Hospital*, he knew people in the movie biz. Then he ran away to Canada to get away from the draft; he couldn't stand pretending he was into college as a way out of it. She stayed. No, she never got any parts. She even tried sleeping with one of the directors.

— I mean what was I supposed to do if that's the only way they'll notice you. You gotta do what you gotta do.

She pulled out the Southern Comfort bottle and a couple of glasses but put it back when I didn't want any. Dan was buggin her again to quit drinking, she said, falling back onto the bed, jolting its saggy springs this way and that and jumbling the bedcovers, then jolting off to the fridge for another Pepsi. By the time she returned she was onto her jewellery business, she got out the trays, and made me sit in the armchair while she draped chains of crinkly beads around my neck, put my hair up to test out earrings, said I should let her pierce my ears, fitted me up with matching bracelets and rings. There were so many girls out there who just needed a little something, just needed to touch themselves up and they'd look like a million dollars, she saw them all the time at the Bilt-more, she'd even helped a few — it was such fun to give them that, to see them walk off looking really stylish, like they really mattered, they could go anywhere, do anything — she just needed a way to find them. What about my dad — she bet he had some artist friends who'd be interested, even men went in for beads nowadays.

— Everyone likes a party — you just throw a party and I happen to have my kits there. Or maybe we could do a party here with some of your U friends.

Dagmar and I must know lots of girls who'd come. Or maybe even a bigger party down at Dad's studio with his friends *and* my friends. And by the way did I know about Dagmar and Dwight getting it on in my bed, which of course I did. Why would a girl like Dagmar go for him, she wanted to know.

— Women can have one-night stands just like men.

Mr. Cockroach, she started laughing, Mr. Cock the Roach. And what if it got stuck in a roach clip? And what if the roach clip belonged to a cockroach?

He reads the same poetry books as her, I pointed out, but she was more interested in her jewellery trays. She rustled through them and clasped a metal-squared choker around my neck, adding huge match-ing squares on my ears and a massive square ring — all in pewter and black. *Soignée* – it was a word she'd read in *Vogue* magazine, she loved the sound of it, she didn't quite know what it meant but she thought I looked soignée. I looked in the mirror, and she was right in a way; it was a costume I could put on like a role in a play – my black hair piled up and my battalion of pewter shields – Queen of the Amazons. But I didn't know the rest of the lines.

Rummaging for the bracelet, she couldn't find it and started pitching out all the trays onto the bed, she couldn't have lost it, with the bracelet I would be perfect, she couldn't stand losing things, she'd have to pay for it and she was already behind.

There was no bracelet. She opened another cupboard and poured herself a Southern Comfort. Even if Frankie wasn't drinking, Frankie was still here and she could drink. Drinking's only a problem if you do it alone, right? She wasn't drinking alone like some loser, she was drinkin with her best friend. She got me another Pepsi, lit another ciga-rette, then told me something that no one knew about except her mom, who was dead. That she once had a little girl like Janey, well not like Janey, she was only a newborn baby, and she, Carla, was seventeen, she thought she could keep her just like her mom kept Carla, but her mom made her give her up for adoption, she'd have a better life, a way better life. Carla would finish high school and when she found the right man she could give her babies a proper home. While Carla talked, I slowly undid the choker and earrings, slid away from their surprising weight. No, she couldn't have gotten married because the father was her moth-er's boyfriend. Her long fingers with their long frosted nails tapped her cigarette. Her eyebrows arched. Her slim leg crossed over her other slim knee, casually dangling a silk slipper. You're the one that's soignée, I said – I'm just a fake. I laid the jewellery back in its tray, dissolving its magic into shiny beads and glittery chains.

– Who adopted her, I asked.

Carla had no idea. She signed everything away.

– People nowadays sometimes find their birth mother, I said. They put ads in the paper, or they get some clue from the adoption agency. Kids always want to know who their real parents are.

— Maybe ... maybe one day she'll find me ... and she'll tell me all about growing up in a big rich house up in Kerrisdale, how she even has her own horse and her own car and she's so bright and beautiful she's now a model for the top magazines, her father owns a forest company and her mother has beautiful parties, and she'll tell me that even though she has the best parents in the world she's always had a special place in her heart for her *real* mom. That's why I want to have kids, Frankie (she was bawling now, and I put my arms around her), so I can make it up to my little girl — so I can be a real mom, before it's too late.

CHAPTER 8

About a week later Nigel and I sailed out of English Bay for our trip up the coast. We headed out of the harbour on a westerly breeze, genny and main tight as soaring gull-wings. Charts on the galley table laid out depth readings and wavy contour lines around islands and mountains. Choppy swell splashed against the bow. Wind dashed my hair, streaming it out behind me; blowing away sweaty buses, baked asphalt, and dusty concrete office towers; blowing away the dingy lunch room at the insurance company, the hunched-over days sorting files, the tiny deposits at the bank, leaving me free as an eagle circling the white-flecked waves spreading to distant smoky foothills of Vancouver Island.

Nigel put me on watch for boats, deadheads, and marker buoys, and I posted myself on the bow, determined to crew so well that he would never think of taking anyone else. Seaspan tug one o'clock, I announced, pointing at two barges mounded with sawdust. I called out the white fortress of a government ferry, a fishing boat trolling a line, and a swirling mat of tangled kelp.

He gave me a turn on the tiller, put his arm around my waist, and smiled. We congratulated ourselves; our journey begun. Yes, I thought, he's relaxing. We looked back at the anchored freighters and the blocks of university towers on their sandy headland shrinking to toys. Nigel's enemies in the department shrinking with them, or so I thought. He went below, just then, and started opening lockers rummaging for something, chucking books and papers on the galley seats and the sleeping platform. Don't worry, he said, I'll find it. And he did. It was the chapter of his book on Lawrence he was working on; it had to be done in two weeks.

He wedged it into the shelf above the tiny galley table, with binoculars, charts, spare blocks, tide tables, *The Magus* by John Fowles, and several other novels.

We pulled in close to shore for lunch, near a corral of logs. The water was calm in the lee of a headland, the air full of pungent lemony cedar. Nigel ordered me onto a boom log to tie up to its big iron ring. Would they roll? Would they tip? I stepped out and felt it solid as a log on the beach, secured to its mates by fat chainlinks big as telephone receivers. What would it be like to walk across the whole field of floating trunks to the tangle of trees and salal on the shore? Did I dare? Would they spin me off like they did in the logger contests, or would it be like walking on water?

A solitary raven rorked. Water slap slap slapped against the logs. Then I remembered my vow of crewmanship and climbed back aboard, put fenders between us and the boom, and cracked him a beer.

We sat in the cockpit. Never had we tasted such cheese, such grapes, such beer as the feast of our lunch. He lounged against the cabin, grinning at me from the shade of his boater's cap, his shirt open to his chest, his trousers rolled up, his stout capable feet propped on the bench.

– This is what you must get into your novel, he said, waving a beer toward the tangled forest that lurched and tumbled down the bluff to the water. This and those islands sticking their backs out of the water like Loch Ness monsters. A novel about a woman like you, Frances, a woman sprung from the land, sprung from forests and rocks and sea – who can she love who's a match for all that, and what does she do with the flimsy town and the little tatters of ideas she finds at the university?

Was U Girl really a woman "sprung from the forests," I wondered to myself. I wanted *Turquoise Room* to be about language, about people speaking different languages, living in different worlds that bounced off each other in strange ways. You crossed their frontiers like molecules in filtration experiments. Did you get through or did you become a different person on the other side? Don't talk about your novel till you've written it, Dagmar always said, if you talk, you won't write. So I asked Nigel about his book on Lawrence, what was it about?

He didn't want to talk about his book either, he'd come out sailing to forget it. It was all codswallop, anyway, he said, dusty old trinkets for a position in the priesthood. Then he said it was about Lawrence's idea of darkness and light — we think we see the universe with our vast scientific knowledge but really we're just shining a flashlight in the middle of the night, lighting a candle in a midnight jungle — it was Lawrence's version of Plato's theory of the cave; people think they see reality when they're only seeing shadows from candlelight on the wall.

Yes, I said (this was the conversation I'd longed for; I'd studied Plato's cave theory in philosophy), people only see the supposed reality they've been exposed to. Take them outside that, and they can't believe their eyes.

– You, Frances, he said, you're already outside the university.

– But university's the most exciting thing in the world, I said. Ideas — thoughts — writing — all the books in the library talking to each other. Why did you go to university if you think it isn't?

– That's what you do if you have good A levels; you go on.

After lunch, he kept the sails down. He made me start up the motor and steer away from the boom. Time to teach you something, he chuckled. When we were out in the strait, he undid the coils of rope to the life ring, tossed it overboard, and told me to go back and pick it up.

– Lower the throttle first.

I got the boat dead slow, turned around, and headed back, thinking the ring in the waves could be Nigel, he could be losing strength in the cold water, he could be ...

Where was the ring? It kept disappearing in the swell. In the cockpit, I turned the small wheel that steered the outboard, but the road I was driving slithered and shifted; it was never where I thought it was. I missed the ring and had to turn around and take another shot. It wasn't like driving a car on a street where the grip of the tire always told you where you were; on the water nothing resisted, nothing braced; there was nothing you could count on. On the third try I picked it up after almost plowing it under, the ring that could be Nigel drowning.

An eerie feeling stuck with me for the rest of the afternoon as we tacked steadily up the coast to Sechelt, pointing the bow to the distant islands on the west, then veering back to the rocky bluffs to the east, the forested slopes above them scarred with clear-cut patches of logging. Our course so certain and predictable; me uprooted and lost like a clump of tidewrack in the waves.

I kept wondering where I'd had that feeling before, and the closest I could come was running into the house from school to tell Mom I'd got an A in math and finding Dad shoving all the tea dishes into her lap.

I shook myself out of it at Sechelt, hauled in the main and genny, and leapt onto the dock with the line — proud that I knew just what to do, proud that I could earn my keep since I'd thoughtlessly contributed nothing to supplies and had almost no money on me. The marina was jammed with boats — red-faced men carrying bags of ice and charcoal briquettes, women in halter tops flipping burgers and hotdogs, boys shooting each other with water guns, boozy men in cheap aluminum deck chairs, the air full of barbecue smoke, lighter fluid, gas fumes, cigars, and burning fish skin. A speedboat hooted at a fifty-footer edging itself past the eggshell hulls of pleasure-craft, and parents yelled at kids to *Keep your life jacket on if you're playing on the dock.*

The store door creaked and flapped, and we fumbled around in dim lights from a cooler of wilted carrots and celery, past walls of fishing lures, rods and reels, revolving racks of postcards, and shelves of picnic coolers, rope, and tin buckets. I held a shopping basket while Nigel picked up a steak, then put it back, picked up a tin of soup, then put it back, and stood in front of the dairy cooler studying the packages of orange mild cheddar.

— So how do we do this, he finally said.
— Do what?
— Figure out what to buy?
— What do you want to eat?
— I think, as skipper, I'm going to designate that a crew job.

He planted a kiss on my forehead, chucked a twenty at me and left me to fill the basket. I didn't know what to make of this. Joe and I had always planned food together; if he was cooking spaghetti he liked to pick out the mushrooms and onions. Could Nigel really be one of those men who can't even boil an egg? Even Dad had often cooked meals when he was at home. But I was crew, and he was paying for everything; managing the galley was another way to earn my keep.

With food on board, we took the boat out in the bay to avoid moorage fees, which meant Nigel running the motor dead slow and me at the bow holding the anchor on its chain till he yelled *drop*, and we hoped it caught on the bottom. It took three tries till he was satisfied.

The shadows of headlands crept toward us over the glassy water, where a pair of grebes arced their swan necks to elegant crested heads. Nigel studied the distance from our hull to the rocky shore. Were we far enough, he wondered. I thought so. But what happens at low tide, he said, those rocks'll be closer. He studied nearby boats. Were we far enough away from the *Jenny Lynn*? And I realized there were boating things that Nigel too had never done like use an anchor. He'd always moored at a dock. The *Jenny Lynn* rocked rhythmically and suggestively, sending small wavelets in our direction.

After dinner, Nigel wanted to know if I'd gotten any cake in the shopping, but of course I hadn't, and the store was long closed. I'll make some, I said.

— How could you possibly do that, we don't have an oven?

Snugged in behind the galley table, he gazed at me cool as cool through his round specs.

— Cook it over a slow heat in the frying pan, I said.

I rummaged around for sugar and flour and eggs, but he said he could manage without, and it wouldn't be cake anyway.

— It would be like very sweet bannock, I said.

— What's bannock?

— It's biscuit dough you fry in a pan.

— Fried bread isn't cake.

— I can make it like cake. Delicious with lots of butter.

— Pancakes aren't cake either, he laughed, and anyway it'll take hours.

— Just let me do it, you'll love it.

— Then we'll have to do dishes again, you'll be up all night.

— It's my job as crew.

– Right then, as your skipper, I order you to stop cluttering everything up, and come to bed.

Later I wondered if the *Jenny Lynn* people saw wavelets coming from our rocking boat. Although they might not have lasted long enough for anyone to notice.

My first order the next morning was to haul in the anchor. *Do not bang it against the hull or grate it into the deck.* Which meant cranking in the chain by the hand-winch till the forty-pound beast could be lifted, dripping with seaweed, over the edge. I slogged away at the winch, mashing my kneecaps into the deck. Nigel offered to do it, but I was damn well not going to let him. I was going to be as good as a guy. No difference on a boat between me and James.

– Crew's job, I yelled, and slung the clunker over the rail, my back screaming. I lay flat on the deck. Are you okay, he yelled. Fine, I said breathing into my back.

I set the main, then hoisted and cleated the genny, checking with Nigel whether I'd done it right. He stood, arms crossed, the tiller jutting out between his legs, gazing at the water, as certain as a lighthouse. You figure it out, he told me, you can't always rely on me to check everything you do. There's a book of knots in the bow locker.

Of course he was right. If I was as good as James I had to figure it out myself, know when it was right, just do it. Stop trying to please the teacher. Please the teacher by stopping pleasing the teacher. So when was I just me, not somebody pleasing someone? And when was he just Nigel, not the teacher? Who decided who we were anyway?

I searched for words that would swoop us up in a flight of togetherness. *A penny for your thoughts*, I'd read in books. I'd have paid dollars for his. I would've talked like a book, and what would we say in the book? The book of silences – that would make a good title. What would it be about? I thought of the grebes floating on their reflections last night. *Soignée* – the word that Carla loved – it even sounded like a swan – a white question mark swooping out of a giant gliding peony blossom. I thought of asking Nigel whether his words made themselves into swans or some other thing like castles or teacups. Exam papers or pyjamas.

No, I thought — too silly; for Nigel, I needed a real idea like you'd put into a book, like Lawrence's theory of science as a flashlight in a cave.

And what kind of ideas could I put into my novel? What could be as grand as the whole of science as a flashlight and the whole of the universe as a cave? Carla kept bounding in with her thoughts. I had to get control of her, but she wouldn't let me. Edith Wharton said I had to make the story come out of her character, and what was that? A character was a bit of a clown or someone who said crazy things or wore crazy clothes. Or a character had backbone, stood up to things and stood for things. A character knew what she wanted, she led people on quests. A character would know how to write this novel. She'd be a captain. Whereas the real Carla wanted to be swept off her feet by that sea captain in *The Secret Woman*, so she could marry him and live happily ever after, while *he* was the captain and braved the storms at sea.

Novel-Carla refused to work in telephone soliciting surrounded by rows of cubicles; that was much too dull. But she wasn't a nurse either, she was too much of a partier. Nor could I make her want to be a fashion designer even though she was good with clothes; she'd never sit in a classroom taking notes, making sketches, working away at sewing projects so she'd get an A. A star on a TV series was what the real Carla wanted; but the real Carla wouldn't go to acting school either. The real Carla was a cocktail waitress but I couldn't let novel-Carla be that; she had to be made up, invented.

I stared at the hummocks of Thormanby Islands, overwhelmed again by slithery uncertainty, the queasy feeling of stabbing away on a Spanish exam with only holes where words should be.

The white flash of a powerboat skimmed across us from the port side. I called to Nigel and he veered off.

— Why didn't you give me more warning?!
— I'm sorry, I said, kicking myself for daydreaming.
— What were you doing anyway?
— Looking through the binoculars.
— *Watch* means watch. Not go sightseeing.
— A powerboat has to give way, doesn't it?

– Right of way doesn't matter a damn – you must know at all times what's around you. Avoid collisions.

– I didn't think we were on a collision course.

– Do you think your thoughts matter if someone hits you?

Was it that easy to displease him? I wasn't that wrong, I thought. Why did I want to please him anyway – please the teacher? But I *did* want to, more than anything. The magic would happen, I was sure of it, we just needed time. But when would I *know*, when would I be as certain of the rules as he was? When would I say things he would write down and put into a book?

The wind dropped as we approached the islands and the headland above Halfmoon Bay. Motor or spinnaker, he said, which would you like?

I supposed he was still cross. I would have to make up for it somehow. I got the genny down and folded on the foredeck, got the spinnaker up. It swelled over us, silent and powerful.

I kept myself to myself, kept the spinnaker from luffing, tightening it this way and that. In between adjustments I studied the knot book. You're so earnest, Nigel grinned, you work hard, you study your knots; you're a good kid, you know. He held the lever of the tiller in that sug-gestive way between his legs.

I said nothing. I wouldn't let it show that his grin mattered, that pleasing him mattered. I was no different than James. He wouldn't have called James a *good kid* anyway. But I was secretly glad that he'd said it. He knows he's been unkind, I thought, it matters to him too.

We cleared the islands and headed toward the forested slopes and rocky bluffs of Texada Island, which stretched north as far as we could see, headland after headland of trees and bluffs swooping down to the strait on our port side. On our starboard, headland after headland of forested mainland coast and before us a vast expanse of sea stretching north to shadowy distant islands.

– Is there nothing here besides trees, Nigel said, as we neared Texada, I mean not even a few towns?! Or even a village.

I pointed out that the chart showed no towns, only a mine.

– No roads or houses?!

He seemed incredulous.

– No roads, but lots of mountains, I said, hundreds of miles of them.

Which is what I'd always known, that my country was hundreds of miles of trees and mountains that no one owned, it took forever to get to Princeton from Cultus Lake, cuz there was nothing much east of Cultus Lake except the moonscape of the Hope Slide, where half a mountain fell down in 1965. After that, we drove for hours and hours of forest to Princeton to pick up the last load of chests and tables and dishes on the move to Cultus Lake. Climbing slower and slower up the mountain pass, grinding down into a ravine, to a rushing torrent, dead slow around the hairpin turn, and slowly grinding up into the pass again. Meeting no one but the occasional logging truck, not a fence or a house, the only sign of humans, the bridge over the water rushing down the mountainside. Then more forest, another ravine, another hairpin, another climb, again and again.

I stood on the bow, letting the wind ripple my hair, and billow out my shirt around my naked chest. The shoreline held not the slightest mark of human contact, just a solid wall of bush above barnacled rocks.

– Not like England, eh, I said. Hell, the whole of England's only about a sixth of B.C.!

Still, I thought, England must have wild stretches outside the towns, where only the animals lived, places like Sherwood Forest.

– Hedgerows and fields, more like, Nigel said, giving me one of those cool John Lennon stares. We started in on the beer then and tacked back toward the mainland, Nigel grumbling we'd probably never reach Desolation Sound. Now, he said, he saw how it got its name.

I studied the chart, and for a while drifted around its folds and tongues of contour lines that reminded me of the woodgrain on the walls of Mom's cottage. Shapes echoing shapes, islands within islands, lines winding around each other, each time billowing a little differently from the sister lines, with the wavering strands of streams threading through the contours from tiny lakes, like fragile rootlets, or very long tails of sperm.

The chart showed we were headed toward Nelson Island and Agamemnon Channel that linked to Sechelt Inlet and the Skookumchuck

Narrows that Dad had told me made walls of water six feet high when the tides came through, boats falling off the edge or mowed down in avalanches of boiling sea. Good thing we aren't going there, Nigel said.

Who was Agamemnon, I asked. I wanted to roll the name off my tongue, the way he did, knowing what it meant, knowing who Agamemnon was, knowing what Agamemnon said. It sounded like agony and memory – something to do with Troy – men in ships rowed by oars, like the Vikings who found North America, in wooden boats with square red-striped sails in my grade four textbook. Men who snuck into Troy inside a horse in the land of *Zorba the Greek*. There's a famous tragedy about him, Nigel said, hadn't I read it in high school? The *Oresteia* by Aeschylus. Remember the *Odyssey*, he said, where Odysseus meets Agamemnon in the underworld, and he says, *Never tell a woman all you know, the day of faithful wives is gone forever?*

Of course I didn't remember.

– Never tell a woman all you know, he laughed, giving me a pointed look.

I said nothing. Did he really have to see me that way, as though *Woman* was a foreign country, full of tricks and sneaks? How did I get to be a whole person to him, like James? By working beside him every day, I thought, every day till he sees I'm just like him.

He finished his beer and grabbed another.

Of course I didn't remember this stuff about faithless wives, why would I? I *did* remember Scylla and Charybdis, the Cyclops, and Odysseus tying himself to the mast for the Sirens, and I knew Persephone'd been carried off to the underworld by Hades. But so what! I said I wished Canada had a religion that allowed you to visit the underworld, a religion with all sorts of gods and goddesses you could meet almost anywhere. It would be so much more interesting.

– You could do that in your novel, he mused, you could make a Canada where that could happen. And you will, Frances, you will, I know you will, you'll write the great Canadian novel.

Flattery. What was the use of that?

We headed toward the mainland shore, dense with fir and spruce and tangled undergrowth, and as empty of human buildings as Texada

Island. Trees fell against each other. Headless trunks with wind-snapped branches clung to cliffs. Rocky bluffs dropped straight into the waves.

— I tried writing one once, Nigel went on, but it was all complete codswallop. A complete fucking botch. You'd have laughed. You, Frances, would have said I can do better than that. And you'd be right, Frances. You could.

I wanted to know about his novel, who were the characters, and how had he planned it. You really don't want to hear this, Nigel said, but I pestered him, and I guess the beer had loosened him up.

— Everything starts out cool and exciting, he said. When you're a kid, you know, and you roam around with your pals, you read the same Biggles books, outsmart the same silly teachers, build crystal sets together, trounce all the other kids with your conkers, beat up the school bullies, and no one can stop you, like you're all one animal, like whatever your mates do you are doing it. Then one day something clicks shut, and you're on the other side of a wall.

— It was going to be about that, he said. It was going to be about three boys who started out like that and how one of them got shut on the other side of a wall. Why had it happened? Why had one of them acted unforgivably? So that he sealed himself off, and the others carried him around like a rat in a glass box? Why did they even bother?

— I had it all mapped out, he went on, how the boys got on like billy-oh. Invented themselves as scientists and explorers, calling each other things like Charles Darwin or Dr. Livingstone. They carried hammers and chisels, created digs in derelict buildings and old bomb sites, collected ancient medicine bottles, deduced the local diet from a trash bin, looked for bits of history: Jase we called him for Jason; Min for Minim, he was smaller than the others; and Nick. One day they see a shard of a bomb casing (we'd got others like it, none this big), it was down a stairwell into what had been a cellar, half the floor above it caved in. Min went down to get it. The floor fell on top of him. They called Min but no answer. Nick said they should get someone with proper equipment. Jase said they should go down too. And then he just went down. And Nick couldn't follow. He couldn't go down the tiny hole in the pile of caved-in floor boards.

– Wait a minute, I said. You said *we*. You mean you were ...?

He chucked another empty beer tin into the cockpit.

– Yeah, he said.

– And Min – did Min ...?

– Min was okay, but nothing was ever the same after that. Min and Jase were always on the same wavelength, Nick always not, because he wasn't brave enough to go down that hole. It was supposed to be how they got back together, I made Nick rescue Min and Jase in a boating accident, but it didn't work, it was too pat. I couldn't get past that moment. I couldn't make it matter enough. Couldn't make them into a novel, just kept writing about Nick in his glass box, the way they always looked at him on the other side of the glass.

Nigel said he'd thrown the whole lot in the dustbin, and I thought of pages of words in a metal can all covered with grey powder. I thought of each of us, unsure in our different ways, wandering together in uncertainty. I brought him a Marmite-and-tomato sandwich and the tea Thermos, and he grabbed me in a sideways bear hug, almost tipping us both overboard.

– Anyway your novel, he said tightening his arm around me, your novel's going to be completely different.

We sailed steadily toward the wide mouth of an inlet cutting deep into the coastal mountains, which the chart said was Agamemnon Channel. Once, I thought, sailors came here all the way from Europe, looking for the Northwest Passage, but all they found were channels like this one that snaked around jagged headlands, channels that had once been rivers gouging away mountains, now become gorges and ravines in a massive coastal wall. How grand were the forces that heaved up and sculpted this wall of coastal peaks! How giant and relentless and bigger than any human evil!

Yet how different the mountains seemed here lurching up from the sprawling sea, compared to my old friends around Cultus Lake, who had always sheltered and protected me. I'd crawled their forests like a flea in the fur of a bear. They were refuge and sanctuary. But here I wondered, if we were shipwrecked, would these mountains shelter and feed us or wither us to nothing in their faceless rock and timeless snarl of forest and deadfall?

– I don't think Agamemnon belongs here, I said pointing to the channel cutting into the mountains, I think I'd call it the Mouth of Agony and Memory.

We got into a game of naming all the headlands, islands, and inlets around us, things like Mushroom Backpack, or Crusty Roll, and arguing about whether we could use proper nouns, which I said should be banned, and he said you had to use because they were proper. It was hilarious.

Nigel told me I must read Proust, because he showed how magical names were, and how in a name you can find a whole world. Proust showed you how sounding a name was exactly like biting into a madeleine, a kind of French pastry, he said, just like one your aunt gave you long ago which you dipped in lime-blossom tea, and now when you bit into it, it made the whole town where she lived, and your bedroom in her house spring up like a stage set before you, along with the streets of the town and the paths where she sent you on errands.

Maybe I could find a recipe for madeleines in Mom's cookbooks, I thought. I could make one, and bite into it and find out what it made me think of. I could go to all the tea stores in Vancouver and find lime-blossom tea.

We zigzagged north back toward Texada Island, and Nigel told me how the name *Parme* always made Proust think of violets, and *Florence* made him think of lilies, whereas *Balbec* made him think of a shard of old pottery depicting feudal rituals.

I said that I, on the other hand, thought of Lorna's red-and-green shaker of powdered cheese, Florence Nightingale carrying a lamp, and nothing at all for *Balbec* except it sounded like sharp rocks. *Madeleine* was magical though because *madeleine* made me think of *Twelve little girls in two straight lines*, living in a house *all covered in vines*. Naughty Madeline, the youngest girl, and Miss Clavel, her neckless head bolting up like a carrot top under her bridal-headdress bed-canopy. *In the middle of the night Miss Clavel turned on the light. Something was not right.*

Proust made his life into a huge novel, Nigel said, which I thought was amazing, the exact opposite of what Edith Wharton said novelists should do. In fact, Nigel went on, Proust thought that you'd only ever lived your life when you wrote it into a novel. He stayed lost in thought after that, and I wanted to ask him if he'd try his novel again or another one, but I too remained silent. Didn't want to spoil our counterpoint of ideas — what I'd longed for with him, I thought, it meant so much more than sex.

Though the sex was puzzling. I'd never really had to think about it before, it just seemed to happen. I came. I climaxed. I reached orgasm, as Mom called it. Mom said it had to do with the clitoris, not the vagina. I didn't think about it. Guys always seemed to know more or less what to do. Some were kind of clumsy, others more considerate. Now I was going to have to think about it, maybe show Nigel a few things I liked, but how did you do that without being selfish? Then too he was so tense and skittish, it would put him off.

Behind us stood Nelson Island and the huge mouth of Jervis Inlet, ahead the bluish peaks and gulches on Texada. I studied the chart and sighted headlands with the compass.

— You can't just eyeball it, Nigel said.

I pointed the compass over the bow — we were heading north-north-west. Supposing we charted a course, I said, drawing straight lines to points where we had to change direction, sliding the parallel ruler over to the compass rose to get our bearing. We'd know where we were on the course. But Nigel said chart bearings weren't compass bearings; you had to find true north. I thought of school maps showing magnetic north drifting over the Arctic islands instead of neatly pinned to the north pole. Earth slipping and sliding in a net bag of grid lines, like a giant melon in an onion sack.

To know where you are on the chart, he said, you have to add or subtract magnetic variation; twenty degrees west — east is least, meaning you subtract on the east — add on the west — twenty degrees to your compass bearing. He made me draw five columns marked True, Variation, Magnetic, Deviation, Compass.

If my true direction on the chart was 300, I had to add twenty under Variation to get 320 under Magnetic and then another one degree of deviation caused by the boat, metal objects, radios, engines. *Finally* I would know my compass bearing to stay on course. If you took a compass bearing on a landmark, the whole thing had to be done in reverse in order to mark it on the chart.

I took some bearings and wrote out my calculations, then plotted them on the chart. By then our position had changed. So where were we? The whole thing seemed absurdly complicated.

— So if we just look at landmarks, we can't really know where we are on the chart.

— Not if you're using compass bearings and not true bearings.

— But you can still see where you are.

— You could be twenty degrees wrong; nowhere near where you think you are. Right on a reef instead of safely past it.

He tossed an apple core to a gull in the water.

— So why aren't we doing it then?

— Because I've got you to keep watch!

When we got to the marina at Powell River, Nigel started the motor and told me to take the boat up to the closest spot on the dock. Just go dead slow, like parking a car, I thought, reverse, if you want to stop, then neutral. I eased down the long channel between the floats packed with boats on both sides. There, Nigel said pointing to a spot in front of a motor launch with a row of portholes along the side and behind a fourteen-foot dinghy with tipped-up outboard. Along the dock, a man ran a belt sander on his deck, another hosed off his dinghy. Men cleaned fish and yakked to the owner of the launch, sitting on deck with cigarette and drink. He'd left his inflatable in the water alongside his boat.

I eased the bow toward the dock, but we were coming in too fast, headed straight for the blades of the dinghy motor. I pulled the throttle into reverse. My stern swung toward the delicate shell of a runabout on the next float. Neutral. Forward. The boat was a blob of mercury on a sheet of ice, a slithering ice cube in a hot pan. It was now pointed straight at the dock. The belt sander stopped, its owner gazing at our predicament. Keep your motor off my inflatable, the launch owner grouched.

I tried to pull the boat back into the channel, make it parallel to the dock again, by reversing and turning right. Our stern squeezed into the inflatable. Launch Owner, out of his chair, peered over the edge of his bow. The fish men put down their catch and the hose stopped splashing. Nigel stood on the bow with the line. I would not ask him what to do; I would learn by doing. Neutral. Forward. The boat rubbed along the inflatable. I turned the wheel to pull it off and ended up headed right for an iron bollard.

The hose man ran down the dock and down the next float to the runabout. He stood with a pole, fending off, and pushing the stern back toward the inflatable. I centred the wheel to straight ahead. Reverse. Neutral. Forward. Neutral. Like looking for footholds in air. Skidding on the slightest bite of the motor. *Whoa. Whoa. Easy* – from the dock. All of them had poles. I was squeezing the inflatable between us and the launch, Launch Owner trying to fend us off with a pole that wouldn't reach. Toss us a line, men on the dock shouted.

Put her in neutral, Nigel muttered. He threw the line, but it didn't quite reach the dock. One of the men fetched it out of the water from the dinghy, handed it up to the men on the dock. They pulled us in. The launch owner went back to his deck chair. Nigel jumped onto the dock. Training session, huh, one of them said. Nigel gave him a terse nod as he tied the bow line, and told me to cut the motor, toss him the stern line. One of the fish men wandered over with a gutted salmon. Pretty nice rig you got there, guess you'd call it a sloop, eh, he said. Nigel nodded, and busied himself testing lines for slack and kicking at a fender. Staying or going, he said to me. Going for a walk, I said, grabbing my wallet, and leaving him to lock up. The fish man stood there, admiring *Windsong*. I'm going to the pub, Nigel said, if you want to come after.

I stumbled up the dock through the barbecue smoke and rock 'n' roll radios, the balding sunburnt boat-owners and their fat, pastel-and-white clad wives. A beach stretched a few yards either side of the dock. I tramped over its rocks and broken shells — if I had turned the wheel port instead of starboard, if I had reversed sooner, cut toward the dock sooner. If I had glided the boat into the dock and it had been as easy as parking a car.

I reached unpassable boulders and turned, crunching back toward the weedy creosote pilings of the pier. I kicked some rocks. I felt like skipping out, like grabbing my stuff and hitching back to Vancouver, fuck sailing, fuck trying to be as good as Nigel and James.

At the other end of the beach, I turned back to the discarded motor-oil jugs, plastic bags, and cigarette packs under the pilings. I thought about that road I'd be hitching, where women disappeared. After a few more turns back and forth, I climbed the steps to the pub.

Nigel, the fish men, and a woman in a sunflower tank top all had beers. I squeezed in to their table, shaking hands with Merv and Wally and Wally's wife, Lola. Merv's and Wally's hands felt hardened and rough. Lola's was softer with long scarlet nails. Her bosom sagged a little over the edge of her tank top and Wally's chest bulged out his faded shirt. Scalp showed through the hair on Merv's head.

— Sorry I made such a botch of it, I said, keeping my eyes on the cartoon tugboats on the table's oilcloth.

— Not to worry, Nigel said. The damage was under a hundred.

— What damage?!

— Merv's pole chipped some paint, Wally chuckled.

— Inflatable got squeezed too, Merv said, grinning. Yacht Man suffered a conniption; there's serious damage there for pain and suffering.

Lola said she didn't intend ever to learn how to dock a boat, just left it to Wally.

— We have to learn, I said, looking into light-brown eyes under her blow-dried hair, otherwise, they'll keep lording it over us. There's no reason we can't do it just as well as they can, I said, trying desperately to smile, take it all as a joke like they did.

Wally leaned back in his chair and studied Nigel, who said nothing and drank his beer. The waitress came by. I ordered scotch on the rocks.

— You'll get it, Merv said. He glugged some beer.

— One day.

The men laughed.

— Nigel here was just tellin me you're a novelist, Merv said. He was being polite of course, and I couldn't very well embarrass Nigel by saying I wasn't. So I said I hoped to be, and they wanted to know what it was about, and then when I said a bunch of people living in a house, they said, oh, one of those hippie houses, where they smoke pot all day, and everyone laughed, even Nigel's eyes twinkling through his round specs, waiting to see what I'd say. Which was nothing.

— Yeah, we got a few of those up here, said Wally, don't we, Loll? One right on our street, eh, Loll?

Loll changed the subject to Nigel's London where they'd all gone last year, Merv and his wife, and Wally and Lola, got their picture taken with a guard at Buckingham Palace (Merv imitated a stiff, poker-faced guard and everyone laughed), and with Pierre Elliott Trudeau at Madame Tussauds (here Merv got another laugh by looking down his nose and preening about an imaginary rose in his buttonhole).

They got onto London pubs, Wally wanting to know if Nigel'd been to this one or that one, Merv saying they searched high and low for some pub where Queen Elizabeth the First danced around a cherry tree, and Nigel saying he went to river pubs mainly, out in Hammersmith. I thought how they'd all been all sorts of places I hadn't. What a fool I was for thinking I could hang out with them, but maybe one day Nigel would show me those English pubs, and I'd be able to say I'd been to all sorts of places too, and anyway why didn't Merv and Wally talk about places around here?

But they didn't. They got onto Vancouver pubs and how they were either really seedy like around the porn strip on Granville Street or vast dull barns or stuffy and hoity-toity. The hours were terrible, and you could never get a drink on a Sunday. The Biltmore wasn't bad, they went on, but had Nigel tried The King's Head, which Wally thought was the most English pub in all of Vancouver, a real gem, with its wood panelling and porcelain taps? And Nigel had tried it, now that he was living on his boat near there, but he thought the beer selection wasn't as good as the Biltmore's.

A roar of airbrakes sounded on the road above the marina.

– I suppose that's a *logging lorry*, Nigel said. We don't have lorries here, Lola said, and what the heck was a *truck* in England? Nigel amused them by saying *pants* were underwear and *gas* was *farts*. It's *trousers* in England, or *knickers*, but he supposed they'd say *panties*, just like they'd probably say *wax* when it should be *paraffin*, or *trunk* when they meant the *boot* of a car, and what you put in the car, he said, is *petrol*. Makes me think of lubricant, Lola said, and everyone laughed, even me, though I didn't know exactly why it was so funny.

Later when we got back to the boat, Nigel told me Merv and Wally worked at the mill. Like their fathers before them and probably their grandfathers. Men of brawn and belly-laughs, Nigel called them, men driving logs into chippers, cranking valves on vats of pulping liquor, feeding seas of pulp into stacks of interlocking rollers. I thought of the stink of the mill. And all the trees mowed down, chopping the mountains bald.

– Watch out for the *nip points*, Nigel said. Merv and Wally's word for all the rolling parts of the mill where they meet other rolling parts and could suck in an arm or a leg or a whole man. I thought of a boy I went to high school with setting chokes; the chain sucked him into the skidder.

The sea was flat calm as we headed next day through the channel between Harwood Island and Powell River, not even enough wind for a spinnaker. Already the sun had bleached the sky to a pale aqua, and dulled the distant hulks of Texada Island and other headlands up the coast. The water's glassy surface spread out before us, glaring back at the sky. Forest fires and the rotten-egg vapours from the pulp mill filled the air with haze. It was one of those days when you wanted to be in the water, not on it.

Nigel set the throttle at four knots and steered toward a glimmering mirage that might be Savary Island. He stood at the wheel, fixed as the mast, the motor droning behind him, the boat dragging a widening V of ripples like a giant royal train. After Savary we would pass Bliss Landing, then head around the northern tip of the peninsula into the sun-warmed bay of Desolation Sound. In the meantime, chores. No, not replacing the battens – he didn't want the sail spread out everywhere. Clean the head.

No bleach. No Dutch Cleanser, no Spic and Span on board. Just use seawater. I went below and scrubbed with a rag at splatters of shit on the underside of the seat. Women's work, dammit. I wanted to take the wheel, learn to be skipper. The bowl was worse, probably never washed. No rubber gloves and no toilet brush.

Hemingway said in one of the library books on novels, *the first draft of anything is shit.* My novel so far. Impossible. Fake sounding, trying to be like something I'd read, not a real novel, like you'd buy in a store, like something by John Fowles or Virginia Woolf or D.H. Lawrence.

My next chore was pumping bilge water. For some reason the long hose would not attach to the pump. I took the wheel while Nigel fiddled with it. The sun pounded down, and the motor droned on, pushing us through a flat sea. Nigel tossed another wrench back in the locker, poked at the pump with a different screwdriver. That didn't work either. You're just going to have to pump it into the bucket and then toss it, he said. But the bucket wouldn't fit under the spigot, so I held an empty Pepsi bottle over it, wedged the pump between my feet and pumped up brown water. After about fifteen minutes my arms gave out. I had half a bucket of bilge water. I lay back on the cool floor of the boat. Maybe we could stop at Savary and swim.

– What are you doing down there?

I hoisted myself up and carried the bucket out to the cockpit. Four Pepsi bottles later, he told me I could take charge. He was going to work on that chapter he'd brought along. Yippee, I said.

We plowed steadily on. Hazy bluffs to starboard, wide stretch of Georgia Strait to port. No sails in sight, since no wind. The motor ground and hummed, Sargasso Sea, Sargasso Sea, Soupy Sargasso Sea. Turquoise room, turquoise room, novel of turquoise room. I gazed through the binoculars at Savary's finger of beach arcing across the strait. White flat sands collecting drift logs below low forested hills.

Like *Windsong* through the Sargasso Sea, I had to plow on with my *Turquoise Room*. I had to make Carla and Dwight fall in love, even though she thinks he's a scumbag dreaming stupidly he'll one day write the next Beatles song. What could Dwight do to make Carla change her mind? Bring her flowers or chocolates? You asshole, she'd say, what the fuck's this for?

Did guys really bring flowers to women they were trying to impress, or did that just happen on TV? Because the TV writer was making his character act in this hokey way so you knew the character supposedly cared? Whereas real love carried you away; real love made you give everything you've got, not just a bunch of tulips. TV writers made characters give flowers even if the character would never do that because he didn't give a shit about Carla and just wanted to stick his dick into Dagmar. Which Dagmar didn't seem to mind, as she told me on the phone before heading back to her island. He went down on her, she said, whatever that meant, I didn't ask. Whatever it was, it was a mighty fine time, her big O, as she called it, was off the Richter scale.

TV writers made people do things on TV and then people in the real world did what they saw on TV, so what was real?

Nigel drifted around the deck for a while, then went to the galley table to work on his chapter. I could see him down there looking things up in Lawrence books, making notes on a lined pad. Lists of page numbers. Then for a long time he just sat there, gazing at pages of notes spread out in front of him. His shoulders hunched. His chin rested in his two hands, his elbows propped on the table. After a while he scribbled something down, then went back to chin in hands.

Afternoon droned on. I took my shirt off, like a guy, why not, it was so hot. I had nothing on underneath. Down in the cabin, Nigel put his head down on his arms folded across the table, like I'd seen him do that day in the Safeway parking lot. I wanted to put my arms around him, wanted to make up for whatever it was that discouraged him so much.

When we came to the mouth of the sound, I cut the motor to one knot. Nigel jolted up out of the galley, and stood beside me directing us to a sheltered cove where we could anchor. He flashed a smile at my shirtless chest, wrapped his arms around me, and whispered in my ear he couldn't have done the trip without me. Oh, I love our sailing together, I told him, kissing his ear, pleased that, after all, my efforts mattered to him, I'll crew whenever you want, there's so much we can explore.

As soon as we anchored, we chucked our sweaty three-day clothes and jumped in the water. You could see all the way to the light sandy bottom, fathoms below us, see the anchor chain and the anchor hooking into the bottom, aqua-coloured water like you see in pictures of the Caribbean. Nigel swam around the boat once, then hauled himself out. He watched me frog-kicking and rolling as he towelled himself. Go ahead, stay in longer, he said. I soaked in the balmy water, sweeping my arms through its buoyancy, pulling belly and breasts through its ribboning muscle. I swam to shore and back. Then climbed out, hair running rivulets on my nakedness.

After dinner, sitting with our wine glasses in the glow of the little galley lamp, I brought out some cake I'd found at the Powell River marina, banana-walnut, I told Nigel. Aren't I lucky I got you as crew and not James, he said. Though, he went on, it doesn't really look like cake, it looks more like wholemeal bread. Of course it's cake, I said. It says right on the package; it is *not* bread. He tried a slice. No, he said. It's not solid enough for cake, too spongy. But, I said that's exactly what cakes were supposed to be, light and airy so they spring up. No, he said, a real cake would be buttery white and made in two layers held together by greengage jam, with a little dusting of sugar on top. It's very nice though, he said. I'll even have another piece, but I would call it more of a loaf than a cake. Don't look so crestfallen, he said. Really, it's very nice.

I asked him if I could help him with his chapter, and he said it was sweet of me, but he needed someone who'd read pretty well all of Lawrence. He'd had an editor but they'd moved away so it was taking him a lot longer. I asked who it was but he said nobody I knew, just someone who'd helped him before. I offered to read the books, but no, he just wished he had his other editor. Maybe you could mail them your chapter with questions, I said, but he said it was more of a thing where you got ideas by talking.

Finally he admitted it was about Ursula Brangwen in *Women in Love* and the other two novels in the sequence. He thought Lawrence had named her Ursula because she was like a bear, like a force of nature, something utterly powerful and wild. But she was also a constellation, Ursa Major; she was one of the constellations in Lawrence's cosmology, she was his pole star. *Cosmology*, I thought, what a gorgeous word – knowledge and universe all in one, as though things you knew were clusters of stars like the Big Dipper and Pegasus.

At Cultus Lake, I said, bears would come around in the fall and raid orchards. High school boys would take a day off school to shoot them. I'd eaten plenty of bear stew. Nigel had never seen a bear except in zoos.

Morning brought the rorks of ravens and the scolding of squirrels from the forest tumbling down to the water where *Windsong* gently bobbed. The setting sun of the previous evening had bathed the sound in apricot and rose; now the morning sun bleached the pine, cedar, and Douglas fir to a seaweed brown that tilted every which way in a tangle of salmonberry and salal. At the edge of the forest lichen-covered rocks jutted steeply into the glassy water, where we drifted with our coffee.

The plan was to spend the day enjoying our destination, but of course there were no roads, buildings, or human presences of any kind, and only a small opening to a rocky beach at the foot of the thick forest. I was all for exploring the beach and looking for the little lake the charts showed about a half mile from the shore. Surely there must be a trail of some sort to that. Unwin Lake it was called. But Nigel said he wasn't much for hiking. I started washing breakfast dishes. Nigel squeezed past into the galley table and rummaged through the storage ledge, sorting charts, flashlights, compass, his chapter. Leave the dishes, he said, take a break for the day.

I straightened the sleeping platform, stowed clothes in lockers, squeezed past Nigel to the cockpit, flipped open a book. After a few pages, I asked Nigel if he was sure he didn't want to explore the lake, it wasn't a hike, it was really close. You go, he said, he wanted to look again at his chapter, last night's chat was so helpful, and he wanted to get that down. He promised we'd explore the beach together later.

— What did I say that was helpful?

— Nothing in particular, but it *was* helpful.

— Tell me what books to read; let me look things up for you.

— Look, Frances, you can't just bone up on it like that. It would take you months.

So we were here at last, but separate. Once again I'd blundered into his forbidden territory, and now I skidded around in slithery uncertainty outside his walls. But fighting about it wasn't going to fix this. Only time could fix it. You couldn't make trust to order.

I shut up, kept to myself, and arranged to get away from *Windsong* as quickly as possible, taking my journal, a sandwich, and a towel. I would wash off yesterday's salt in the lake. I would work on my novel. I would think. About what? Not about us. Not about trying to be *us*. I would *not* cry.

Nigel sat in the galley staring at his chapter. I said nothing as I left the boat.

I found a narrow trail through a thicket of Oregon grape, salmon-berry, and juniper so dense the sound seemed no longer to exist once you were in it. A raven swooped low over my head; I could hear its wings raking the air. My nose filled with the scent of sunbaked pine needles.

I hummed a tuneless tune and whacked tree trunks with a stick, in case of bears. Some people wore bells to warn them off; others said bells just made them curious so they followed you. Why wouldn't humming and tree-whacking have the same effect, I wondered? The only bear I met, though, was a paunchy man in a ball cap and palm-tree shirt, behind him a Doberman and a young boy carrying a plastic squirt gun. Howdy, the man said. Hi, I said.

— Goin up to the lake?

— Yeah.

— Y'all watch for bears.

— You see any?

The kid squirted the bushes with his gun. The man said not particularly but he'd ahearda some around here.

— Y'all keep alookin. They liketa go after a young thang like y'all.

— Okay, I said.

Not long after that, the trees thinned out, and the trail wound around
some rocks and over a ridge to the edge of the lake. I looked for a place
to jump in but the shore was buried in a wreckage of felled trees. These
were the trees the loggers hadn't bothered to haul away when they sawed
off the forest around the lake. All that remained now, stretching away
as far as I could see, were stumps and smashed branches, everything
brown, blackened by slash-burning, everything dead.

I scrambled over the mess of weathered, broken trunks to a dog-
house-sized rock and stuck my feet into soupy water. Whole trunks,
their sides and branches coated with slime, sank into the muddy depths
around the rock. Algae clung to my toes, caressing them as though it
would grow on me. There would be no fish here.

It truly was a cultus lake, I thought, a dead, useless lake, whereas
my Cultus Lake was just a silent lake. My Cultus Lake was full of fish
if you knew where to find them. My cultus lake, Indians said, held the
mouth of an underground tunnel to the ocean; the Shla-lah-kum lived
there who swallowed a man and spit him out on the tide flats forty miles
away at Mud Bay.

Dead Lake at Desolation Sound, I wrote in my journal. Then stared at
the blank page. What could be poetic about such a place? Dagmar in her
island cabin would have filled a page; whatever she was doing became
a poem. *Underwater trees,* I wrote. *Forest of algaed limbs.* Another fifteen
minutes of blank page drifted by. Then: *You won't be in anyone's painting of
a lake.* The algaed water threw a brown blank at a hazy sky. I peered over
the edge of the rock but saw only a dark hole for my head and shoulders,
cut out of a ghostly ceiling.

When I got back to *Windsong,* Nigel wrapped his arms around me and
said he was sorry he'd left me to fend for myself, he knew it wasn't fair,

I'd come all this way and worked so hard, but then he said he was sure I'd have enjoyed reconnecting alone with my mountains and trees. As though they couldn't ever be his trees, I thought.

I kept cool as James. Damn him.

– I'm sorry, I really am, he said kissing my ear, I'm all yours.

He poured me a beer and told me about a visitor. The paunchy palm-tree man with his Doberman, in his eight-cabin motor launch. He pulled alongside. He was a little worried about me up there on the trail alone, Nigel said. I told him not to worry, you were half bear yourself and had shot and eaten a few; so you'd know exactly what to do.

He was from Texas and had a summer place in Lund, around the point from the sound, thought Nigel should come into town, take me out to dinner at the restaurant. Then he had a better idea. Told Nigel to come on board. He'd caught too many crabs, so he gave Nigel a bucket of them along with a bottle of wine. Of course he had to tell Nigel all about his "small" fifteen-thousand-acre ranch, and show him his new depth sounder. He said the lake was *plug-ugly*, and I'd be *matty* disappointed.

I had to smile at Nigel's Texan accent. He was having such fun with it, and he was so affectionate, I couldn't carry on my "cool as cool." For the rest of the day, we goofed around together, asking each other things like what *tam* was dinner? didja want to *clam* into the dinghy and go to the other *sad* of the bay? wasn't that stump over there *jis' plug-ugly*? and should a *brang* a beer?

Things were okay again, and we made love, and it was good.

The next day we headed south. At Bliss Landing, we swam off the boat and walked on boom logs. A killer whale breached near us at Savary Island. Nigel coached me into safely docking *Windsong* at Secret Cove, where we drank white wine and ate scallops in a floating restaurant. Back at Kitsilano Marina, I even docked the boat with no coaching. I vacuumed the cabin, washed down the deck, stowed the sails, and kissed Nigel goodbye. Get that novel finished; let me read what you've got so far, he said. He would call at the end of the week after he'd been out to UBC, or so I thought.

CHAPTER 9

I reported the swimming, the whale, and the Secret Cove dinner to Lorna and Kitty during mail opening. Kitty wanted to know if he was going to propose. Her boyfriend proposed on the Dine & Dance Harbour Boat. Got right down on his knees. Handed her a blue velvet box. Lorna wanted to know whether I'd be in his class again in the fall and what kind of books he liked. Would I go live with him on his boat and give up my room – that was like a boat anyway, just one room. Except for all the icky other people you have to share the bathroom with, Kitty said, touching up her frosted lipstick. She said she'd keep a can of Lysol in her room and spray everything every time she went in there.

Back at the sorting racks in the shadowy supply room, Lorna said, no, she hadn't gone before the abortion committee, and Steve hadn't got a job. Let's go for a walk at lunch to Stanley Park, Kitty's dad's taking her out.

But just as we'd got safely out of the building and headed past the Bayshore Inn, Kitty came trotting along in her red taffeta and red heels, calling wait up, wait up, and, breathless, accusing us of both knowing something secret, so what was it?

– What, Lorna looked at me.

– I don't know. What?

– It's not fair, you two are keeping secrets.

– It's Lorna's glasses.

– What about them?

– They're on backwards.

– Oh, get out. Oh my gawd, lookit that cute jumpsuit with the pink shorts, Kitty pointed at a woman ahead of us, that is sooo cute.

— They have them at Eaton's, Lorna commented.

Beyond the Bayshore Inn, we set out across the clipped grass toward a flock of geese billing for grubs or worms or whatever they ate, Kitty trying to dodge goose turds in her new red shoes, Lorna munching a chocolate bar. There were no benches and Kitty was definitely not going to sit on the grass. We stood on the bridge over the lagoon — Lorna the giant redwood with Kitty the lollipop on one side and Frances the squirrel on the other — gazing out at the red brick mansion with its white-trimmed windows of HMCS Discovery Naval Training Station. A uniformed man opened the gate and waved in a black car fluttering little flags. Why's it called Deadman's Island, Lorna wanted to know. I don't know, Kitty said, but I wouldn't mind living there.

A week drifted by with no word from Nigel. I rang his office, but he didn't answer. On the Friday, I headed for my shift at the Biltmore, but I was darned if I'd put my hair in a beehive. I braided it down my back. Harry said he didn't want some peasant hippie girl as a waitress in his bar. Get it fixed and hurry up. Carla's ghost in the blue light of the can missed an earring. Shit shit shit. Why? Because they're Coolique earrings, and I owe them a ton of money. She dug out a Coolique hair-clasp from her bag — a red plastic bird. The stick running through it had a peace sign on its end. I wound my hair into a bun for the clasp. They came to my room today. Who? Harry opened the door and yelled, Carla, ya left half an order behind, get with it. She'd tell me later.

No Geers or Aggies in the Biltmore that night. Instead men in brown or checked Dacron jackets and perma-press pants. Brown striped ties. Some had zippered binders or glossy folders stuffed with papers. Sweet deal, I heard them saying. Yeah, and if you buy a case you save 10 per-cent a unit. I should be going. We just got started — it's on me. Wife's cooking, it's Friday night. Hey, it's on me — no — absolutely — no strings attached — get us another round. Hey sweetie (to me), whaddaya doin after work? Wouldn't you like to know, I said.

Five or six bikers came in and threw their skullcaps and studded leather jackets along some benches. Their women wore tight, crotch-high miniskirts, low-cut frilly blouses, and spike heels. Flames, eagle wings, skulls and crossbones, souped-up bikes, and Maltese crosses spewed along their arms from ripped black T-shirts. The men ordered Molson's and Ginger Ale Wiser's; the women, peach coolers. Jack and Cheyenne joined the biker table, Cheyenne's eyelids muddy with smeared mascara, her black lace bra poking out her tank top. Jack's arm below his clean white T-shirt sleeve said *Live to ride.*

Dwight eyed me over a book from the back table by the washrooms. Dad had come by to score some dope but he was two bucks short. Dwight gave it to him anyway. Thanks, I said. Maybe he'll make it up next time. Dwight's book cover said, *Run with the Hunted* by Charles Bukowski. He wanted to know if I was a blue-water sailor now.

– What're you ordering?

– I see your limey friend's here.

– What's it to you?

I turned and Nigel waved from a table across the room.

– Didja get that, Dwight said.

– What?

– A pint of Moosehead.

– Okay.

– Aren't you s'posed to say that with a smile, and *I'll be right back with your drink?*

I headed over to Nigel's table.

– Sorry I haven't called, Nigel said. I've been kind of under the weather, throwing up and all that.

– That's exactly why you should call, I said. I'd bring you soup, keep the cabin tidy.

I sat down opposite him, took his hands, and asked if he'd seen a doctor, did he need clean sheets, did he need food, was he okay on the boat without a proper washroom? James had taken him in for a couple of nights, he said. He was better now, he'd call me if he needed anything. I guessed he probably didn't want to take the boat out, and he said, no, not this weekend, and maybe not for a while, the head left a lot of paperwork in his box; he had to get ready for classes and finish ... He stopped midsentence, looking at someone behind me, which turned out to be Harry ordering me into his office. Now!

Where did you grow up, he demanded, did they have restaurants out there or did I live in a teepee? When you wait tables, he went on, you do not, EVER, sit down with the customers. Got it?!

— Got it, I said.

— I will not tell you a second time. I don't care whether it's your fiancé, your baby sister, or your dying grandmother. Your job is to hustle, not sit on your ass.

— Sorry, I said.

— Okay. Out.

Back in the lounge, I saw Nigel had left, not even ordering a beer I guessed. Dwight waved me over. Reminded me that about twenty minutes ago he'd ordered a Moosehead. I ran to get it.

— I see your limey friend took off, when you tried to seduce him.

— Piss off.

— So what'd the manager rake you over the coals about, he smirked.

— None of your business.

— Would it be seducing your boyfriend isn't part of your job?

— I'm busy, I told him and strode off, smiling at the bikers.

Nigel didn't call but a few days later I wandered down to the boat anyway. The gate to the floats was locked, and I could see all *Windsong*'s hatches closed and the padlock on the cabin door. I hung around the wharf overlooking the floats, picking out *Windsong*'s mast in the forest of sticks. A wooden mast, Sitka spruce, not aluminum like so many of them clinking their rigging in the breeze. *Windsong*, with her teak deck, when so many were just moulded plastic. On the way back, I looked in at The King's Head, which was easier to get to than the Biltmore from the boat; maybe he was there, but he wasn't. Buckets of flowers stood outside the corner store across the street. I would buy a single rose, I thought. I would take it down to the boat and wait till someone unlocked the gate and leave it on the cabin door. I would wrap it in wet paper towel from the beach washroom.

At the floats, I waited with my rose in its soggy towel till a man with a barrow of supplies unlocked the gate. I squeezed past him and held the gate for him, felt his eyes on me all the way down to *Windsong*. I propped the flower between the lock and the door, wandered around the floats for a bit, but finally had to head for my room.

On my balcony with a book, I left the door open in case he phoned. My eyes slid over shapes of words, but the words drifted off into thoughts about our dinner in Secret Cove: breaded scallops and tartar sauce, mashed potatoes and peas. The tall glasses of white wine, with ice cubes cuz they'd run out of chilled. It was the first time anyone had taken me out to dinner in a really swish restaurant. I thought about all the other dinners we would have, talking about Lawrence or Proust or Virginia Woolf. All the islands and channels and inlets we would sail to, we would name them for whales and ravens and mushrooms, we would name the spirits that haunted them, the tree spirits, the bear spirits. We could write books together. I would look up things in the library for his book on Lawrence and he would help me finish my novel. And one day he would take me to England and France and Italy. And I'd speak his language of *lorries* and *trousers* and *knickers*.

He did not call. I went to my shift at the Biltmore. He didn't come in. During the week I tried calling his office again, but there was no answer. Maybe he was in the library working on Lawrence. Or worse, maybe he was in hospital.

Another week went by. I walked down the hill past carts of Kellogg's Corn Flakes at the Safeway lot, past mats of Coppertoned arms and legs parked on towels at the beach. I drifted through the chestnut trees dropping their crinkled brown leaves on clipped grass behind the Maritime Museum. The gate to the marina floats was open, but *Windsong*'s cabin door was locked. The knots on the mainsail cover looked just like I'd left them at the end of our trip. My rose was gone.

I tore a page out of my notebook. *Dear Nigel,* ... But what could I say? He either loved me or he didn't, and if he did he would come to me. Love was free. Love was either there or it wasn't. Love was a magic energy that sprang out of nowhere and if everyone would just let it do its work we would be fine, we wouldn't have the Vietnam War. We wouldn't have people trapped in mean marriages; they could follow their hearts, and when the marriage was over they could go where love was. You couldn't make love happen. You couldn't tell someone, love me, and if they didn't, make them. All you could do was give them flowers ...

And you could be the flower that you give. Give him everything there is to give.

Dear Nigel, I thought, here is a rose. *Dear Nigel,* I wrote, *I miss you. Hope you are all right. How is the Lawrence work going? I've got half my novel typed. I'm dying to show you. Love, F.*

I went back to the beach for a rock, then back to the boat and weighed the note down in the cockpit. I dawdled around the floats for a while, picking the boats I liked, the wooden ones with windows in teak cabins to shiny brass barometers and compasses, the sloops with names like *Heart's Ease* and not the fibreglass speedboats with names like *Adventurama.* Then instead of heading west back to my room, I walked east along the gravel path toward the Burrard Bridge, until I was under it in the dusty weeds and bushes of the overgrown Indian Reserve. I sat on a rock for as long as I could with cars and trucks roaring overhead and looked at boat traffic in False Creek, the red coast-guard boats, the yachts with their many dark-windowed decks, the fishing boats with stout wheelhouses, and spools of nets, a tug towing a Seaspan barge. Then headed back past *Windsong's* marina. Maybe he'd returned.

And indeed he was just returning, almost at the top of the wharf. He was with someone too, a woman with curly red hair, I'd seen her in the same plaid skirt and saggy pullover, but where ...? They walked toward me, close together, arms around each other's waists. He saw me and pulled away from her just as we stopped face to face.

– My old friend Sandy's just arrived in town, he said. Quite unexpectedly, just got here today, about two hours ago, wasn't it?

He looked at her, then at his watch.

— Yes, because it was three o'clock when you got down here, and we've been strolling about for at least an hour, haven't we?

She said nothing.

— Anyway Sandy, this is Frances; Frances, this is Sandy.

Sandy held her hand out, her face unsmiling. I did not take it.

— I was just going, I said, and pushed past them, putting as much space as I could between myself and them. I pounded along the beach back to my room. I knew where I'd seen her before: a photograph that'd fallen out of a book on the sailing trip, a book called *Birds, Beasts and Flowers* by D.H. Lawrence with poems for things like pomegranates, mosquitoes, she-asses, and bats. A photo of the same plump woman in a plaid skirt and saggy sweater, beside one of the lanterns in the Nitobe Gardens at UBC.

All the time, I thought, when he had supposedly been sick or too busy, something else was going on. All the time when he was stroking my cheek and looking longingly at me and saying we'll go sailing as soon as I've finished this department work, all that time he was seeing her. And of course Sandy was his editor too, who'd read all of Lawrence, who'd gone away, *nobody I knew*, no wonder he didn't tell me, and now she was back, and he was all over her.

I threw myself on my cot and didn't move for the rest of the day. He'd played off the two of us, and Sandy had won. I had lost lost lost. Now I was nothing. I lay there soaking my pillow, drying my eyes on the sheets, and feeling dull as cardboard, dull as the muggy air. The sun sank. Silhouettes of pots on my hotplate and clothes on my chairs loomed up the walls.

Why had he taken me as his sole companion through all those channels, to all those islands and harbours, through all those glorious days, telling me about his novel, about Lawrence and Proust and Agamemnon — didn't it mean anything that we'd lived together full of freedom all that time? that we loved sailing together and *she* hated it?

Shadows blackened my turquoise walls, smudging out the sailing men and Toni Onley's chaos of abstract shapes, till a last streak of light faded from the glass of the bookshelves and a patch of street lamp zagged up the wall.

He was so real – this man I loved – his intelligence – so real – I wanted to tangle in it – forever. I wanted to give him everything. I wanted to talk to him, dance with him up to the stars. How could he walk away like that without even caring what I felt? Without saying anything at all, just letting me meet them together and then introducing us like we all could be friends.

Dwight tapped on my door, saying he knew I was in there and why not come over for a beer. He rattled the knob back and forth, the door solidly locked. I remained silent, waiting for him to go back to his room. I certainly wasn't going to show *him* my tear-streaked face. Some paper slid under the door. The fridge opened and closed. His lock clicked.

Nor was I going to give Carla the chance to say *I told you so*. Her heels clacked across the hall, her key snapped open her bolt. The TV mumbled through the wall, then went quiet. I lost consciousness. Woke again, my arms, legs turned to slabs of lumber.

That he could just end it with nothing – not even a word – was I that stupid, that much of a hick, a bumpkin, dressed in my faded bumpkin clothes, that I meant so little? A twit, a fool, a klutz. I *was* that, I thought – a goddamned fool – daring to think I could match him, when I knew nothing, talking in my tongue-tied bumbling way, my starry-eyed stupid flower-child way, daring to think my wildness could match his Shakespeare, his world wars, his kings, his castles, his Captain Cooks. Whereas really I was no one, from nowhere, as Dagmar said. Really I was no one. And how would I ever find my way to that world without him?

A glimmer of light from a passing car slid across the ceiling. Then earliest grey morning bleached out the yellow stain of lamplight. Now it was nothing, only grey-turquoise wall, flat and empty, stupid as the flimsy paper of a page in a magazine selling some Hawaiian holiday.

Later, footsteps descended from the attic and down the outside stairs, doors slammed, heels clopped along the sidewalk, Jack drove off on his motorcycle. I stumbled over to the phone. Cardboard head. Thick numb fingers dialing. I croaked into the receiver. The manager warned me I wouldn't get paid for sick days. I fell back on the cot. Why go back, I thought, what was the point? What was the point of anything? Horse-faced Tiny Tim leered off my wall in his ridiculous plaid and striped jacket. Beside him bright T-shirted men raced their sails, in their trim team of muscular arms and legs, their rightness of being, their mattering in the world, the team that Hedda Thorston told us we could be on too. I ripped down the sailing poster and scattered shreds of sailboat, T-shirts, and muscular team around the room, then ripped up university notes and essays, flinging my green notebook and typed novel pages into my closet.

The phone woke me up. For a tiny second, I thought it might be Nigel. Maybe he at least wanted to talk to me alone. Maybe Sandy was just friends and she'd gone back to Prince Rupert.

But it was Lorna. Was I all right? Something must really be wrong for me to miss work. She'd bring me something when she got off. She said, uh-oh gotta go, and hung up. The manager must have come by. I fell back on the rubble and lay there stupidly. Thinking I should get up. I shouldn't let Lorna see this mess. Thinking, who cares?

The first thing Lorna did was make me sit up and drink a glass of water. She folded clothes. She opened my window and washed cups and bowls in the bathroom sink. Dwight nosed by on his way to the laundromat, offered to help. No thanks, Lorna said, blocking him out of the doorway with her towering girth. She gathered up all the scraps of paper, and sorted the poster pieces, essays, and course notes into different piles on the table. You can't just throw these out, she said. Everything you've studied is in here. She wanted to smuggle some Scotch tape from work and tape them back together. She said she'd take them home with her and read them after she'd done taping. It would be like being there with me in the classes. Of course I was going back to school; how could I even think I would not when I got all A's last year?

She didn't know what to bring me, she said, but she found some beautiful peaches at a Chinese market on Fourth. And a chocolate bar. She dug out a paring knife from the hotplate cabinet and peeled one of the peaches. I flopped back on the cot and sagged up against the wall, watching her pull skin from the glistening fruit. She'd missed me when I was on the sailing trip. What would she do after I went back to school? She could help me with my homework; I could work two afternoons a week, instead of one. Steve had found out she was pregnant. He would go to the hospital and complain if she went for an abortion. He wanted them to get married. She didn't know what to do. Didn't you have to buy a licence to get married? Make him buy it, I said, or no dice. Don't tell him you're going to the hospital; tell him you're going to work. She didn't feel like eating any of the peach. It was for me. I must promise her I would eat it. Promise to come back to work the next day. She was reading *Martha Quest*, from the library. We could talk about it at lunch if Kitty wasn't around.

She gathered up the torn essays and notes and left to cook dinner for Steve. The peach was turning brown. Beside it she'd laid a letter – it must have been what Dwight slipped under the door. A letter from Lindegaard on Hornby Island.

I dropped the letter on the piles of poster scraps, and gazed at the rusting peach on the table. I gazed down at the street – dusty leaves hanging in trees, faded humanless houses, a dog slumped across the sidewalk, too hot even to wag. Some noises from Carla's room seeped into my dullness – voices arguing – voices repeating things louder the second time – it reminded me of my parents' fights – low at first, like they were talking through clenched teeth, like they didn't want anyone to hear, then rising with accusation and outrage till the whole house was awake. No you CANNOT come in, I heard Carla shout, I KNOW MY RIGHTS.

– Lady, we know our rights too. You have property belonging to Coolique.

– I've talked to Coolique and everything's fine. Get lost.

It dawned on me that Carla was in some kind of trouble.

– Look, lady, you can let us in to pick up the merchandise, or would you rather everyone in this building knew you're a thief.

I opened my door.

– Like for instance your neighbour here.

He smirked at me under his shag hair, which sprang up on top and bristled out like plastic doll-hair down to the lapels of his brown polyester jacket, his mouth so small and encircled almost by his moustache, it looked like a vacuum-cleaner nozzle.

The other one merely stood with his arms crossed, his wispy sideburns fanning out over a pasty jaw, his pale eyes suspended in eye white, as though the bags under them pulled down the lower lids.

– I'm dealing with Coolique. Now get lost.

– Did you know this lady was a thief, Shaghead turned to me, I'd watch out for your property around her.

– She told you to leave.

Hang-lids shifted his thumbs to his pockets.

– Coolique's going to take you to court, you'll have to pay for that or quite likely go to prison for failure to pay.

– Tell you what, lady, Shaghead leaned into Carla's face, you take that TV and whatever else you've got down to the pawn shop, and you get the cash back here tomorrow.

Jack opened his door, What the fuck's going on?!

– Your neighbour here's a bit of a thief.

– Piss off and leave me alone, Carla spat, I toldya, GET OUT.

– How about we garnishee your wages?

– You stay away from the Biltmore.

– We'll go to the Biltmore anytime we want, have a drink, talk to your friend Harry.

– She told you to leave, Jack pushed in beside Carla, the three of us now facing the men, so get the fuck out.

– Nice friends you got, Shaghead sneered at me.

– I said, GET THE FUCK OUT. Jack had some sort of leather thing with spikes on the back of it wrapped around his fist.

– Don't worry, we'll be back, Shaghead twisted out of his nozzle, when your sleazy friend here isn't around.

The men left. Jack slammed the door after them, muttering, stupid fucks, how'd they get in here anyways?

The door must've been off the latch, I thought, or maybe Lorna let them in on her way out.

Carla's hands shook pulling a cigarette. Jack flicked his lighter. She grabbed onto me and took a drag. Youse all wanta beer, Jack offered. We shambled into his room with its one chair and neatly made bed that reminded me of summer camp cots all tucked in along the sides. He cleared his work clothes off the chair and made Carla sit there, telling her he had some Wiser's, and looked like she needed it. He poured her a couple of fingers, and she wondered if he'd got any ice. I rushed from my spot on the cot to the frost-thickened freezer box and dug out an ancient tray, bashing out cubes in the bathroom sink and running back to bring Carla some water.

I bummed a cigarette and glugged beer. Hate those bastards, Jack said, flicking the butt of his cigarette with his thumb so the ash dropped into a tuna-fish tin between us on the cot. Carla said she never borrowed money from anyone. Her mom'd taught her that. Her mom'd taken her to other people's funeral wakes when she had no money for food. Jack said debt collectors were slime, and if they came around again, just let him know, he'd kick the shit out of them. Carla dabbed the corner of her eye with a Kleenex, she was not a thief, she would never steal things from anyone, especially not from me or Jack or even Dwight.

Jack said one of those dirtbags told his gramma they had police outside that'd take her to jail if she didn't pay. His dad took a crowbar after him. He never came back. She'd ordered a toaster oven from the catalogue, and it never came, so she didn't pay. The company said fine, no problem, then three years later this scum shows up.

Carla wouldn't steal, she said, let's get that straight, she didn't take things that weren't hers. Her mom'd taught her that, and her mom'd had a pretty hard life. Carla downed her Wiser's and Jack poured her a little less. I brought more ice from the freezer.

A guy at work'd told Jack, these bastards had come after him about a funeral bill, his wife and daughter had died in a car accident. If he didn't pay, the bastards said they'd dig up his wife and his daughter and hang them from a tree in his front yard. He grabbed a whole dozen eggs, opened the box, and smashed them into the guy's windshield. I asked if they ever came back, and Jack said for sure not, it was completely illegal. Carla said, just so we knew, that she *did* owe Coolique some money, but that didn't make her a thief – she was selling their product – she just hadn't sold enough yet to pay for the last shipment.

Talk drifted around: borrowing money versus working for someone, selling their stuff so *they* made money while you got a tiny cut, dirtbags that threatened to take away people's kids, illegal telephone calls five times a day, round and round through the smoke and lipstick-coloured butts of Carla's Rothmans – Carla's song and then Jack's song, as though we were riding a needle round a vinyl disk that every so often started over – on the sad-sack eyes, the poodle-puff sideburns, the Zellers polyester pants, the vacuum-nozzle mouth.

Jack lit another Player's, blew smoke out the side of his mouth. Brown paint-peeling clapboard on the house next door completely filled his window frame. A wire dangled in front of the clapboard as though it might once have been attached to a TV aerial on the roof. I felt giddy on tobacco and beer and not eating all day. I brought the peeled peach over from my room, apologizing for its being a little brown and saying I was just going to eat it when the scumbags arrived. Carla thought it sweet of me, hon, and went on about Dan making peach coolers at the Biltmore, she should try one, bet it didn't taste like a real peach. She took a bite and a drag of her cigarette. Beer and peach, not for me, Jack said. You have it. Carla's piece slid onto the floor, and Jack quickly mopped it into his waste bucket with some paper towel. Peaches reminded him of the time his mom made a peach pie – the kind with no crust on top but whipped cream instead. She left it on the kitchen table but the dog climbed on a chair and licked off all the cream. She cut off all the dog-licked peach tops but no one would eat it except her – every day till she finished the whole thing. She wouldn't make any more desserts till the peach pie was gone.

Frankie's writing a novel, Carla announced, on her third and even smaller Wiser's by then (each time Jack poured, he held up the bottle and eyed the level; I was on my second beer). Jack thought he'd read a few of those but then it turned out he thought a novel was the story part of *Playboy*, about guys chasing low-life, or fighting over a girl or something. Carla told him it wasn't just some little magazine thing – this was a whole book, about a bunch of people living in a house, Frankie's writing about us, she's makin us into people in her book. I'm gonna be an actress called Tiffany, just getting little parts, so I'm gettin by on waitressing at the Penthouse, and then an aunt I didn't know dies and leaves me a mansion in Bermuda, and one of the guys plans to marry me, then steal the house but the other guy thinks I'm his, so whaddaya gonna call Jack, Frankie, you should callim Grant.

I told her it wasn't going to be about that any more, it was about a girl who goes to university but flunks out so she ends up working in telephone soliciting, and she gets it all wrong and the boss makes her have sex with him, otherwise he'll fire her.

– Aw hon, that's not what ya said before. I liked what ya said before, I gotta perfect name for Dwight, callim Johnny Dallas like that ex-con on *Edge a Night* that tries to murder Adam. And you, Frankie, ya can't be Frankie, yr the author, honey, ya haveta have a really glam name like Victoria Holt.

– Or Liz Taylor, Jack chimed in. So what do I get to do, he went on, beat up Johnny Dallas for hittin on ya?

– Yeah, Johnny tries to kill ya ... by overdose of smack (Carla had it all figured out) ... first he gets ya hooked, but meanwhile my director says, hey, you'd be great in this movie role of a cop ...

– So Liz Victoria (Jack smirked at me), what does *she* get to do?

– Well *she* ... (Carla dragged on her cigarette) ... she ... finds needles hidden in the can ... she figures out they're Johnny's ... she's a detective ... like Nancy Drew ... she knows Johnny's just a bit player, she tails him, private eye, knows he's linked to a whole network of trouble, and she's gonna track them down before tipping off the police ...

Jack's girlfriend Cheyenne drifted in about then, followed by Dwight. I lurched up toward the door. You don't look too good, hon, Carla said in the midst of Dwight wondering how come the party was breaking up just as he arrived. She clutched onto me, falling off her heels and

154

surrounding me with bangles, frosted nails, and honey-coconut scent as we reeled into the hall. It was like I was already some famous author on TV when I hadn't even finished the novel, maybe never would, it was still at the bottom of my closet. I told her I was fine. Yes really. Fine. Really.

I dragged myself back to work. Eventually I read the letter from Dagmar. She told me about sitting on her front porch watching *seals nosing up their dog heads in the bay.* She told me she'd read all the novels for Hawks's course. She already had her term paper planned out, on how novelists make themselves up as certain characters in their books *like* Portrait of the Artist. *Or like Rupert Birkin in* Women in Love, *who is really Lawrence himself.* She even had her title figured out: "The Fictional Double." She told me she got her best lines after smoking Murray's hash. She'd almost finished her manuscript; Boyd would tell her where to send it. She said I should come and visit; we'd talk about the novels for Hawks's course. We'd take him on together.

I hadn't even signed up for the course. How could I ever keep up with her, I thought. *A cat can look at a queen,* I thought, staring at the golden trees shimmering on their reflections in Dad's painting of Cultus Lake. All Dad's friends kept telling him to paint, to be an artist: Richard Weaver, his Gestalt encounter group guru; Hans, a cable TV producer who lent him an MG; Joyce, his girlfriend; Walt Wiseman, his architect friend who got him to do pictures of his building proposals. There were always these shacks and sheds where he would supposedly paint, always these moves to other places that would really be better, the shed had better light, or he'd build a shed with north windows, which would be his studio, and this time he'd really paint, this time he'd go into his studio and paint pictures and become a real artist. And he'd actually build it. He'd pour the foundations and raise the posts and beams and get some local guys to help him sheet in the walls and roof, and I'd help him put in the windows. And then the studio would become storage for a candle-making project or a place to make Fuck the Pigs protest signs. As though anything but painting was the thing he had to do in life. As though he was missing the piece that got him from painting pictures to showing them in a gallery. A piece that Dagmar's dad had plenty of, with his family roots in Denmark, his corduroy jackets and gold rings, and Dagmar had it too with her trips to Italy and Greece and France and her Danish grandparents. Dad would never have this, just as I would never say *wartah* like Nigel and not *watur* like someone from Cultus Lake.

If I wasn't going to be trapped like Dad, I would have to be part of something bigger, a world I could only imagine as though it were a fairy tale – the world of Romans, knights errant, the Magna Carta, Wars of the Roses, where Chaucer and Tennyson were real human beings, not storybook heroes. Dagmar was already in this world so far away from where we lived, Dagmar already knew how to rattle off bits of it like it'd always been part of her. Like it was all connected – the knights and Tennyson, the rosy wars – to what was here where we lived – the mountains and sea and salmon and fishboats and forests that went on forever – that Dagmar folded into her poems, knowing exactly how to look at them, how to link them to Hermes or Aphrodite. She already spoke the language of that fairy-tale country.

And yet Dagmar enclosed in her letter a poem all in my language, a poem that seemed meant just for me:

> *fireweed flames*
> *daisy meadow lick*
> *be-ness bumble bee*
> *to starfish sky*
> *to ancient curtained trees*
> *to you and me*
> DL

Light tapping sounded on my door, Dwight I guessed. I opened it a crack. He had a new painting to show me – how about some KFC and beer. And by the way, what was everyone doing in Jack's room a couple of days ago? Across the hall, Jimi Hendrix detonated tangled explosions of buzzing chords, hurling out "Purple Haze" like ricochets off graffiti bricks. I followed Dwight into his shambles of dirty socks, ragged paperbacks, record albums, fried-chicken containers, painted skulls, and burning cities. A quiver of excited guilt ran through me as we talked about the sleazy debt collectors, Carla's drinking, Jack's knuckle buster — an electric badness of gossiping about people living in the same house, people I wanted to have think of me as always on their side. It was the guilty pleasure of sneaking cigarettes after telling everyone I'd quit. Or doing more and more crossword puzzles instead of studying. The kind of guilty and hideous pleasure of masturbating. Where I fell into a self I kept invisible to others. I knew I couldn't be on Carla's side and on Dwight's side at the same time, and now I was pretending to be on Dwight's. A self I couldn't let Carla see.

The new painting on black velvet showed Janey and her mother sitting on jagged rocks beside a moonlit lake. Last week, Shirley had stayed in bed most of the time, while Janey was with Dwight's mother, although Dwight thought that since Shirley was well enough to go to the movies and then downtown to Eaton's to buy a new TV, she was well enough to take care of Janey.

I said nothing. He watched me comparing the new portrait to the photograph he had used. It was a picture of Janey and Shirley in matching sundresses, dangling their feet off a dock at Cultus Lake. He'd put them on grey rocks and streaked moonlight across the water; he'd bleached out their faces, hands, feet, and dresses; he'd painted silhouettes of broken trees along the shore.

— I feel you know what I'm going through, he said. You're about the only person who does.

I said nothing. He'd painted Janey holding her mother's hand and looking up at her mother, who was looking out across the lake.

— Like you really notice my pictures, Dwight went on, like you know where they're comin from.

— Anyways, he said (waving toward a box of KFC fries and chicken near a scummy cup of forgotten coffee), you look like you could punch someone; I thought you needed cheering up. He cracked a couple of beers and told me not to pretend I didn't know what he was talking about. Why hadn't I answered when he slipped Dagmar's letter under my door last week?

– He dumped you, didn't he? Don't pretend; you think I don't notice things. He hasn't been around here for at least three weeks. You were cryin, werentcha?

He leaned over the table grinning into my face, his eyes bulging as though they had burrowed into my brain, read my every thought, and even been present at my secret masturbations.

– He just needed free labour, he went on with his toothy grin, free labour for his sailing trip. Probably too chicken to handle the boat on his own. Just used you for labour and sex. Sooner you wise up, the sooner you'll get over it. I know his type, I've been watching him at the Biltmore. The type that lords it over you with their limey accent and hoity-toity manners. They come into the shop, he said, mosey around like they own the place, trying to make me think they know engines so I'll give them a better price, when they wouldn't know a gear-puller or a transmission jack if it smacked them in the kisser.

He bet Nigel was a dufus in bed. Bet he was a wham-bam-thank-you-ma'am type who hadn't a clue what women like.

– What, you think I don't know? Or are you just too squeamish to talk about it? Too squeamish for Masters and Johnson?

He sprinkled ketchup and vinegar on the chips and told me to eat up the chicken – he got it specially for me. He was sure a smart girl like me had read Masters and Johnson. Whereas guys like Nigel didn't even know women had orgasm, or could care less. He was one of those people who said *could care less* when they meant *couldn't*.

He lit up a chunk of hash and passed the pipe. I assured him that although I hadn't read the report, I knew about Masters and Johnson's four stages of sex. Four stages of sexual response, he corrected me. When I heard their names I always thought of slavery and Band-Aids but I didn't mention this. He changed the record album to Paul Horn and lit one of his beeswax candles surrounded by its phantasmagoria of runoffs. He switched off the ceiling bulb, and Horn's flute echoed and warbled around the cave of toolboxes, grubby clothes, and dried-up paint palettes, as though its long sighing notes were moonlight on water, and a hand dangling from a skiff scattered the moonwater to moonchips, let them fly back to their silvery disk only to stir them away again in cascades of stars.

Your ex, he went on, wouldn't know the first thing about the clit or the G-spot.

Dwight's eyes in their white sockets loomed larger than normal in the candle under his chin; his three-day growth blotched his pasty cheeks.

– *The* most important part of sex for women. You know what I'm talkin about, eh? You're givin me that look.

I said I was just into the music. Metal glinted around the edge of his stained teeth, and the candlelight reddened the flesh of his nostrils. He bet Nigel knew nothing about sex, bet he was no match for me.

– Am I right?

He leaned into my face so the candle made his nose even redder. Just admit it. He didn't have a clue did he? I bet he got off in less than ten seconds. Didn't he? And left you high and dry? Didn't he?

– Nigel was fine in bed, I said, although I thought to myself he wasn't a patch on Joe.

A stiff clenched little body like my ex's, Dwight said. You could tell how uptight he was. You have to be loose and relaxed, you have to focus on the woman, give her lots of foreplay, and kiss her where it counts.

Paul Horn's flute pretended to be dolphins shooting skyward in the shadowy room; they dove over and under each other shattering moon reflections.

– What? (Dwight's crazy grin leered across the table.)

– Whaddaya mean *what*?

He demanded again that I admit what a shit my *ex* as he called him had been. Like that time Dwight heard him right through closed doors going on and on about Shakespeare, lecturing me for at least ten minutes.

– He wasn't lecturing me. We were just friendly arguing about whether you could have a great writer like Shakespeare in a place like Vancouver where there were no kings. It's an important question, but you wouldn't know about that, I guess.

Dwight laughed, then lit three more candles and smirked at me, swirling beer in and out of his cheeks.

— Okay, he was a shit, I said. I told Dwight about Nigel introducing Sandy at the marina.

— So quit mooning over him, Dwight said. Quit thinking about what could have been.

Paul Horn shot off playful flocks of swallows but in among the swallows was a sparrow reminding me that I'd promised Lorna I'd bring her a book on essay writing tomorrow which I would have to dig out of a box under my cot.

I stood up, thanking Dwight for the beer and the chicken and the hash and the Paul Horn album, which at that moment was pretending to be a volley of juggler's balls, sinking back into a melancholy pool of old carp. What's the rush, he wanted to know, don't you care about your friend across the hall, your friend who cheers you up when you're down; I need company too, you know, like I said, and like you know, better than anyone.

Dwight stood between me and the door, wondering why I was going so soon — the night was young — work, shmirk, what was to get ready — it was at least twelve hours till I had to be there — I could at least listen to the rest of the album — he'd bought it specially for me. Or was he just the hash and beer supply, take the goodies and run?

— I know what you want, I said, and I don't want that with you.

— What? What do I want? Nothing — I want what you want.

It was totally okay for me to go. It was a free world. Of course we were just friends if that's what I wanted, but could we just give each other a sympathy hug — for my breakup and his Shirley hassles? On the other side of the door I heard Jack clump into the toilet. (Had he left Cheyenne with her skirt up in his cot? What would he do with her when he got back?)

Getting dumped was the worst, he went on. Specially getting dumped without him even saying anything and then waltzing up and introducing her. That was just mean. Only a real dickhead would do that just to make me feel bad, just to make me feel like I was garbage. I didn't deserve that. I had to remember I was really a very beautiful woman who deserved the best.

— Thanks, I said.

— Seriously, he went on, he wasn't just saying that to suck up to me. I had to believe him.

— Okay, I said, I believe you.

He put his arms around me.

— Don't let him make you feel like a shit.

— I'm not. I'm fine.

— Really.

— Yes really. I'm fine.

He reached an arm around my waist and pulled me in. I kept my face into his shirt buttons, breathing sweat, car oil and ashtray. He slipped his other hand up my shirt. His fingers ran over my breasts like limp ropes of putty.

— This isn't *just friends*, I said.

— I'm your best friend in the world, he said, pulling my face up and swallowing my mouth with the sloppy hole of his. It worked away at my lips among snippets of Paul Horn that spiralled down like leaves drifting off a tree. One hand pressed my head in to his kiss, the other worked my shorts down to my ankles. I thought of Carla and Jack, if I shouted would they come? Had he locked the door?

That it had come to this. That I'd let his putty fingers touch me. Let his lips on mine. That I'd stupidly acted like we could be equals and friends. That I'd let myself fall into his story — become his piece of ass, his cunt, his twat. That I was no longer I, no longer the person I imagined others could see, the university woman with dreams and ideas, the person who could write a novel. I'd let myself become legs and tits.

He swung me down on the bare mattress and stale grungy sheets that smelled of hair and skin grease, my back crunching on something like potato chips. That it had come to this. But then I thought, it was only sex, only that stupid thing we all had to do, because we all needed to, it was natural, and people who didn't do it were twisted; everyone nowadays slept with anyone and it didn't matter, it didn't mean anything if they weren't your great love. It was only that stupid thing that would soon be over, that I had done with other guys, one of whom had been so gargantuan around the middle that his dick dangled like the vestigial nozzle on a moon-sized balloon, and we never did figure out how to make it reach my vagina – his enormous weight on top would have crushed me and I couldn't straddle him. Or the guy who stabbed my labia with his fingernails. The guy who twiddled my nipples like stereo dials. The one who mushed his tongue into my mouth as though there were nothing in there. The guy who held onto my breasts like they were hand loops on a bus. The one who watched me and calculated adjustments like an engineer with a Geiger counter or an astronaut with a robot. And a guy once, before the pill, who thought I had taken care of it, as though I could have put a condom on him without his knowing it.

Dwight splayed my legs off the edge of the cot and filled my crotch with the frizzy bush of his afro, his hands reaching up to finger my nipples, while Paul Horn doodled his flute over paintings of burnt-out skyscrapers and haunted women. He licked me and played his tongue around my clit. It probed and caressed, shimmered and rippled, slithered and sucked till I pulled wildly at his arms to drag him onto me. He pinned me open and kept his tongue on my clit. Okay, I was ready for him to fuck me. Yes, now I wanted it, didn't I? I clutched at his frizzy skull in my crotch. I was going to want it even more. He tongued my clit, played it, circled it, stroked it, finger on a light switch, flipping it, flipping it, flipping, till it filled his mouth, it filled the whole haggard, candlelit cave of his skeletal women, burning towers, broken trees, and poster moonlight. Yes, I really wanted it now didn't I, okay okay okay – till I was nothing but a huge throbbing, undulating hole, writhing into his tongue, writhing into his arms splaying my legs, his fingers rubbing my nipples – I was nothing but clit and my clit was exploding, and he was on me thrusting his cock into my hole and my clit was exploding and my hole was collapsing, my hole was a flapping shirt sleeve, an old feed sack, and he was banging at water in a worn-out pillowcase, squeaking the cot springs, banging the cot against the wall, banging a wet dishrag waiting for him to come. Banging and banging and banging, working himself up, panting and groaning till he came and rolled off, and his cum oozed out on the mattress.

I yanked on my shorts, stumbled across to my room, grabbed a towel, and headed to the bathroom. I stripped and sat in the empty tub. No baths after ten o'clock. Supposedly. No noise, no visitors after ten. But what about Jack? He and Cheyenne made plenty of noise. Did the landlady do anything? I bet not. I bet she didn't give *him* funny looks with her creased face and painted eyebrows, bet she didn't ask *him* where he met his friends. And what kind of marks was I getting in my courses. Mentioning, when I brought my cheque, that she'd heard noise in my room. It was right after the Dagmar and Dwight incident. For me, I bet she had different rules. I sat in the empty tub, filling the hair-washing jug and pouring it over my crotch, hoping Carla next door wasn't bothered.

Lying in my cot, I tried to make sense of what had happened. The horrible banging with this pasty-faced, tooth-rotted man in his dingy room, this creep who supposedly I was just friends with, an equal, just someone I smoked dope with and yakked to, like a brother, how he'd made me a nothing, a hole, a vagina for him to fuck.

But before that, I had to admit, he'd made me feel something no other man, not even Joe, had made me feel, and certainly not Nigel. My body still glowed and tingled with it. How was it possible this pleasure could come from sleazy Dwight, instead of Nigel, whom I loved? But then Nigel had brushed me here and there in a bemused kind of way, as though he were embarrassed to touch my breasts, as though he knew he shouldn't touch me, and of course he *was* embarrassed, he was feeling guilty, I thought, because he damn well knew he was betraying Sandy.

A week later, my crotch smelled like putrid meat. I bathed morning and night. I stood in the feminine hygiene aisle at the drug store: should I get the cream, the gel, the capsules, or the aerosol spray? Packages talked of fungus and bacteria. Foul odor. No laughing matter. Keep fresh.

Once-a-day spray increases your freedom. Woman running through fields of flowers. Be confident. Wear a fig leaf of roses. Smiling man on a pillow beside her.

Harry at the Biltmore called me into his office. A customer said I smelled like a hog farm. I went to the doctor and found out I had VD; I should inform all sexual partners I had trichomoniasis, and tell them to see their doctor.

CHAPTER 10

Dwight had Janey with him when I knocked on his door. She did not remember auntie Frances. She wanted to visit the other lady in the other room. She swung back and forth off Dwight's leg, and he promised ice cream after he talked to auntie Frances. Just hang out on the bed for a minute. Why's it secret, she called through the keyhole after he'd shut the door and we stood in the hall.

— Thanks for giving me VD, I muttered, adding that he'd better tell Dagmar and the rest of the women he'd fucked all over town.

— Aye aye, captain.

— Piss off okay!

I closed my door on him.

It goes two ways, he said through the door, you might think about the fact that you probably gave it to me. You probably got it from your limey friend. I hope you're rushing out to tell him.

— Piss off, asshole!

Fuck Dwight. He could go to hell.

Dagmar's letter still sat on my table. I still hadn't signed up for the modern novel course. Tomorrow it was back to work at the file racks. Was this where it was all going to end? A stupid meaningless job? And then I'd end up like Dad, never getting anywhere, or like Dwight — trapped in his life, thinking he was so cool and hip but not even knowing how crass it was to paint on black velvet. Why did some people get to be painters and others get stuck in their own little glass paperweights? Why did some people like Dad give up, and others like Toni Onley keep on till everyone said they were real painters? Carla too — trapped in her world of dolling up, looking like a million dollars, thinking she could make money selling mail-order baubles, instead of trying to become an actress.

And maybe I too was like them, trapped by things I couldn't see, that I just assumed were right. I too would never become anything. But then Dwight and Carla never seemed to think about what was happening to them; they just thought they knew the way the world worked. Maybe that's what happened to you when you got to your thirties. You just stopped looking for what you once wanted.

Maybe I was the same as them. I'd gone to the same high school as Dwight. I'd never been anywhere. My dad, like Dwight's, was a nobody. Dwight's dad had run a service station till a hoist broke, dropping an engine block on his feet. Now he just sat at home waiting for Janey to come visit.

I'd even slept with Dwight. Who would ever read anything I wrote? But if I didn't write what was the point of my life?

Kitty was away so Lorna and I had the lunch room to ourselves. Rain beat against the high window with its tiny patch of grey sky. The rain and the fluorescent light made the beige walls even duller than usual, the holiday couple running along the beach above the clapped-out couch even more garish. The coffee percolator, a large urn with flapping plastic spigot, stood empty on its rickety trolley, having filled the room with a fug of singed brew and the wastebasket with a heap of soggy grounds, plastic sticks, Styrofoam cups, and Creamo thimbles. Lorna flumped down on one of the two metal chairs at a battered Arborite table; I took the couch. Lorna liked the way Martha Quest saw through her parents' attitudes to blacks, but why was it always so easy for characters in books to get good jobs compared to real life? She runs away from home and instantly gets a job as a classy secretary; and she doesn't even know how to type.

An adjuster in a pink suit and pink heels came in for coffee. You know, girls, the person who gets the last cup is supposed to start a new batch percolating. Sorry, Mrs. Bingham. I'll do it, Mrs. Bingham, Lorna lumbered over to the urn, threw out the old grounds, opened a new package, dumped them into the basket, then headed out to the washroom with a couple of juice jugs for water — three trips to fill the urn. Yes, the book was good, it was about Africa, I told Mrs. Bingham. She liked a good bodice-ripper, but well, she didn't need to stand over us making the brew.

Lorna wondered whether Martha had cum all down her dress when the book said it had been spoiled, and why the mother of Martha's boyfriend just ignored it. And why Martha didn't get pregnant when she kept having sex night after night.

Lorna moved from the chair to the couch, sagging it almost to the floor, and gave me half her Oh! Henry bar. She felt under a cloud and didn't want to eat. I was the only one she knew who understood about this thing growing inside her — she was three months already — she didn't know if she could sneak off to work, then go to the hospital so Steve wouldn't know. But it's *your* decision, I said, it's *your* body, not his. She was scared of the hospital committee — what if they were all like her doctor — he made her feel dirty and bad — it was her fault and she deserved what she got — she wished she were smart like me — she wished I would let her do my homework so she could learn. She wanted me to tell her all the books I was reading for school so she could get them out of the library. I told her not to worry about the committee, my friend Dagmar'd had more than one; no problem. It was pretty routine.

Dagmar hit town for the start of term, arriving at my room without warning, throwing her arms around me, and filling the room with the smell of tobacco, kelp, and canvas backpacks. I really should have come to Hornby, I would have loved it, walking through huge old-growth trees, and every morning the eagles shrieking and plunging off the trees around her cabin. She'd got soooo much writing done. But she supposed I'd done a lot of sailing. Fuck sailing, I felt like saying, but I didn't want to tell her about Nigel, didn't want to admit what a failure it had been, what a stupid mistake I'd made, that she would never make.

I let her deluge me with stories of canoe trips, feasts of oysters and clams right off the beach, Country Joe and the Fish playing great music in the pub, everyone hanging out, dropping acid, growing their own weed. She wandered out on my balcony, calling over her shoulder that she wasn't going to call it *Hornby* any more but *Isla de Lerena*, like the Spanish did; José María Narváez – he was the one who named it that.

She patrolled around my table, gazing at the wall where the sailing poster had been. Had I painted my room; it seemed more turquoise? A truly beastly colour. I should cover up this swimming-pool paint with more art like the Toni Onley abstract. Or why didn't I get some Tak Tanabe landscapes or some Jack Shadbolt – there must be some decent prints around of his drawings of Vancouver – street corners, backyard fences, boats along the shore below the old warehouses on Water Street. Not prints – you know what I mean – reprints, posters. Go down to the Vancouver Art Gallery and look through their bin. Or go down to MacLeod's – what! you've never been! She bet he had a poster bin. Or I could try Falstaff Books on Tenth – just don't mention Margaret Atwood – Bill Hoffer hates Canadian writers. What I should really look for is something by Molly Bobak – a student of Shadbolt's – a neo-Romantic expressionist who painted cityscapes and people scenes. The first woman Canada sent to paint the war.

She lit another cigarette and wanted to know if what's-his-name across the hall was around, so she could score some dope. I blocked her path to the door, demanding to know whether she'd got VD this summer, which she had, so why hadn't she told me about him?

– Why would you have cared, I thought you were out sailing with Nigel? Anyway it's just a few pills and its gone, nothing serious, what did you think it was, syphilis or something?

– You didn't think if we were living in the same house something might happen?

– You told me you despised him, and anyway I didn't know it was him.

She told me not to get my knickers in a knot, it was no worse than getting a cold, and she was glad I was playing the field, which we had every right to do. And was I getting it on with wife-beater too? I told her of course not, and asked what her boyfriend Murray thought about it. Murray screwed around plenty, she said, so he couldn't very well complain, anyway she was off Murray at the moment.

Knickers in a knot – it sounded like something Nigel would say or something out of a book, which irked me; no one in Canada said that, so I asked her if she had a lovely time with Cleo on Hornby Island and had Cleo won any more writing contests lately?

– Oh she's quite clever about it, we had an amusing little lunch today at Mozart Konditorei, she's quite determined to get into *Ms.* She sends out stories every week to every magazine she can think of.

– You, she said, winding her arm around my waist, are jealous! You should have come up to the cabin, it would have just been the two of us, and it's your own fault if you didn't.

– And you, I said, talk like something you've read in a novel. What's this *knickers in a knot* and *amusing little lunches* and your *clevernesses* and *beastlies* and *shops* instead of *stores*?

Dwight knocked at that moment with a *Mind if I interrupt your ladies' coffee klatch?*

He oozed in and grabbed Dagmar – it was so good to see she was back in town. With a scowl at me over her shoulder, he pulled her in and planted a kiss on her lips.

– Boy, you don't waste time getting down to business. Dagmar twisted away, what's the rush? Haven't got laid since I last saw you?

Dwight held the blue cover of Dylan's *Nashville Skyline* album, Dylan's smiling face above the shoulder of his guitar, which switched on a record player in my head crooning "Lay Lady Lay" and a picture of a prince draping his lover over a brass bed. He wanted Dagmar to have the album, he had an extra copy, and he knew how much Dagmar loved that song. Remember, hey, remember? It was so cool she'd come to see him. Of course he had supplies. Why don't you ladies come over and have a toke on me while I divvy it up?

He pulled out one of the two chairs for Dagmar at his paint-littered table and pushed some oily work clothes off the cot for me, smoothing the sheet, sweeping his hands toward it and bowing like some kind of grand butler in a palace. I sat on the floor where I could look up at Dagmar's arched eyebrows and sharp blonde Twiggy hair across from Dwight's pasty, bug-eyed face. I couldn't actually see her kissing him.

I couldn't see anyone kissing him; even during our ridiculous sex, I had avoided his mouth. But then his wife, Shirley, must have kissed him lots, and they had had Janey, and he still painted pictures of Shirley. It was sad really. Nor could I stay mad at Dwight over what had happened. He seemed just as determined as I was to maintain the new fence between us: no more casual chats in his room; no more passes at me.

– When did we get to be ladies, Dagmar said, are we back on some nineteenth-century pedestal?

Dwight thought it was just a sign of true respect and humbleness. Women should be honoured to be called that. Under the table he nudged his knee into Dagmar's. She shifted away and balanced her sandaled foot on her other knee. He lit the hash pipe and passed it across.

– The best Dylan, the really best – the thing he'll be remembered for, Dagmar dragged on the pipe, was "Ballad of a Thin Man." That song totally defined sixties counterculture.

– Is that a fact, Dwight leaned back in his chair dangling his hands behind it and spewing a long stream of smoke toward the bare bulb on the ceiling.

They began arguing about whether "Leopard-Skin Pill-Box Hat" was on *Highway 61 Revisited* or on *Blonde on Blonde*. All his real poetry is on *Highway 61*, Dagmar went on, with *Blonde on Blonde* he got mushy and sentimental – instead of surreal social lyrics, he gives us pop stuff about sad-eyed ladies – break-up-with-your-girlfriend songs like every other pop band.

They passed the pipe back and forth, apparently forgetting I was in the room. Dagmar waved at one of the haunted portraits of Shirley, and asked what all the apocalyptic stuff was about in his paintings. He told her he was from Sardis. She didn't get it. Book of Revelation, he spewed out another long drag of hash, Sardis was one of the cities in Revelation.

– So ...?

– So I guess that's why my painting is apocalyptic.

– You should try art school, she said, and get a different model. Who is she anyway?

– No one special, he said. A lady I know – a friend. (He tossed a glare in my direction.)

– I want to paint you, he said. Paint you while you read your poems to me. Paint those high cheekbones and chocolate eyes.

He grinned dreamily under his poof of frizz, then asked, how about this weekend?

Dagmar ignored him, turned to me, and announced that we had to get started immediately on Hawks's course. Make sure I was ready for his quiz. Had I got into the course yet? Had I read Conrad? Had I got Coles Notes? Had I made lists of all the characters in Forster, Huxley, and Lawrence? Don't mention sexism in Lawrence. Hawks hates feminists. Why do you think there's no Woolf on the list? Horrible. But he knew more than anyone else in the department about novels; his lectures were full of anecdotes about writers and the period. It'd be really good for me. I must get Coles Notes immediately – get the plot outlines and key passages – I could mark up the books and take them in to the quiz – I probably wouldn't have time to look through them though.

Dwight nudged Dagmar's foot off her knee. Hey, how's your poetry?

She kept on at me. Don't tell me you're not going to take it – we'll study together – ace the quiz – proofread each other's essays; he's a stickler for punctuation and spelling. Coles Notes – they're everywhere – UBC Bookstore or go to Coles downtown.

Under the table, Dwight hooked his feet around Dagmar's chair and pulled it toward him. Hey poetess, when're you doing another reading?

She yawned in his direction, then said, so how much have you got?

Then she was off on the subject of yoga while Dwight dug around under boxes, record albums, and mechanics overalls for his leather pouch. She laced her fingers together and stretched her arms over her head. They glowed a deep honey colour from her summer of canoeing and beach-combing, whereas mine had already faded with work every day. Had I ever tried yoga – we should do some together – cobras and downward dogs. I wanted to shake her; she was always dangling something in front of me that she knew and I didn't.

– What's *downward dog?* I said. She didn't answer. Instead she announced to the room in general that she was reading in a couple of weeks actually.

– Can I read some in the meantime? Dwight leaned across the table and thrust his grin into her gaze. She looked at me and rolled her eyes. Here's one of my favourite of your poems, he said, grabbing her pamphlet from under his pillow. He read a piece called "Trees of Hades" – *shadow trees that stalk you / insomnia trees that tangle you / jealous trees that turn you green.* I bet that pamphlet was under his pillow the night we fucked, I thought, and was Dagmar any different, with *her* sleeping around?

Dwight flicked his lighter under Dagmar's cigarette. She waved it away and carried on with her match. She was getting a book published she announced, waving the cigarette up and down between her lips as she spoke. Al Boyd said she should send her manuscript to Coach House in Toronto or Oberon or Sono Nis – she might even send it to all three. Dwight thought she should read them aloud to him – see whether they felt right on air.

So how much do I owe you, Dagmar wanted to know.

For her, Dwight had a special price: $10 for five joints. She stuffed them in her wallet, stood up, reached her hands down to mine, and yanked me to my feet. Then toodle-oo, thanks for the Mary Jane, and she was out the hall door and clattering down the outside steps, leaving us standing in the hall, Dwight still holding his gift copy of *Nashville Skyline. Al Boyd*, he grunted, what happened to *professor?* Or is that just the way you girls get an A? He slammed the door to his room and moments later cranked up *Purple Haze* full blast.

Somehow I got through Hawks's quiz. It was all questions like, Which character allows himself to be killed while a Beethoven string quartet is playing? Which characters are painters? Whose son dies of meningitis? Who is his mother's father? I even got a couple more marks than Dagmar, though I hadn't read *Point Counter Point.* Last time I'm going to help *you* study for an exam, she harrumphed, and don't look so hurt either.

A few days later, she took me down the trail to Wreck Beach where last term we'd stood at the jagged rocks of the breakwater, and she'd told me all about Virginia Woolf's diaries. How do we get to be like Woolf, I asked. Woolf invented the modern, she said, now we write the modern, same as the men.

But what exactly was *the modern*? Was it just that we had science instead of god, women's rights instead of women chattels, or cars instead of horses? It seemed too stupid to ask since I myself was modern.

Now, plunging down the trail, she was on about her meditation workshops with a new teacher Lucas Lynn, who'd studied with Alan Watts, and even looked like Alan Watts, she said, with the long hair, the moustache and goatee, and the bemused smile.

The trail ran along a dried-up creek gully. We tunnelled steeply down through giant maples and Douglas fir toward a brilliant glow at the bottom, meeting people coming up carrying towels, inner tubes, hibachis, or boxes of food. Browned salmonberry bushes and sword ferns snatched at our clothes. We crunched leaves big as dinner plates. A float plane zoomed in low landing in the harbour.

– Lucas says the mind is always concerned with dualities, Dagmar shouted over her shoulder. Is this watch too cheap or too expensive? Is my house too big or too small? Did I have a good weekend or a bad weekend?

She charged ahead of me down the trail, leaping from step to step on round slices of trees. Rustling through bushes and sliding along skinned saplings holding us back from the creek gorge – daring me – racing.

Who was nimbler, I thought. Who could fly like that raven to the high branches to rork, rork at the tiny pink-and-brown humans? I charged after her.

– You can't experience life and think about it at the same time, she went on, this is the mind that keeps us on the wheel of *samsara*, repeating our karma over and over.

– How do we ever figure anything out, I yelled, as we pelted down the slope. How do we do science?

— We have to find our essential mind that exists outside all thoughts, she shouted back. Lucas says life and death exist only in thoughts, nowhere else.

— When I'm dead, I'm dead, I said, I'm no longer here.

— That's exactly what Lucas says is the wrong way to think.

Pell-mell we hurtled from the trail out onto the sand to a vast blue bowl of sky and the sea lapping lazily at the shore and spreading out before us in ever finer chops and crinkles sparked with afternoon sun, an enormous open space out to the hazy outline of Vancouver Island and beyond that the Pacific Ocean, an even vaster space, of the forever possible like the shimmering mind-space of eastern meditation where even death disappeared.

I was never going to buy this stuff about death, but there might be something in Watts's ideas just the same. For years Dad had been bugging me to follow him. Going on about freeing myself from attachments, letting go, and living in the present. You already are that thing that you're seeking, he said. The harder you pursue that future goal, the faster it runs away from you.

So how would I ever write a novel then, I thought, or get my degree?

We settled against a log and shimmied out of our clothes, and Dagmar taught me Meditation 101.

Men, women, couples, and families strolled around or lounged on towels, or logs. Avoid gawking, said a crudely painted sign on the trail, but I couldn't help noticing how some breasts sprawled over curvatious midriffs, while others clung on flat chests like slight hills. Some nipples lazed out of huge reddish skirts, others shrivelled to dolls' thimbles. Some thighs squished together; others passed each other like swings in the playground. Some bellies spilled in overlapping folds, others drew sleek ovals between ribs and pubic bone. Some men nestled pink tips in luxuriant growth, some dangled cucumbers from curly meadows. Some cocks cloaked, others exposed and ringed. Some bum cracks snugged up tight; others splayed out, like bibs on a line.

Dagmar was the lanky type with small brown berries on her chest. Don't gawk, I told myself but looked around to see if anyone else was gawking. Many had devised any number of ways to avoid it, to both expose themselves and to at the same time seem nonchalant about it. Three boys with long skinny legs and tiny fragile willies hurtled past, dashing into the water. The fat-puckered thighs and sagging bums of a greying couple wearing nothing but tennis shoes ambled along the shore. Some bronzed young men scrambled for a ball, bunching and unbunching themselves, their backs glistening. They froze wide-legged – their thighs, crotches, and armpits thick with hair – faces up, hands spread for the next bounce, then burst into motion again, reaching for the ball that bounded away across the sand.

Men and women sculpting a sand tower with packed buckets gathered around for a photo of their brown limbs and whiter crotches. Another group danced to bongo drums and flute. Long-haired women emerged from the sea, coated their wet bodies in sand, and joined the dancers. They smoked joints. They drew hearts and peace signs in the wet rippled tidal flat. They photographed their bodies spelling LOVE.

Dagmar sat cross-legged, pulled her back straight and her feet on top of her calves and, resting her hands on her knees, gazed as though in a trance at a disintegrating crab skeleton in the sand. Empty your mind; think of nothing at all, she instructed. Of course as soon as I tried to think of nothing, I thought of a whole lot of things, including that thinking about not thinking was still thinking. Lucas says, Dagmar instructed, just say to yourself, *thinking*, and let the thoughts slip away. Keep your eyes open. Just be like a mountain that lets the clouds come and go and doesn't change. I thought about whether I should ask Hawks if I could do my term paper on Virginia Woolf. Then I said in my mind, *thinking*, and gazed at the crab skeleton.

I pictured Hawks on a dark rainy day the previous week, when he switched off the classroom lights and lectured to us in the gloom of our small-windowed, tree-darkened room. *Thinking.* Back to crab skeleton. Dagmar glowed beside me in the late afternoon sun, her face underlit by the sun's sparkling path across the water. Then I saw Hawks's face, gouged with lines as though a rake had run furrows from forehead to chin and dragged his mouth to a permanent frown. Dagmar told me his daughter hanged herself in her father's garage a couple of years ago. *Thinking.* Crab skeleton. Sky. Water. Just be like a mountain.

Then for a moment, it seemed, I had stopped thinking, as though a crevasse had opened to outer space. An impossible void that lingered as a memory of mind's unity with sky – which I might find in the crab shell. Was this what the eastern monks spent a lifetime practising?

Heels and toes rubbed along the sand in front of us. Shadows crossed our gaze. What if Dwight hung around down here? I was pretty sure I'd seen a couple of the students from Nigel's *Godot* class – the longhaired brooding guy and the peasant-blouse girl. One person who wouldn't hang out down here was Nigel. Do you go in for nudism, he asked, when we came down that cold spring day. I kinda grew up with it, I said. He hadn't. He kept his underwear on even when it was just the two of us swimming off the boat.

Thinking. Be like a mountain. Gaze at crab skeleton. Sound of throat clearing and snickering. Bodies blocking the sun. Rosie from the Women's Auto Collective – thick arms, muscled from heaving wheel rims, cranking jacks, and lugging oilcans – planted herself like a phone box in front of us, her hand around the waist of a woman with small breasts and big thighs, whose face was almost hidden in curtains of chocolate hair. I could see the outlines of her panty elastic and bra printed on her pale skin. She wore the high-waisted type, not bikini, probably waist-high slacks too, no hip-hugging bell-bottoms. She kept her knees demurely together, the way we'd all been taught for photographs if we were wearing short straight skirts and sitting in chairs facing the camera, whereas Rosie planted her iron pilings like a brigade commander. Nippled mounds on her barrel chest loomed over us. I nudged Dagmar out of her trance. Rosie ground her foot into the crab shell and whirled her friend into their breast-bouncing march. She had a crush on me, Dagmar said. She'll get over it.

About ten yards off, Rosie and her girlfriend wheeled around and marched back. That your next victim? Hey get a life, Dagmar yelled. You better run the other way, Rosie tossed over her shoulder at me. They rubbed away down the sand, banging their hips together and swinging bum cheeks side to side. Just beyond them I noticed Dad's grizzly haired chest beside Joyce, his headbanded girlfriend.

Dagmar pretzelled her feet back on top of her legs. It hurt just looking at her knotted limbs. I stretched mine out till the blood flowed again; then dragged them back to a half lotus and tried to think only of the sun dancing across our skin from the sparkling sea. If you don't want to write on these topics, Hawks said, you can pick an author from the alternate list and I'll assign you a topic. He couldn't completely despise Virginia Woolf if she was on the alternate list, could he? I was thinking again. I gazed at crab legs and pink shards of shell. Theories of education in *Women in Love* and *Portrait of the Artist as a Young Man*; Philip Quarles, Stephen Dedalus, and Rupert Birkin as portraits of authors; the "new woman" in *Point Counter Point* and *The Rainbow*; modern industrialism in Conrad and Orwell; morality and decadence in *What Maisie Knew* and *Howards End* — these were the main assigned topics. Did I need a theory of something in order to write a novel about Dwight and Carla and Jack? Did I have to read Freud or Marx? Should I make Dwight into a "new antihero" or make his paintings into self-portraits? Make Carla a lesbian and Jack a union man? Or did they have to have endless affairs like Walter Bidlake and Lucy Tantamount? And there I was, puzzling over my novel again, trying this move and that move in its chess problem, wandering around in its chattering conversation, its labyrinth of questions, blind alleys, and sudden *aha*s that evaporated like ghosts as soon as I grabbed them.

Who was afraid of Virginia Woolf? Why was she so scary? Sweat trickled from my armpits. People lay about in sun-baked water in the long shallows spreading away from the beach. A chubby guy, pink from too much sun, rammed his inner tube into a bearded guy on an air mattress. A longhair turfed Chubby off the tube and he turfed Beard off his mattress. Water streamed their thick-haired legs and bushy crotches. Chubby was Hal — the painted wooden egg-doll on that first sail with Nigel, writing his thesis on Hermann Hesse. The air-mattress fight paused — Rosie and her girlfriend strolled into the water, and all the men's heads turned as though pulled by invisible strings attached to the women's nipples. Don't gawk, yet I was as guilty as they were of checking out dicks and cheeks and cleavage. Above it all, hovered Lucas's floating island of bliss – a shimmering possibility of everything unfolding as endless golden sunshine and love. Anyone and everyone could have it. All you had to do was open your mind.

For the next few evenings, I wrote furiously at my novel. After losing his song to Country Joe and the Fish, D goes into the mountains back of North Vancouver looking for a cabin he built on public land when he was still in high school. He picked the site by following a creek gorge off an old logging road. He felled young cedars with an axe, whacked off the branches, and slid the axe blade under the young bark, peeling off long strips. He made A's out of the smooth yellow cedar trunks. A couple of buddies helped him raise the A's and sheet them into a wooden tent with lumber scrounged from construction sites. They even lugged in a tiny Franklin stove and a window for the front.

When he didn't feel like teachers nattering at him or his father pestering him to work in the family grocery store, he went to his cabin and wrote songs. Sometimes his buddies came and the three of them crammed themselves into the wooden tent and smoked dope. Maybe they could all start a farm together, just grow enough to live on, fuck the job grind.

How'd they ever clear all that farmland out in the valley, D asked the others, I mean like they did it by hand, eh, with axes and handsaws, like my grandfather, eh, he cleared fifty acres with just hand tools and horses. Not like the chainsaws, bulldozers, and skidders they have now. He thought of a song about choppin trees till your hands bleed. One of his friends said you could still get homesteading land up in the Peace River or the Kootenays, all you had to do was farm it. Yeah, get a bunch of us together, it wouldn't be that hard.

D tells them about his grandfather's barn, how one post had carved into it, *man buried 50 feet nw.*

– Guess they didn't have rules about cemeteries, someone said.

– Probably not, but it wasn't that, it was cuz he killed a guy.

– Police get him?

— They knew about it, but they never charged him.

— What'd he do, pay them off?

— Nah, the guy was messing with his wife, they figured he had it comin, he was some prospector guy who'd ripped off a few people.

Maybe if he went back to the cabin, D thinks, he could write more songs. He straps the guitar and a sack of food on his back and heads up the old logging road.

Meanwhile, C quits her job with the sex-demanding boss. She goes to the public library and reads *Anne of Green Gables*; like she had, again and again, as a girl. Now especially, C feels like Anne, an orphan, far away from her mother, who lives in Calgary. Her grandmother is dead, but when C was a girl, she used to stay with her grandmother on the other side of the Rockies at her farm near Invermere, B.C. Gramma got out the big canning kettle, and C helped her stuff cherries and peaches and raspberries into the jars. They lowered the rack of jars into the boiling water and later listened to the pings of lids sealing as the jars cooled. They ate Gramma's butter tarts and Gramma got her crossword out and asked her, what was a five-letter word for *mountain goat*, or what was a six-letter word for *hit or miss*?

C takes a job in the packaging department at a factory that makes Indian totem poles and statuettes out of crushed marble and plastic, cast in moulds. She wraps them in tissue paper and stuffs them into cardboard boxes along with a slip of paper labelled Killer Whale or Salmon or Hummingbird that also gives the name of the carver whose work had given the mould its shape.

At the end of the day, she counts up all the boxes like she used to count the jars she and Gramma had put away on the shelves of the root cellar. The more there were, the better. What would I carve if I were a carver, she sometimes wonders. What would the little piece of paper say if I were a carver?

Her favourite item is something called a Spirit Box, a small, lidded container shaped like a frog or a bird or a fish. Not for any Bible God, reigning from his throne in the clouds, she thinks. But what, then? What spirit lived inside a frog?

CHAPTER 11

I decided to ignore Dagmar's advice to choose a safe topic for my term paper and instead set out for Hawks's office. I was certain that in private, away from the elevated performance of lecturing, he would smile like a normal person. He would be pleased with my initiative, he would even be friendly, and soon I'd be talking to him the way Dagmar had chatted amicably with Hedda Thorston or Allen Boyd, and the way I had with Nigel.

The elevators in the office tower were always jammed, on the one hand with students talking up professors, and on the other hand with professors avoiding looking at or talking to anyone. As the doors clunked shut, then opened squeezing out people, then shut, then clunked to the next floor, I realized Nigel was separated from me by only one person: a heavy-set professor wearing a cap and gown. It was the first I'd seen Nigel since the terrible meeting with Sandy at the gate to the dock. He was so close I could almost smell his Yardley shaving soap.

Of course I wasn't going to say anything. I wanted him to see me as I got off the elevator one floor below his, to see my thick mane of black hair — my mountainish, wolfish self — to reach for it, run his fingers through it, follow me off the elevator into the shadowed winding corridors of offices, tell me it was all a mistake about Sandy, she was gone forever, tell me he missed me on the boat, missed our talks, missed reading books together. He would cover me in passionate caresses instead of the absent-minded fingers I blamed on Sandy waiting in the wings. The elevator stopped at my floor. I strode off, stiff and aloof, certain of his gaze, certain of his fascination with my wildness. But he did not follow me, and I had to walk around all the corridors several times in order to calm down before I knocked on Hawks's door.

His desk faced the door, his back to the window. The closed blinds blocked the only light into the room. He pointed to a chair. What have you come to see me about, Miss Nelson? (Dagmar might call Professor Boyd *Al* – everyone did – but in Hawks's class everyone was Miss or Mister. Mr. Nelson, Hawks called out my name on first-day roll call, to snickers around the room. Do you always spell your name the masculine way? No. Then see that you get over to the registrar's office and get it corrected.)

Neat stacks of texts stood at one end of his desk, and three files across the front: English 200, English 380, English 452. No coffee cups. No kettle. No typewriter. No photographs. Just a pink pad for telephone messages, but why would he need that since if he was here he would answer the phone, and if he wasn't, no one would take a message? His eyes burned like black flints out of his shadowy tomb.

– I'd like to choose an alternate topic.

– You choose the author. I choose the topic.

– I'd like to write on Virginia Woolf.

– Very well, you may discuss *Orlando* and its connections to Lytton Strachey's *Elizabeth and Essex*.

Not having the faintest idea who Lytton Strachey was, I scribbled this down. Most profs were only too anxious to help you get started. I dared to meet the flinty gaze in its clawed face and ask if he had any suggestions.

– No.

That was it. No. Not *No* with an explanation that it was up to me to find out for myself how the topic worked and perhaps we could discuss it after I'd read the books. Instead, just plain *No*. A shut door.

– Well I guess that's all, I said.

– Goodbye, he said.

Dagmar drifted into Hawks's next class wearing a rust suede jacket and did not sit in the empty seat beside me, choosing instead the one beside Cleo, whose arm was so coated with bangles that every time she brought her pen down to the page in her notetaking they clanked and caused Hawks to glare at us midsentence and eventually comment that if he had to stop every five minutes he would be unlikely to finish his lecture before it was time to move on to the next novel. Which would not change what would be on the final exam.

Now he was lecturing on *Heart of Darkness* and the device of framing Marlow's story within another story, which allowed Conrad's views on imperialism, civilization, and savagery to remain in the shadows behind a screen of fiction told by a narrator who believed in England's glorious knight-errant explorers but who recounts a story of imperialist savagery told to him by the character Marlow.

What did *my* narrator think about imperialist savagery, I wondered. And anyway who exactly was the omniscient person narrating my novel? Who was she talking to? Was it Dagmar? Or Lorna? The novel swirled in a vortex of relics from my turquoise room. As though I were a night sky, where Narrator and U Girl, D, C, and J, floated like constellations. At the centre of the vortex a black hole tugged to another universe. Yet each time I tried to dive through, the tunnel shifted and beckoned from some distant galaxy, where wisps of story petered out into deep space.

Something ruffled the outer regions of my consciousness — a rustle of pages, a shuffling of shoes around the bolted pedestals of our seats. I missed Hawks's last point about Conrad. He'd moved on to term papers. It was the last day to choose an alternate topic. So far two people had chosen, one on Graham Greene, and one — it seems we have a feminist among us — on Virginia Woolf — isn't that right, Miss Nelson? I looked up — still lost in my vortex. Everyone followed his gaze at my seat. Or should that be *Mister* Nelson?

— I don't think writing about Woolf makes me a feminist.

— Why else would someone write about a bluestocking?

The students thronged out to the hall. Dagmar, Cleo, and I drifted into the coffee room with its pumpkin-coloured settees that had once been slim, modern, rectangular invitations, but were now battered, chipped racks of coffee stains and cigarette holes. I staked out some seats while Cleo and Dagmar headed to the trays of cinnamon buns and giant chocolate chip cookies beside the coffee urns. While they chattered away in the lineup, Cleo waving her bangled arm and blood-coloured nails, I thought of ways to take Dagmar somewhere Cleo would never go — a hike into the UBC Endowment Lands, for instance, to collect plants for my botany course. We'd find badge moss and crane's bill moss, deer fern, licorice fern, and if we were lucky along the open edges, we'd find moonwort. I bet she'd never seen it; I bet she'd put moonwort in one of her poems; she'd love the ancient lore that said it could unlock doors and make you invisible. We could look for chanterelles too and maybe cook them up together afterwards.

Cleo slipped a Virginia Slim into a gold-and-blood cigarette holder. Since I was Frances, she wanted to know whether I should be Franny Glass or Frances Earnshaw? Cleo was one of those women who liked to wear rings on every finger.

Dagmar started singing *Franny and Zooey were lovers*, to the tune of "Frankie and Johnny" — the two of them grinning at me from the other side of a table littered with napkins and crumbs. Clusters of silver snakes dangled from Cleo's ears.

— Frances Earnshaw's too boring — just there to give birth to Hareton so he can marry Catherine Linton and end the feud.

— Cleo's father's the editor of the *Province* arts section, Dagmar announced, as though this explained these comments.

Cleo brought the cigarette holder to her lips, holding it the way people held roach clips — thumb below, fingers on top. She didn't inhale, whereas Dagmar dragged heavily on a Player's and streamed smoke out her nose. Cleo attracted a stare from a shag-cut buying a sticky bun.

— So you have a choice between a J.D. Salinger character and an Emily Brontë character, she went on, unless ... unless you spell your name with an *i*! Then you could be Francis Drake and be knighted by Queen Elizabeth. Or you could be Francis Bacon and discover the scientific method. Or a famous movie director and create *The Godfather*.

Dagmar said that of course I would be writing my term paper on the Bloomsbury group, which I vaguely thought must be something like beat-niks living in Paris — all staring defiantly from berets and dark glasses, or drinking martinis at midnight parties beside huge tangled canvases of abstract art.

– No, I have to write on *Orlando* and Lytton Strachey's *Elizabeth and Essex*.

– Strachey – *Eminent Victorians* – definitely Bloomsbury, Cleo sipped her cigarette holder. He was gay, wasn't he?

– Duncan Grant, the painter, Dagmar said.

My stomach growled at the chocolate cookies beside the coffee urns.

– In a way, Dagmar thought, Orlando's really Elizabeth and Essex rolled into one. But you know what it's really about, don't you? Virginia's affair with Vita!

Cleo's bangles slipped up and down her arm. Each one thin and silver, each one decorated with a different pattern of vine leaves, curling waves, monkey faces, or eagle eyes. She thought that obviously I should be Francis Drake. You've been knighted by Queen Elizabeth for sailing around the world and capturing Spanish pirates. All you need is a spyglass, a waxed moustache, and a pointed beard.

– And a lace collar.

– Or an Elizabethan ruff fanning out pleats around your neck.

– Must have a sword and a globe.

– And a leather doublet and britches.

– For your term paper, you could actually *be* Orlando.

– A one-act play.

Cleo and Dagmar egged each other on. How did they remember all that stuff from high school history? All that stuff about a country we'd never seen and that was mainly about kings and wars you memorized for tests? Dagmar would just laugh if I asked her on that moss hike, I thought, with the two of them going on like that. I said I had to go. You're not pissed are you, that we said that, Cleo said. Then to Dagmar, she's pissed. They looked at each other and it was like at the Women's Auto Collective when Cleo couldn't stop laughing. I'm not pissed, I just have to go, I said, heading toward the long hall of lockers and classroom doors. Dagmar grabbed my arm as I swept past, making me stop and look at her. I'll call you later, she said. I could still feel her grip as I walked between rows of combination locks, past the square windows to rows of students listening to teachers' voices.

Leaves came down. Campus grounds-workers raked them into mountains of brown, red, and yellow on the dew-soaked grass shooting up its last vibrant growth before winter. October sun cast dark shadows of branches and trunks across the malls between the stark rectangles of Psychology, Commerce, Education, and Biological Sciences and the older vine-covered Math, Chemistry, and Old Auditorium buildings. Students thronged out of classrooms into the sunshine, tossing a soccer ball, linking arms, grabbing coffees, chattering about graphs, theories, parties, social injustice, moving like shoals of fish between the buildings, or lingering alone on a bench or in a sheltered nook, storing up solar energy in their brains to sprout like cedar fronds into chemistry and poetry.

Dagmar strode along in rust suede jacket and black sultan trousers, taking me to her little Fiat in the distant B lot, while informing me that she and Cleo thought Cleo's dad — the editor of the *Province* arts section — would let me review books for him. I should do this. It would be good to get my name in print. Then people would have heard of me when I came to publish my novel. No, she hadn't done that. But then she had Al Boyd, his name carried a lot of weight with editors. I must therefore come with her to Cleo's party, it was at her parents' house.

She switched to Hawks's novels course, how Lawrence was rehashing Freud, fitting characters into class and psychological types to illustrate theories of a healthy society. Inventing a whole new way for people to imagine themselves; showing them you could break class boundaries for healthy reasons, though of course breaking class boundaries was what the First World War did.

How did she know that, I thought crossly. It was just a war about African colonies. What do you mean about the war breaking class boundaries, I said. Before the war you had servants, after the war they went out and got jobs, she said, Woolf's always going on in her diary about the difficulty of getting servants.

Orlando invented new ways of being too, she went on. In its complete tongue-in-cheek, high-camp way. So real in its unrealist fairy tale. Dagmar's ramblings showered over me. What did she mean by *camp*? I didn't ask. I wasn't going to let her idea of *Orlando* influence my essay.

I pulled her into the piles of raked leaves, and we began plowing through, knee-deep. We rustled and sloshed, kicking them up in clouds in the crisp sunshine, and her words cascaded over me, so unlike the pressed formalities of the professors at their chalkboards and overhead projectors, hurriedly scribbled by rows of writing hands. I wished I could respond with similar outpourings, but it seemed I could only do this in letters that somehow never got down on paper.

Her voice rose and fell with the calm certainty of a narrator in a novel, the voice that made a door to a novel's journeys and imaginings. In reading you opened the door and fell onto a velvet couch that drifted through underground caves and rivers. And I thought of telling her this idea, telling her I wanted to make this happen in my novel, but I thought it would sound silly and romantic and definitely not camp. And I thought how uncalm and uncertain my own U Girl narrator was about everything, not like a Lawrence or Hardy narrator.

Dagmar's narrator never doubted, never wavered. She was writing her paper on the author self-portrait topic, reading biographies of Lawrence, Joyce, and Huxley and matching them up to Birkin, Dedalus, and Quarles. A dead easy topic. But why had Hawks made me write on *Orlando*? Probably he was closet gay, she said. Hideously repressing any hint of his desires, armouring himself in dreary gloom in case it leaked out. *That's* why he was so gothic. She'd done it again, come up with the perfect word for Hawks's dark gaze and fierce scowl.

On our botany collection hike in the forests of the UBC Endowment Lands, she told me her favourite fern was maidenhair because the leaves were shaped the same as the ancient ginkgo tree's. She tried out my pocket magnifying glass and looked through my plant key, and said our specimen wasn't in the key because there weren't any spores along the edges of the leaves. Well they've probably fallen off, I said. This is definitely in the key. *Adiantum pedatum*, the only species in B.C. except for a semitropical one that only grows beside hot springs. Then she told me all about ginkgo trees, how important they were in Tokyo, how they were the only living thing to survive Hiroshima. And why didn't they classify maidenhair ferns with ginkgo trees since they were obviously related. Because that's not the way it works, I said. Botanists compare lots of things besides the shape of the leaves, and anyway the leaves aren't the same shape, they're squared off along one side. And we argued about whether the different shape meant they'd evolved differently from the same place or whether it meant they were different things.

Then she remembered she'd heard on Hornby that Indians had eaten the sweet roots of licorice fern. So why don't we try some, I said, and we scooped up a plant. But when we got back Murray was there wondering where she was, they were late for the Arts Club Theatre.

Cleo's family home snugged itself into a hill on a street that ran straight into the forests of the University Endowment Lands. A wide veranda with stone pillars and thick plank steps sheltered its leaded front window and a stout door with brass knocker. I found myself in an oak-panelled hall next to a balustraded staircase. A hubbub of voices sounded from the kitchen. Moulded oak framed an archway to armchairs, couches, and polished side tables on a red-and-gold oriental rug before a crackling stone fireplace. In the crowd draped over the furniture, I noticed Dagmar's boyfriend Murray talking tree planting with a lanky guy, one of those super laid-back longhairs with dreamy brown eyes under a wide-brimmed hat. In his lumberjack shirt and logger boots, he looked like he'd just stepped out of the woods.

Murray was at least thirty and already owned a record store called Grooves, reaching a place most of us could not yet imagine. He wanted to know whether Lanky's tree-planting team used hoedads or dibbles. We used planting shovels for bare root *and* for plugs, Lanky said. A women in red bell-bottoms hung out nearby with a woman in farmer's overalls. Rosie from the Women's Auto Collective leaned against the mantel. She was talking up a woman in miniskirt and thigh-high boots.

In the kitchen, Cleo, in a high-necked metallic collar like you saw in pictures of ancient Egyptians, presided over a long pine table surrounded by friends. Mostly people we know from Lord Byng, Dagmar told me. Help yourself to drinks or other stuff, Cleo waved vaguely over the wall of bodies between us and the table. Bottles littered the countertops along with boards of cheese and crackers, bowls of chips and dip, and plates of brownies. Is Cleo's dad here, I asked.

– I doubt it, I think they're away for the weekend.

– I thought I was going to meet him about book reviews.

– Oh no no no. This wouldn't be the time to do it anyway. You phone him up at the *Province* and ask.

– But you said that was the whole reason for me coming here; now I find it's just a bunch of your high school buddies.

– Darling, relax, I'll introduce you.

Darling, she called me *Darling*, I thought, so maybe I meant something to her after all, more than Cleo, more than this crowd of Cleo's friends.

Arm around my waist, she steered us through the kitchen, and introduced me to a skinny guy with glasses. He remembered me, for sure, yes: I was the one who'd organized the all-girls Shakespeare in grade 11, I was the one who played Desdemona, and Dagmar played Othello, and the next year I played Hamlet and Cleo was Laertes. I wish I had, I said. I felt Dagmar drift away.

Then a curly-haired, smiley woman thought I'd been the one who organized the Loiter-In protesting vagrancy laws. Down at the courthouse fountain. She'd seen my picture in the *Georgia Straight*, me and Dagmar getting arrested. Another woman in a purple jumpsuit also saw my picture in the *Straight*, but she thought I was the woman the cops had dragged over broken glass at the Maple Tree Square protest. All imaginary, I sighed.

I followed Dagmar to the living room, planning to take her for an *amusing little lunch* far from this *madding crowd*. I could be a sort of artist version of Hamlet in *Portrait of the Artist as a Young Man*. I could wear a beret and smoke French cigarettes.

I trolled around Cleo's house through the kitchen, dining room, living room, back through the hall to the kitchen, listening to conversations:

the B.B. King concert. The John Hammond, Dr. John the Night Tripper concert. Ingmar Bergman's *Wild Strawberries*. Howard Hughes at the Bayshore. Just showed up in his bathrobe and pyjama bottoms. Said he'd buy the hotel if they didn't let him stay. Reporters camped out on a roof across the street. Someone flew a glider past his window.

A woman slipped into the living room, her face framed by flowing chocolate hair parted in the middle, her chest and arms carried along as though on wheels. Perhaps her legs couldn't move in her too-tight jeans, which tried to squeeze away the wings at the tops of her thighs. She kept her eyes lowered, focused on a half glass of wine carried like a candle to an altar. It was Rosie's girlfriend from the beach.

She settled into a place just beyond the archway into the dining room. People brushed past her as though she weren't there while she gazed across at Rosie by the mantelpiece, still chatting to Thigh-high Boots. I drifted over, thinking should I mention I'd seen her at the nude beach, but then she'd seen me, so what did it matter? Dagmar and most of these people were ahead of her by one or two years, she said. Dagmar was kind of a bitch, she thought. Then, she means well, I guess, but she's such a little rich kid.

I should hear what Rosie said about her, she went on, telling me how Dagmar and Rosie had lived in an old bowling alley on the east side of town. Sleeping in the office and cooking behind the counter where bowlers used to get shoes, burgers, and hotdogs. Rosie said they used the shoe cubicles to store bread, potatoes, and soup tins and had dance parties on the polished floors of the lanes.

Rosie had been really into 1968, marching against Vietnam, picketing for better minimum wage, deliberately getting arrested to protest vagrancy laws. Dagmar was into it too, but even then she had her bourgeois ways with her $80 shoes, her trips to Italy, her plans to major in art history, all financed by daddy's art gallery of course. Rosie's dad was a longshoreman. What did *she* want a degree for? You didn't need a degree to see what needed doing.

Dagmar was stuck in her class, she said. She did good things, then forgot all about poverty and battered women. Couldn't care less. She told me how Rosie and Dagmar took over an abandoned warehouse next door to the bowling alley and created a shelter for battered women and kids. They raided Safeway dumpsters at night for food, and Rosie's dad helped them tap into electricity. The owner sent eviction notices, but Rosie and Dagmar picketed his restaurant chain. Dagmar even put on a suit and her $80 shoes and cornered him in his office. She said she knew people on city council and they'd block his chain from opening in the trendy blocks of downtown Robson Street, so he backed off on the eviction. Then suddenly Rosie came back to the bowling alley and Dagmar's stuff was gone. She'd got her own apartment on the hill up from the beach. Everyone but Rosie knew she'd been hanging out with Murray.

This wasn't the only story about Dagmar I heard that night. Later Cleo told me about hitching around the south of France with her, how Dagmar wanted to try her hand at the gambling tables in Monaco, but they weren't yet twenty-one. Dagmar dyed her hair grey and made a thrift-store outfit of granny shoes, thick stockings, and a mauve polyester suit with a pleated skirt. She piled on the makeup like she was covering up wrinkles. She even stuffed her underwear so she'd look lumpy, and waltzed in while Cleo waited in a café. She spent all her money on chips, then headed for the roulette table. Of course she lost.

She said she won, Cleo said, but there was a mix-up about getting her chips off the layout and the dealer spun the wheel again with her chips still on there. An older guy in a bow tie gave her some chips and whispered in her ear, play again and I won't blow your cover. Dagmar told Cleo afterwards he was really smooth in his Yves St. Laurent tux. This time she won and cleared her chips off. She gave back what he'd given her. Then headed off to the blackjack table. Mr. Bow Tie followed her. Said she owed him more chips. She said she didn't. She told him to get lost. He dragged her into an elevator, taking her back to his room. He said he knew she was underage and he'd report her if she didn't shut up. She kneed him in the balls and got away. Well, Cleo said, that's what she said, but who knows, maybe she slept with him and ripped off his wallet when he was snoring, but she came back with more money than she went in with.

The words *Fritz Perls* jumped out of the hubbub of voices, Fritz Perls – Dad's idol, he'd read every Perls book and quoted them endlessly, *I do my thing and you do your thing*, or, *I'm not in this world to live up to your expectations* – Murray holding forth from his armchair to Red Bell-Bottoms and Farmer's Overalls sitting at his feet. You can't just write new rules for yourself, Murray was saying, Rules like now I will stop lying. Now I will always be polite and let the other guy go first. All that does is start a fight between your top dog and your underdog over whether you're living up to some phony image of goodness.

– Our psych prof says Gestalt is about how you see the world – what kinds of *percepts* you use. Overalls twirled some of her waist-length silky hair around a finger and thoughtfully pulled it across her lips.

– Yeah, whether-you-see-a-vase-or-two-profiles kinda thing. Murray dug into a bowl of peanuts and tossed a handful in his mouth. I'm talking about Gestalt *therapy*. Different animal. Except it *is* about seeing yourself, seeing the holes in yourself, so I guess it *is* about percepts.

– Yep, live in the here and now, eh, Lanky the tree planter added, stoking up with another joint.

– The thing is, Murray went on, we're only using about 5 to 15 percent of our potential. Living in clichés. Perls gives a way to access 85 to 95 percent of our creativity.

– Human potential, eh, far out, man. Lanky gazed around the room like an angel about to shower everyone with gold coins.

– The thing is we prefer to live in stupid games, being good girls and boys, flattering people about their great knowledge, manipulating others so they'll love us.

– Yeah sure, Rosie scoffed from her post at the mantel, live in the here and now so we can all become geniuses. Live now for the future – no different than any religion.

– Did I say that, or are you trying to goad me into proving you're unlovable?

– That's heavy, man, Lanky leaned back and gazed at the ceiling, I don't know if I can handle that.

Rosie laughed, flashing a smile at Miniskirt, I couldn't care less whether you loved me or hated me.

— It's all about independence — stop playing roles to get what you want. Murray grabbed another handful of peanuts. For instance, Murray turned to Overalls, what are you doing right now with your hair?

— I don't know. What am I doing?

— You tell me.

— Twirling my hair around my finger, she laughed, I always do that.

— And?

— And — I don't know — what?

— Jezuzz! Rosie huffed, what is this — group therapy? You think cuz you've done a couple of workshops with the big Fritz you can go around psychoanalyzing people at parties?

— Hey man, lady, let's not get too heavy.

— You're pulling it across your mouth.

— So does that mean I'm manipulating?

— Don't avoid the question. What are you doing to your mouth?

— Hey buster, leave the chick alone (the whole room listening to Rosie now, others drifting in from the kitchen. Dagmar perched on an arm of Murray's chair. Cleo standing behind her).

— She's probably *wondering*, Rosie boomed, how she's gonna look after her kids while everyone's busy living in the here and now.

— Man, you're sure invested in making power plays, Murray oozed, studying his perfectly manicured nails.

— First of all I'm not a man, and secondly, whaddaya call what you're doing?

— I'm trying to make a point, so she can see for herself how she's repressing something. Why are you so threatened by my point?

— Oh for Chrissake, Rosie rolled her eyes, talk about manipulating!

Gigantic gold disks stamped with Egyptian hieroglyphs dangled from Cleo's ears. They jiggled and caught the firelight as she leaned over Dagmar. Hey Dag, Rosie shouted over the heads of Bell-Bottoms and Overalls, still wearing Gucci shoes? Still too bourgeois to join the party? Too highbrow to do the real work?

— Ah, the glorious worker, Dagmar flung back, we're all supposed to turn into lumpen proletariat, running rat wheel slogans. The state will wither away while Comrade Lenin and Chairman Mao organize us into land armies to hoe fields and grind away in factories. One big union. One big farm where we fuck on the commune plan, have babies on the commune plan, die on the commune plan.

— Yeah, those Gucci shoes are just soooo comfortable, aren't they?

— Work will make you free, huh?! That's what it said on the gates over Nazi concentration camps.

Someone brought in a giant tray of Nanaimo bars then, and someone else cranked up Dylan wailing away on the stereo about all the roads a man'd have to walk before you called him a man. Rosie beamed at Miniskirt, Overalls laughed at something Lanky whispered to her, and the party went back to being just a party.

Dagmar wanted me to read her manuscript and in return she would read mine. Yippee, I thought, neither Murray nor Cleo would be there. To avoid Dwight, we went to her place — a top floor from which you could see the freighters out in the harbour. It even had a clawfoot tub and a proper gas stove, the kind on spindly legs from the forties. Her dad had given her some bookshelves and a long oak table with four oak chairs. There wasn't much room for anything else except the bed. We flopped down on that and spread out our papers.

I asked her if she'd ever eaten madeleines when she was in Paris, and what were they like? Nothing much to them, she said, except flour and eggs and butter, she didn't know why Proust went on about them so much, of course she'd done the whole Proust thing, even visited his room in Le Grand-Hôtel in Normandy, and she supposed if they brought back memories fine, but really the best was to go to Ladureé on the Champs Elysée for petits fours, and no you couldn't really make them, you had to have special scallop-shell pans, but surely I wasn't reading Proust, the new John le Carré wasn't bad, though not as good as his spy novels, Proust was all about gay men anyway, and why was I reading it?

— I'm not, I said, Nigel told me about it. He said sometimes he wishes he'd written his thesis on Proust and names, instead of Lawrence.

— So what does that tell you about Nigel?

— He's not gay if that's what you think.

— All those Englishmen in their boys' schools are a bit gay, you know, and some of them are a lot gay.

I asked her if she'd really dressed up like an old lady and snuck into a casino in Monaco.

— Of course, she said, Cleo was too chicken.

She'd put talc in her hair and got some lisle stockings at a used clothing store, and one of those forties hats with the netting over your eyes. That was the best disguise, she said, not a swish suit, because with the old lady clothes they think you're an addict, you're so desperate you don't care what you look like, you're so desperate you'll wear diapers so you don't have to leave the roulette table and go to the bathroom. That guy who tried to take my winnings, she said, he was a shark. But she'd done the old hand up the nose and knee up the crotch.

— Rosie taught me that, she said.

Dagmar made me get off the bed (*you gotta know basic self-defence*). She grabbed my hand and made me whip up the heel real fast under her nose.

— No! Don't be such a wimp! Surprise me, she commanded. Don't let me see it coming. We danced around the apartment trying to deke each other out.

— Am I going to get you or are you going to get me?

Lurking behind the doorframe, sidling up and whirling into attack, grabbing arms, hands, knocking a chair over. Then she pulled me toward her, surrounding me with her canvassy, wool tweed, cigarette smell.

— Okay, I've got you, what are you going to do?

She pushed me against a wall. Mooshed herself right into me.

— What're you gonna do? I'm all over you. I'm gonna rape you.

I pried her off the wall, laughing, ha, no you aren't.

— I fuckin am.

Her hands grabbed at my pants and breasts, her electrified body smashed me into the wall, her voice muttering into my ear, get your knee going, get your knee going, till I did (*Aha, now you're getting it*) and she let me go. I stumbled back to our manuscripts on the bed, blood pounding – her sinewy arms, her scent of canvas and wheat ...

She was already engrossed in my pages. How glad I was that it was her and not Nigel reading them. How could Nigel ever feel as I felt about university and the city, or even about the mountains and the sea? How could Nigel ever feel what it was like to have someone like Dwight stick his dick into you? When a man reads your story, how can he imagine being seen as an ever-available vagina? But Dagmar would see it as I saw it, Dagmar would feel it as I felt it.

I plunged into her *Landscapes* (an expansion of her pamphlet) and let her words slip around me. Here I lost all my tongue-tiedness and hickdom. Here she stopped lecturing, she showed me her most private sanctuary. Here she spoke only to me, not Al Boyd, the guys at the poetry reading, Cleo, or Rosie. Reading her poems, I became Dagmar herself – I slipped into her skin, a cormorant into water, and if I stayed in her poems long enough they would gloss my feathers.

I swam through *island humps like the backs of porcupines*. I talked her *talk of the raven. To run raccoon,* she wrote, *through fir women and cedar women / saved from their pillaging lovers.* Yes, I too ran raccoon, bandit-like through night woods where trees had eyes and arms and told stories of their past. Raccoons, I thought, that gathered the pillaging and washed it.

But who was the *you* in

> You slink like your music
> gyrating your Bacchus dance;
> you are water while you tell me to breathe
> your cat following me like a Medusa.
> Once your moon was full
> but now your husk is empty.

It couldn't be me because I was her poetry-I. It was someone else —
a mysterious you — offstage, lurking behind the poem. I was supposed
to moon for this loved one the way I did with the pop songs on the
radio, swept along on big sugary waves of emotion, big woolly waves
of cotton batten that lulled me in a cradle of wistfulness, when I could
have been running raccoon. Get rid of the *you* poems, I wrote on my
notepad. Quit name-dropping Greek gods. But what was she getting rid
of from my novel?

Her eyes gazed into my pages as though into a tiny theatre in a shoebox on her lap, the hint of a smile curling the corner of her mouth, her
focus shifting back and forth like she was following the movements of
hockey players zooming around a rink or armies practising field tactics.

For sure she would laugh at this beginner stuff, but maybe if I was nice
about her poems, she'd be nice about my story, but then I wouldn't find
out if it was really bad, but if it *was* really bad how would I ever make it
into something good, that people would like, like Woolf and Lawrence?

What would she think about C and U Girl's experiment in operant
conditioning? To see if it really works on the men's behaviour. They punish J for noisy nights by refusing to smile and chat in the hall the next
day. They reward for quiet nights by offering him a cupcake or a beer.
They punish D for leaving his door open all the time and pestering them
with *how was your day?* They ignore him, they don't smile. They shrug
and close their doors. I know what you're doing, he says, normal people
say hello when they live in the same house. Don't reward the behaviour,
they agree, and then play his most hated music: opera. He drowns it out
with the *Mothers of Invention*. When the door is closed, they tape a note
to it, *Thank you for giving others privacy*. If he keeps his door closed for
several days, they offer him a beer. I know what you're doing, he says.
I can prove it. I can even do it better than you. The next day he leaves his
door open after work. He places a beer and a glass of Southern Comfort
on a chair outside his door and a sign, *Help yourself!* He keeps his door
open to observe the results. It's some kind of game that only girls play,
J says, taking up a second observer position.

U Girl and C shrug and ignore the chair with its bait. They increase their punishment by placing small stones and sticks on D's car and J's motorcycle, then hang out on their balcony suntanning and planning other positive and negative reinforcements. J storms across the hall and pounds on their doors, practically breaking them down: Youse get one thing straight (bringing his fist with its hideous knucklebuster up to U Girl's face). No one touches my bike! I'll fuckin rip you to shreds, if you go near it again. Now who the fuck took my lemon tarts?!

D lounges against his doorframe, smirking.

– We didn't take your tarts.

– Too fucking bad. You've got twenty minutes to get them back, J says.

The men go into D's room and close the door. C and U Girl replace the tarts.

The telephone rang and Dagmar left my shoebox, my *Turquoise Room* of battles and hockey games between D, J, C, and U Girl. She gazed at the ceiling and made plans with Murray for the endlessly delayed trip to Japan. Why did they have to talk about that now?! Why was *that* more important than our reading?!

I supposed he was the *you* in her poem. But why the *husk*? Why were they planning a trip if his *husk* was now *empty*? Dagmar flipped through my pages and told Murray she wanted to go to Hokkaido before Kyoto. I took her poems into the other room and sat at the long table which was a jumble of books, grass-bottomed wine bottles, and old *Harper's* magazines scattering headlines about Albert Camus, Simone de Beauvoir, or the mystery of memory. Marilyn Monroe's half-lidded eyes gazed from the August *Ms.*, which offered new fiction by Doris Lessing and an article on the "Liberated Orgasm."

I scrolled a page into Dagmar's typewriter and typed *a book has a stage*, but it came out *a book as a stage*. The *h* key didn't work. I lifted its long arm away from its companions, poked a scrap of paper between its base and the next letter, pressed the key, but it lay inert, its link to the letter gone. Everything I typed on the broken machine came out in French-Canadian English.

Dagmar was still on the phone. Why was there always something or someone between us, someone else it was more important to talk to? She lay on the bed with her feet propped on the wall, gazing up at some pages of *Turquoise Room* in the nontelephone hand. Could he swing by the stationery store? The one on Fourth. He walked past it every day practically. It was beside the bakery. Not that bakery, the one up the hill. The one where he got cinnamon croissants. Yesterday. It's right beside it. The stationery store – Alice's or Emily's or something like that. She needed a ream of typing paper. Not onion skin. Typing paper. Eighty-pound white. Just ask. Not eighty pounds of paper, that was just the quality. It had to do with how much a box weighed. Of course she didn't want a whole box, just a ream. He was right next to the store, and she was trying to do her final revisions. He was right there and he was coming over tonight. Why not? They'd planned this weeks ago ...

Dagmar liked the title *Turquoise Room*; it reminded her of titles like *Room with a View* or *The Italian Girl*, which made me cross because of course I hadn't read these novels, and it turned out neither had she.

She liked the scene where J got a kitten and called it Velvet. It made him a rounded character, not just a warehouse clerk who reads *Playboy*. She didn't think D could be a shoe salesman. A shoe salesman would not have a huge afro. A shoe salesman would slick back his hair with pomade, but that would make him too much like J so I should make him do another type of work – like record-store clerk or he could sell roach clips in a head shop but mostly be out of work, hanging around on the beach playing his guitar.

She thought J should be meaner. He could lock the kitten in the fridge. C could find it and take it to the SPCA which makes J mad – he was just teaching Velvet a lesson for crying too much, he wasn't going to leave her there – and C better get her back or else!

– But J's already mean, I said. He threatens to beat up C and U Girl; the kitten shows the tough guy still needs something soft.

Dagmar wanted to know whether that guy across the hall who beat up his girlfriend – did he really get a kitten? You mean Jack? Yeah and his girlfriend whatshername Shy ... Shana? Cheyenne. The name *Cheyenne* reminded Dagmar of heroines in John Wayne movies. Women whose husbands had died leaving them in charge of the ranch surrounded by crooks and bandits – not that Cheyenne looked like much of a heroine. More like a drowned rat. Was she still seeing that creep?

– Have you read the whole thing, I said, cuz there's a lot more about J and the kitten; how he gives her milk and the best cat food and washes out the dish every day, and gets U Girl to look after the kitten when he's late from work, how he watches TV with the kitten wrapped in a blanket on his chest. J would never put the kitten in the fridge.

– But you can't stop there, Dagmar said. People don't want to read about nice things, they want to read if the kitten's in danger or if C's in danger, what's going to happen to them?

She wanted to know if it was a love story or a revenge story and what the ending was, was C going to fight with J, then eventually shack up with him. And was U Girl going to go back to her small town with D?

– That would just make it another *Women's Day* romance, I said. Who cares about the ending anyway? What about the fact that she's writing a novel about the novel within the novel? Or the fact that Rice Krispies matter as much as high-class art? Or Darwin or rum and Coke or Karl Marx?

– Don't look so heartbroken. Look, C's got to want something more than anything in the world and J's got to threaten it. Like in *Tess*, the whole story is whether he'll give up his principles and act out of love, instead of abandoning her, or like in *Heart of Darkness*, the whole story is whether they'll get out alive or not, every page keeps you wondering.

– Shit, I might as well throw it all out and start over, I'd have to make C a completely different person, she's not like you, you know, she had nothing growing up, her mom had to get food by gate-crashing funerals, she didn't even finish grade nine.

– All I'm saying is, if you're going to write a novel, you've gotta have a story.

She went to the kitchen and came back with a glass of scotch, saying my face was a raincloud, and I better toughen up if I was going to be a writer, and what did I think of her poems? I took a glug of scotch and I told her she had to get rid of the *you* poems because they sounded like pop songs. That was ridiculous, she said, not using *you*. That was like eliminating love poetry from Sappho to the troubadours and on up. And in case I hadn't noticed, twentieth-century poetry was a whole new ballgame. Look at Ginsberg, look at Creeley. She flipped through *For Love* and quoted a line *If you were going to get a pet ...* What on earth did I mean by a reader *you*? I was just splitting hairs if I thought the *you* in the pet poem was different than the *you* in *you slink*. If you don't like the pet *you*, here's another Creeley: *I did not expect you / to stay married to / one man all your life.*

Twentieth-century poetry uses everyday speech, she went on. Look at Cavafy, *When you set out for Ithaka ...* It didn't have to be any *you* in particular. It was an open-ended *you*. It could be the reader or it could be whoever the reader wanted to imagine the poem is for. No, not necessarily my boyfriend. She wasn't thinking of Murray when she wrote *you slink like your music.* Whatever had given me that idea? I really should read more widely. I should read *The New American Poetry*, get clued in to Charles Olson and Frank O'Hara. Nor did she agree that she was name-dropping Bacchus and Medusa. The point was to speak of them in a modern way, to rethink them like Olson did. She kept tidying her typed pages as she said this.

– Why don't you write a poem about sneaking into a Monaco casino, I said. That'd be way more interesting.

– Because it wouldn't fit. Don't you get it, these are Vancouver poems!

I leapt off the bed with my pages and stared out the window at a couple holding hands and walking down to the beach.

– What're you going to do, because I have to be over at Murray's in half an hour.

– Fucking Murray! It's always Murray Murray Murray!

– I'm sorry about Nigel.

– Fuck Nigel.

– Listen, promise me you won't do anything stupid.
– Like what?
– Like throwing these pages out.
– It's fucking garbage.
– There's good stuff in there; promise!
In the end I promised and threw on my poncho to leave.
– What's the rush, at least stay while I get changed. Have another drink.
She pulled various shirts from her closet.
– No, I said, and raced out the door.

I stomped along the blocks between her place and mine, past the military barracks and the vast green space of Jericho park, past low budget stores, head shops, Indian cotton stores, rolling my thoughts over and over. Cars whizzed by. I glared at cozy people in restaurants, and nearly ran into a woman walking her poodle.

We were s'posed to be best friends, take each other's part, conquer the world together. We were s'posed to dive into each other's lake of words, let the lakes merge, each of us holding the same vast lake. Together we'd find its caves and sunken wrecks. It would no longer be worthless and meaningless. It would be vast and rich and deep. It would hold us just as we held it.

But words fenced us apart. Words like insects marching across the pages. Words like placards people waved at corporations. Not casements to magic vistas. Just so many annoyances. So many boredoms.

Words! And on the other side of them – what? Eyes, hearts, guts – something pulsing autonomically like the swallowing gorge of an octopus or the clawed gullet of a pitcher plant closing on a fly. Something impossible to even think twisted and shifted like the ocean, something no one ever saw. People tossed words in the air every day like they mattered, when they didn't matter a damn. Only what was beyond them mattered.

A few days later after work, I found an envelope slid under my door in Dagmar's unmistakable handwriting. It was a poem:

For FN

You read me
You fight me
You race me to the beach
You tell me not to write you in my poems

I beg you
I plead
I smash you with elbows
You refuse all my yous

But here they are anyway
And this time you means you
really you
not any of the others.

Hope we're still best of friends, DL

So maybe she understood after all, and maybe someday, if we were friends long enough we would find that merged lake ... that place where reading was a kind of loving.

In Hawks's class, people moseyed into the room and homed in on the seats they always sat in, as though on the first day they fell into the rows of identical chairs with their identical right-hand arms for notetaking, all identically spaced and bolted to the floor, and became frozen to those spots. They wandered away till the next class in this room and then returned on invisible strings to their one and only sticking place. Clean-cut guys in V-necks sat in the centre middle rows. A long-hair with a hooked nose slouched into third from the end on the back, rolled a cigarette, and planted it above his ear. A woman in pearls and red jumper cradling a binder and neat stack of books sat two from the end in the front row, beside a woman in granny skirt and bun. Maybe they sat in the same spots in every classroom. Every theatre. Every church.

It was Halloween. The blue-and-white cover of *What Maisie Knew* sparkled on everyone's desk. Maisie who was lost in the maze of her divorced parents' illicit affairs and gaddings about. Sir Claude with something of the bumbling lump of earth about him when it came to human relations. Mrs. Wix who soaked up all the mess and Maisie along with it in her vast broken heart and Miss Overmore, the overly presentable governess, a ripe cluster of grapes, which Maisie's father, Beale Farange, and later Sir Claude were only too ready to pluck. Beale reminded me of beagle, and Farange a cross between far ranging and forage. But Hawks would not be discussing the naming of characters, he would be continuing with his lecture on James's theories of knowledge and education.

Dagmar did not sit beside me. She and Cleo drifted into the far left of the second row, then beckoned me over. Cleo had something for me, something for my term paper. They gazed at me in their city way, Cleo with her dried-blood lips and thick eyeliner that gave her something of the pale-eyed wolf, Dagmar with her blonde hair sliced off above small neat ears. I gazed back, willed myself to remain aloof, cooler than cool. From her bag Cleo pulled a package marked with jack o' lanterns, ripped it open, and dangled a false moustache and a beard. For my Francis Drake thing. They used that cool way of saying what you were doing, as though you had it all wrapped up but it didn't really matter, you just happened to toss it on that day – your thing, like a leather coat or $80 shoes.

– Try it. Dare ya.

I let her peel off the backing and attach it to my face. I wouldn't be the only one in Halloween garb. Down the row, a man in a monk's tunic painted with a skeleton sat next to a cat-eared woman sporting a long tail and cat-eyes mask, her face painted with black whiskers.

Hawks entered the room and switched off the overhead lights. He arranged his papers on the lectern, then started in on James's concern with knowledge in *The Ambassadors* and *Portrait of a Lady*, how Strether and Isobel Archer are trapped by what they don't know because they can't decipher the complex and subtle world around them. Hawks paused, looking out from his lined face into the gloom. What did he see? Rows of heads tilted toward their notebooks, then as the pause lengthened, heads tilted up, eyes gazing at him.

— I suppose you think it's funny coming to class in your silly getups. In my day you'd've been thrown out of university for that. We wore suits and gowns. But then we didn't have this obnoxious American custom of carving up pumpkins and begging door to door for bags of candy. Making fun of death. Making fun of something you know nothing about. You act like you know all about it but you know nothing, and you make fun of me because I *do* know something. Miss Nelson, I find your mocking particularly offensive. Your face is like some nineteenth-century portrait in a book crudely decorated by an ignoramus. You are disrupting this class; please leave the room immediately.

— But sir, one of the clean-cuts said, as I gathered my books and pushed past knees and feet, it's Halloween.

— You can get out too. All of you — get out!

There was a stunned silence. Then a general clumping of books and donning of coats and squeezing out of rows of seats till all the students, eyes averted, or suppressing smiles, had shuffled out of the room and the door closed behind them. I looked back through its tiny window. Hawks stood at the lectern, clutching his notes and staring at the back wall. His lips moved inaudibly.

— Great, what are we supposed to do now, I muttered, tearing off the moustache and beard and chucking them in a garbage can.

One of the clean-cuts said I should complain to the department head. Dagmar said Hawks'd get over it, but yeah the head should probably know what happened, and she'd go with me. Forget it, I said (everyone else gone by then), you can tell him without me. You're not still mad at me, are you, she said. She hoped not, because she'd been thinking about it, and actually I was right about her poems, that thing about the *yous* and the classical name-dropping, I was really a super sharp reader and the best of friends, and any time I wanted her to read my novel, all I had to do was ask. And really the great literary friendships were epic, she went on, they lasted lifetimes, Aldington and Lawrence, Aldington writing Lawrence's biography. Or Forster and Cavafy in Alexandria. Or Vita and Virginia at Sissinghurst.

– So get Cleo, I said.

Well Cleo was a dear friend of course, but Cleo wasn't into poetry, Cleo was a story writer and she was more worried about protagonists and antagonists, and that sort of thing. By this time we were outside, standing near a bust of some university father set into a cedar hedge. She threw her arms around me, saying she really needed me, she couldn't face typing the whole manuscript by herself in the library now that her typewriter was on the fritz, and could I come at least for moral support, and she'd take me to lunch on Sunday at Mozart Konditorei, just the two of us? We'd have a grand literary talk. And I agreed, even though I thought the grand talk highly unlikely. Where would I find my grand talk, I wondered, unless I somehow read everything she'd ever read between now and then? But if we stayed friends, maybe ... maybe one day ...

I went home early and watched *Edge of Night* with Carla, the two of us sprawled on her bed with beers and potato chips, the show punctuated by pops and fizzes from Halloween firecrackers out on the street where kids in witch's hats, Captain Hook outfits, skeleton costumes, black pussycat suits, and plastic masks of Frankensteins and vampires thronged from house to house with their buckets and pillowslips. Downstairs, they were climbing the concrete steps to the landlady's door, chorusing in unison *trick or treat*, but no one was going to climb the long outside steps and bug us, not that we had any candy for them anyway.

But someone did knock. We whispered what if it's the debt collectors, but of course they'd've heard the TV. A child's voice came through the keyhole, I can hear you – singing out the *you* the way one does in hide and seek, threatening to find someone. It was Janey, dressed in a Snoopy sweatshirt and kid's jeans turned up at the bottom showing their plaid lining. Dwight's door was open but he wasn't there. He told her to wait here. He went to see her mommy. Then they were going to trick-or-treat. Daddy said Carla would make her into a princess again – a fairy princess. She didn't know where mommy was. She was staying at Gramma's. She didn't want any dinner. She wanted Carla to make her into a fairy princess.

– Okay, hon, as soon as the program ends, we'll do that.

She gathered up Janey on the bed with us to watch the rest of the show. This lasted for about three minutes. Then Janey started to cry – at first just whimpering, Carla cuddling her, asking if she missed her daddy, not to worry, he'd be back soon – then, looking at me like I was about to beat her with a cudgel, shifting into loud wails, squiggling out of Carla's arms, and yanking her toward the dresser. Choking it out between big sobs, she wanted Carla to make her into a princess now, cuz soon there'd be no more candy.

– Hey okay, hon, but you gotta promise me to dry those tears.

Minutes later she was twirling around in a chiffon skirt made of one of Carla's negligees and a cloak made from a wraparound. I made a wand out of the landlady's stick she used to dust around the fridge, and Carla decorated her face with lipstick and sparkly eyeshadow, topping it all off with a tiara made of tinfoil and one of Carla's plastic hairbands.

We stood in the hall. Janey was all ready. The most beeyoutiful fairy princess in all of Vancouver. Carla knelt in front of her. Janey shook out another sob.

– Hey, fairy princesses don't cry. They wave their wands and make magic happen.

When was daddy coming, Janey sent a tearful gaze toward the outside door.

– He'll be here soon, hon – hey, wave those tears away.

She waved Janey's hand holding the wand, abracadabra, whoosh, tears all gone.

– I had a little girl like you once, and she was real special, just like you are.

– Did you take her for trick-or-treat?

– No, she was too little, but I wish I had.

And that was how Janey got Carla to take her out with the other little ghosts and goblins and a Hudson's Bay shopping bag to collect her loot, while I was to listen for Dwight and let him know. Dwight did not come back that night. Nor was he there the next morning. I phoned his garage but they didn't expect him for a couple of days. They didn't have a number for his mother. Janey sat in Carla's rumpled bed, going through her candies, while Carla thought she should have a proper breakfast. Janey didn't like eggs or toast. She liked Cap'n Crunch or waffles and maple syrup.

– We can go to the diner, hon, over on Fourth.

– Where's your little girl, Janey asked Carla, we can play together.

– Oh, she's with another family now, a really nice family.

– Why did you give her to that family? Why don't you go find her?

Carla said she was probably as big as auntie Frances by now, not a little girl anymore.

– My mommy doesn't give me away, she's just tired, so I stay at Gramma's.

They went off to the diner. I went out to the library to help Dagmar type up her manuscript.

In a windowless pocket of the stacks under dim electric bulbs, the library typewriters stood on long wooden tables too high really for typing – all of them Underwoods, Smith-Coronas, or Royals with bodies like boxy Model-T Fords, chrome return levers winged out like single oars, and huge metal-rimmed keys that plunged down so far my fingers walked through quicksand up to their necks. Thick walls of bound books crammed into metal shelving surrounded the typewriters on all sides and up to the ceiling, so that heat ducts working overtime kept the whole book-lined box on a slow oven setting.

Along the table, a student pored over scribbled sheets, yanked out a typed page and hurled it into a waist-high wire basket. Another man rested his head on his machine completely encasing it in his arms and flowing hair. Dagmar put some new ribbons in ours, and we began clunking away, making nice typed copies of her poems.

A clean-cut type in suit jacket and rayon slacks suddenly filled up the table with himself and four friends, all women.

– Hey mister, he said to the mound of hair, go find somewhere else to sleep, we're taking that machine.

The sleeper shook himself, looked around.

– Relax, okay, I was just thinking.

– Well think somewhere else, I got an important project here.

He and the women laid out papers all over the table, Marketing 305, Business Admin 400. He got all the women typing except one whom he sent off with a typed essay. He himself sat in front of a typewriter, but did not type. I'd seen his kind at the Biltmore, pressing friends to buy into deals. He smiled at me like a young Richard Nixon winning an election and suggested I quit staring at him.

After a page or two, Dagmar yanked out what she was typing and hurled it into the wire basket. What was another word for *landscape*? She'd used it too many times. *Forest, mountains, ocean, geography, countryside, scene, view* – all ridiculous. Too pastoral. What did cities have instead of pretty fields and chirping streams? She forked her hands through her cropped hair, staring at the poem. Sleepy Thinker offered *manscapes*. Dagmar muttered thanks but she didn't think it'd do. She'd have to fix that one later.

We stripped down to shirt sleeves and banged away, stopping every so often to insert correcting tape over wrong letters, plaster them in white and then type the correct letters over top. The pages piled up; we were almost halfway through. Me and Dagmar, allies against the world. We would go on together, I thought, writing, talking, building a bigger and bigger lake of words. Making each other stronger till we mattered, in the world of books by men.

Richard Nixon's errand-woman came back and handed him some bills, which he held under the table and told her to get on with the next one. She held out her hand.

– End of the day, that's what we said.

She slouched into a chair in front of a machine. By now their papers were piled everywhere, some right in front of my typewriter, others mingling with some of Dagmar's pages. I cleared these back and got a bark from Nixon not to disrupt the layout of his project. You don't own the table, I said. Go type somewhere else if you don't like it, he said.

I bashed furiously away, till I got to a line about *rooks plunging to rocks* and another one about *maples quivering.*

— Are you sure you want *rooks* and *quivering*, I said to Dagmar. I mean no one around here says *rooks*. It sounds like, I don't know, not really you, but like you're trying to be Virginia Woolf.

— People here say *rooks*, I say *rooks*. Why can't we have *rooks* here?

— People here say *crows*.

— My dad says *rooks*.

— But your dad's not from here is he?

Sleepy Thinker suggested we saw it down the middle and put *ravens*. Nixon told us to hold our poetry group somewhere else, and Quiet, it's a library.

— Go type somewhere else, I glared at him, then low-voiced, *crows* would work, how about *crows diving to rocks?*

— Say *crow* and you think stupid little bird raiding nests or something, cawing away in a farmyard. *Rook* is dark, powerful.

— Crows are actually really smart, I said. They can count up to four.

— Shit, I'll have to rethink that whole piece, I wanted *rooks* and *rocks*, and then *maples quivering* to echo *skyscraper cartoning.*

She said she had to take a break, just a few minutes to walk around, think. Figure out whether she was going to ditch the whole thing. She left the rook poem in the typewriter, and told me to guard our stuff.

I started in on *Ferry Crossings*, a poem I really liked where she ran phrases together and broke them off midstream and didn't bother with complete sentences:

> *coyote in the night lope*
> *across ferry bows of*
> *cedar under weather oar to*
> *handle careful fishnet*

Another one of Nixon's errand-women returned with money but it wasn't the right amount and they started arguing, finally, after some glares and quiets from me, moving a few feet into the stacks. Someone tapped my shoulder. I turned to face Nigel.

He beckoned me away down an aisle of books. Nixon's typists hammered on at their tasks, eyes on their work. I followed him under the back stairs into a side room with no carrels, no studiers, just glimpses above the books, of distant necks or jackets trolling through the stacks. He said I had every right to think he was a shit. He *was* a shit, and he was sorry for the way he'd cut me off without a word. I deserved better, a lot better.

I stared speechless into his blue eyes in their round spectacles, then at his sailor fingers grasping a notepad, a pile of books and a copy of *The Rainbow*. Hands I wanted to caress me, books we could read together, pages we could write together, the lifelong friend I wanted, maybe I still could, maybe we could still find our great love.

If it was any consolation, he said, he'd broken up with Sandy too. I'm such a stupid sod, he said, never was much good with women. He said he'd understand if I didn't want to be friends, I probably should tell him to completely bog off. But as a way of saying how sorry he was, he'd got something for me at his office, a book he really wanted me to have, and he hoped I'd come by.

Never much good with women — like we were some kind of skittish horse or dangerous pet snake or some kind of excitable foreigner or Martian alien you had to handle with kid gloves. Nothing had changed. He was giving me books just like before, looking at me with that John Lennon cool, same as before, only now it bugged me, because I thought, there's nothing behind it except more and more cool. More and more keeping me at arm's length.

Yeah you're right, I said. You don't know about women cuz you think we're aliens from outer space. You and your fucking Lawrence books, I said, all about how men see women, men know everything about women, and women just need sex with men. And I went back to the typewriters, leaving him standing there with his *Rainbow*.

In front of my typewriter, I couldn't see the words on Dagmar's page. She still wasn't back; her poem waited, half-typed, in the machine. Nixon muttered to one of his typists, hurry up, it's supposed to be ready in half

an hour. Then I saw *Ferry Crossings*, and gradually the rest of the poem.
I started pressing keys.

Dagmar returned smelling of fresh air and autumn leaves. She rustled through her papers.

– So what'd you do with it?

– What?

– The rook poem?

– It's in your typewriter.

– I mean the original.

– Nothing, I've just been working on this one.

– Shit!

She flipped through her pile again and then my pile. It was the only
copy of that poem.

– Shit shit shit!

– I thought you took it with you.

– No, why would I do that?!

– Because you were thinking about it.

We both started looking through Nixon's piles of papers.

– Get your hands off my stuff, get your hands off or I'll fucking arrest
you for theft.

– You fuck off. Your papers mixed up ours. We're getting ours back.

– Well if your friend hadn't left them lying around while she took off
with her boyfriend.

– You what?

– Nigel. I was gone two minutes.

Dagmar hunched over her machine trying to remember the poem.
I looked again through Nixon's piles. Then pulled out every sheet of
paper from the wire basket, stuff about endorsements vs. fear appeals;
eye-catching colours for the counterculture; aim, target, media, and competitors – the four rules of advertising. I unscrunched Dagmar's *landscape*
page and pages about the sonnet form in English literature, Aristotelian
logic vs. Buddhism, cetaceous vocalizations in killer whales. I spread the
entire contents of the wire basket around the table and along the aisles,
but the rook poem wasn't there.

– I'm going down to Lost and Found, I said, maybe you did have it and someone picked it up.

Dagmar said okay, but she doubted I'd find it. She was still hunched over her machine writing things down by hand.

A lost poem, the student on duty said through the wire mesh of his cage behind the circulation desk, don't get many of those. He rummaged through hats, coats, bookbags, and binders on the shelves, unearthing an essay on operant conditioning in preschool behaviour problems and some pages of an essay on *Paradise Lost*. I said thanks, and trudged back to the typing tables. When I got there, Dagmar had packed up everything and gone. She said to tell you she couldn't do any more today, one of Nixon's bunch told me. So she was going to find you at Lost and Found, but if she missed you, she would just go home.

CHAPTER 12

Back at my room, I telephoned Dagmar, but no answer. I threw myself down on the cot and sat, lead-hearted, in the darkening room. My eye drifted over the constellations on a star chart Nigel had given me when he moved to the boat – Cassiopeia, Andromeda, Ursa Major, and Pegasus, white dots on a black sky. He'd torn them out of a magazine and tacked them on his wall and now they were tacked on mine. Fuck Nigel. I lurched off the cot and ripped them down.

Maybe I was done with men. Maybe I'd just love women from now on like that *Georgia Straight* article said. But how did you do that? Okay, you started by kissing, and then what? Did I even want that? How could I kiss Dagmar, just supposing I wanted to? She'd think me an idiot. She knew all about it.

Tiny Tim gave me his hair-over-the-eye wink, strumming ukulele strings into my brain, dancing the points of his toes on peaks of tulip petals, and singing in his high falsetto, tiptoe through the freak show, in the garden, through the window; moonlight with a pardon, in the window of a pillow, tiptoe through the freak show ...

I got out my notebook and wrote down everything I could remember of the rook poem but it was only about two lines. I guessed she'd be too bummed out to remember our lunch plans.

Jack knocked on my door, still in his workboots and carpenter's belt, just to let me know that Dwight's ex was in a coma, that's why he disappeared yesterday. Jack didn't know where Janey was, probably with her gramma.

A few days later Jack asked Carla and me if we'd seen Dwight. He needed to get his Allen wrenches back. We ended up with beers in Jack's room, Carla in the one chair flashing her high-laced boots and her frosted nails, me cross-legged on the cot. Dwight'd borrowed the wrenches weeks ago to fix Janey's Pinocchio puppet. Carla said she'd seen him the day before from her bus on the way to work — standing on the street near the hospital, just standing there like a lamp post, doing nothing. We talked about people who lay in comas for months and then suddenly woke up, people who doctors said had no brain activity but the relatives refused to unplug them. That isn't going to happen to Dwight's ex, Carla said.

— When did you get your M.D.? Jack leaned against the wall doodling with a pair of red clacker balls.

— Trust me, I know.

— So what happens?

— My mother didn't just die instantly with her heart attack (Carla snapped her fingers). She was in a coma for two days. You talk to them when they're like that. They can hear you, even though they can't talk. I talked to my mom the whole time. I knew she wasn't coming back. Hardest thing I ever did. Or maybe second hardest.

Jack wanted to know why Dwight would talk to his ex. Carla rolled her eyes. Told him he'd figure it out sometime. Wouldn't say what the hardest thing'd been. Why, Jack asked, would anyone give his little girl a puppet with a hard-on for a nose? He got the clacker balls smacking and clapping, pleased with a row of ten clacks before they went off-kilter. Delusions of a dirty mind, Carla scoffed. From someone who plays with his balls. She loved *Pinocchio*. She remembered her mom taking her to see a free show once. The blue fairy was her favourite.

Just a dumb kids' movie, Jack thought, about a stupid little birdbrain in a bow tie that ends up in a birdcage. The whole thing just saying, be a good little boy and go to school.

— So do you wanta be a puppet or a real person, Carla said. Just play games all day, or think for yourself?

Carla sang the Jiminy Cricket song, and I remembered Mom playing it on a thick pink seventy-eight when I was about five.

— When's your conscience gonna give a little whistle, Carla said. Or do you even have one?

— Ah, don't be such a goody, Jack said. School's just a puppet show, for sure. He swung the clacker balls into a frenzy of thwacking. Then bet Carla and I couldn't do it.

We were all standing around playing with them when Dwight appeared in the doorway and stood there not really looking at us but through us. Unshaved stubble made his face even pastier than usual. He took a beer and fell into the chair. Carla settled herself on the floor leaning against the wooden cabinet of Jack's Magnavox TV that Dwight had helped lug up the outside steps from a secondhand shop. Shirley was dead. Died hours ago, in the morning sometime. He chugged some beer. Don't worry if it doesn't really hit you for a couple of days, Carla offered, that's normal.

I didn't know what to say. I focused on the chain-link patterned cloth covering the speaker box under the grey bulgy screen of the TV, while Carla went on about how she didn't really get it at first when her mom died; she just carried on doing all the things she had to do: getting the death certificates, arranging the funeral, closing the bank accounts. She didn't break down much at the funeral, but two weeks later it suddenly hit her, they were never going shopping again. Her mom was never going to make her favourite scrambled eggs again. They'd never again watch *Edge of Night* together. Never read their horoscopes and do their nails on Saturday afternoon. She bawled for days, she said.

Dwight said he didn't really know what to do at the end, didn't know if she was dead when he felt her hand. The nurse rolled up a little wash-cloth and propped it under Shirley's chin so her mouth didn't hang open. Nurses carted away the IV. They said he could stay there as long as he wanted; the doctor wouldn't be around for a couple of hours. To sign the death certificate, they told him. He hadn't thought of it. Nurses told him he'd need that in order to take care of her affairs. There wasn't a will, he thought. That didn't matter, the nurses said, there were still things he had to take care of. He supposed they meant her funeral.

He stayed there for a while inside the curtains around Shirley's bed, trying to figure out what had changed now that the nurses said she was dead. Wasn't she still in her body just as much as if she'd been sleeping? He wished he'd brought a sketchbook. He would have drawn her face. It was peaceful, he said, except for the women in the ward on the other side of the curtain, groaning or farting or complaining to their relatives about the cold toast and watery porridge in their breakfast, and how it was so noisy at night they couldn't sleep.

Then Dwight's father-in-law showed up. He'd remarried after Shirley's mother died in a boating accident, but Shirley didn't like her stepmother, didn't trust her around Janey. Dwight said you could hear Shirley's step-mother way down the corridor before she even got to Shirley's room telling her husband he'd better check into that Seaview funeral place, which was more than that drip of a husband of hers would do, that snake that turned Shirley against her, Shirley would never have chosen cremation if he, Dwight, hadn't conned her into it. Because it was the cheap way, she said. Dwight could hear the nurses asking her to keep it down. Then she was into the room with Dwight, complaining there was nowhere to sit, ordering her husband, whom she towed around like a moping dog, to get chairs, asking Dwight if he was pleased now that she was dead. Like it was my fault she got cancer, Dwight said, telling us he'd never mentioned anything to Shirley about cremation, he didn't really think she was in the final stages yet, but then about a week ago, Shirley had told him she wanted to be scattered off the breakwater on Wreck Beach where they used to swim, and he'd promised he'd do it. He'd get a boat and go right out to the end of the breakwater and let her go on the waves like she wanted.

If anyone killed Shirley, Dwight said, it was her stepmother, always telling her how to cook and clean and bring up Janey. He called the step-mother the Sawmill and said she once washed all the family bedsheets in Sani-Flush. They had to throw them out afterwards. They almost had to throw out the washing machine. Her idea of cooking steak was to burn it in ketchup. If they left Janey alone with her, she'd send her to the store to buy magazines and cigarettes, or leave her in a corner all afternoon because she wouldn't eat a raw-onion sandwich.

Dwight grabbed another beer from the hall fridge. Jack wanted to know if Shirley was still in the hospital room. Dwight guessed not. Probably down in the morgue, he guessed. I thought of her lying on a metal table under a sheet, this woman who was Janey's mother. This person who just a few moments before had been a field of energies and thoughts now identified by a tag wired to her toe, like on the body of Jake Berman in the coroner's lab on *Edge of Night*.

The Sawmill had said Dwight would have to let Janey see her more often now, cuz he wouldn't be able to manage on his own. No fucking way, Dwight told us, was he going to let Janey over there without ... He broke off and stared out the window at the wall of the next-door house. Jack studied his fingernails, looked at me, then back at his nails. Carla watched Dwight, but she didn't get up from the floor. No one said anything. The moment passed, and Dwight said he'd appreciate it if any of us felt like coming to the memorial service.

The day before the service, Dwight tapped on my door. Could I help him with something for the memorial? He leaned against the doorframe grin-leering his usual bug-eyed smirk, and by the way he was still really sorry for what had happened – the you know – the VD thing. A cloud of sour sweat hung around him, underpinned with rotten eggs or meat, and I realized his purple shirt and pinstriped bell-bottoms were the same ones he'd had on the day Shirley died. He wanted me to help him choose the clothes Shirley would wear in the casket. It was going to be open-casket – the Seaview Home near the beach. They needed the clothes today.

A fug of cigarette butts and empty beer bottles stifled his room. I left the door open. He unlatched a blue vinyl suitcase, and lifted out a dark paisley muumuu made of some shiny delicate fabric, carried it across his forearms, and laid it lengthwise on the rumpled bed, then laid a pair of pink heels at the bottom. We should ask Carla, I said. I don't know a thing about clothes. But he didn't want Carla's advice, he wanted to know what *I* would choose; *I* would know better than Carla what Shirley would want. He lifted the muumuu back into the lid of the suitcase and laid out a mauve bell-bottom pantsuit with white slippers. She had worn that when she taught grade three, he said. She was a different person then, he said, but I didn't know whether he meant before she got sick or that she wasn't the same as when she stayed home and did housework. He got down on his knees, folded the pants so they kept their crease, and tucked the slippers back into the silk puckered pockets of the case.

Even I knew the next dress was a Laura Ashley print covered with little blue flowers, its pleated front gathered into a stand-up collar trimmed with lace. He carried it across his arms to the bed, slipped his fingers along it to straighten the full-length skirt to its flounced hem, and arranged each long puffed sleeve. I don't know what shoes, he said, I don't know what shoes. She wore this the last time we sat in her kitchen, but I don't remember what shoes she had. He pulled out the kind of sandal with a braided leather band across the arch of the foot linked to a leather ring for the big toe, and laid them at her imaginary feet. A moment later he'd gathered the dress and all the crumpled bedding into his arms, and buried his face in its pool of little blue flowers.

Carla came in then, as he crouched over the bed and shook and rocked. Aw hon, she said, kneeling down beside him and putting her arms around his shoulders, it's gonna be okay, hon. We're all gonna be there tomorrow.

The Seaview Memory Home was a white stucco building with leaded windows and fake brown shutters stuck on either side of the windows. It looked like a low-slung manor house except for the large chimney behind it. The same brown wood as the shutters decorated the chapel inside with little fleurs-de-lys along the tops of its white wall-panels which held a picture of Christ on the cross, a photograph of a waterfall cascading through a forest, and a sunset over an ocean. One corner of the room held a glass cabinet of china teacups. Rows of padded stack-able chairs, divided by an aisle, filled most of the space on the brown carpet, leaving an open area at the front for two huge vases of lilies and the casket which rested on a platform leading into a wall of gold drapery.

In the front row a woman bulging out of her black sateen dress chattered loudly about the casket to a shorter slight man with thinning threads of hair and a sharp nose. *He* would've buried her in a cardboard box or an old bed sheet if I hadn't done something, I heard over the recorded organ music. She had rust-coloured permed hair. I guessed she was Shirley's stepmother. Across the aisle on the other front row sat Dwight, clean-shaven and wearing a black sports jacket, next to him Janey in blue velvet and little white gloves, with an older woman I guessed was Dwight's mother. Carla and I and Jack sat a couple of rows behind Dwight. Cheyenne had come too, and a guy, in jeans and black windbreaker, from Dwight's garage. He marched up to the front of the chapel, said hey man, gave Dwight a hug, then disappeared to the back row of empty chairs.

The polished wood casket stood on its stout moulded base that reminded me of carved feet on heavy forties sofas and armchairs. Its walls looked as thick as a refrigerator's and were heavily decorated with carved trim and brass handles. Its lid, like an open refrigerator door, displayed pillowy white satin held in place by white upholstery buttons. I decided not to view the body. I wanted to remember Shirley as she was beside Janey in the summer photograph, full of sunshine on the dock at Cultus Lake. They chose the Laura Ashley dress and the white slippers, Carla told me, and they gave her a wig. Too bad the hair doesn't look real, she said, too dark, too shiny.

But what was real?

Who're all these people, Shirley's stepmother belted out, Shirl never knew *them*. Shirley's father stared ahead at the golden drapes, stock-still as though she hadn't spoken. She lumbered in her too-tight black sateen over to Janey, took her by the hand and told her to come sit with your gramma for a while. Janey pulled her hand away and clung to her father, beginning to wail, and the woman spat out, you're gonna hafta grow up pretty soon little girl, and lumbered back to her chair.

The chaplain emerged from a side door, whispered something to Dwight, then disappeared again. Dwight took Janey over to the casket and stood her on a chair so she could see inside. She fingered some of the hair, Dwight explaining that it was to make mommy pretty, but mommy wasn't going to wake up, she wasn't sleeping, she wasn't even breathing, she couldn't feel anything now. Carla grabbed my arm and bawled on my shoulder. We were all choking back tears, even Jack. Even the Sawmill dabbed at her eyes with a Kleenex. Dwight's eyes had darkened the way a sky does when a storm moves in, his face flushed and twisted.

Two men in suits came in and closed the casket. The organ music stopped and the chaplain began the service. He called her *the deceased*, then checked another sheet of paper and slotted in the name Shirley Williams. He talked about her close and loving family, her father and mother here today. He said she'd be missed by all the students at the high school where she taught, and by all her friends here today. Then he began to call on the Holy Power by His glorious resurrection and ascension to have mercy on his servant and deliver her from eternal death, to pardon all her sins and give her a place of refreshment and everlasting blessedness, joy and gladness with the saints in Your holy kingdom. Calling on the Lamb of God and redeemer of the world to have mercy on a sheep of Your own fold, a sinner of Your own redeeming, to deliver her from all evil, to set her free and give her everlasting peace. Praying also for those who mourn, that they may give themselves up to the mercy of Your heavenly grace and know the consolation of Your love, and that He would remember them and look with pity upon the sorrows of His servants, and nourish them and comfort them with goodness, and that He would lift up his countenance on them. Wherefore we commend to Thy hands Merciful Father the soul of this our sister and we commit her body as ashes to ashes, dust to dust ...

The casket moved toward the wall of drapes on a muffled rolling of belts on rubber wheels until it parted the gold curtains and disappeared beyond them. Janey wanted to know where she was going and could she breathe in there. She doesn't need to breathe now, Dwight told her,

She's going to become ash and dust like the man said, like sand. And then Janey wanted to know if everyone in heaven was made of ash and dust and sand.

Whatever Dwight said, I didn't hear it. I slipped out of the row of empty chairs, past the Memory Home's spiral-clipped shrubs. I crossed rain-sodden grass and matted heaps of fallen leaves till I got to the beach. When would Janey understand? How would she ever understand that darkness where her mom had gone?

Grey drizzle fell from clouds so low in the harbour you could almost reach up and touch their tattered hunks. The sand stretched out to the leaden water. A solitary man wearing a red poppy threw a stick for his dog. A gull poked at a clamshell. No one else found anything of interest on the beach at that time, the concessions having long closed, the August bathers now hunkered down to November jobs. I sat on a log and studied the freighters on their anchors. Not in Nigel's "roads," no, there were no roads, only ocean, only a vast writhing animal that let the ships slither along its back or thrashed them to bits.

I felt someone behind me put their hands over my eyes and say, guess who. What was I doing sitting on the beach staring forlornly out to sea?

It was Dagmar. I grabbed her hands, such small plump lively wrens, so much not the stout protective paws of Nigel or Joe or any other man I'd touched. She yanked me off the log and along the sand close to the water, arms around each other's waists – I taller, I the protective one, she a bundle of energy and talk. She hoped I wasn't torturing myself over that rook poem, and, sorry for just going off like that from the library. She'd written a new poem called "The Lost Poem." She couldn't wait to show it to me; and we must have our little lunch at Mozart Konditorei.

Was this when I kissed her, like the men in the movies making a pass? Was this when I made the pass, and she laughed? But if I loved her I would, wouldn't I? I'd do anything for her, even the most scary and humiliating thing. I did love her, but no, I could not make a pass – it was impossible. It was not that kind of love.

– I don't want a little lunch, I said, I want a big lunch.

I launched a flotilla of driftwood with my toe.

— We'll go to the Hotel Vancouver, then.

— Okay.

— We'll go tomorrow.

— Yeah, tomorrow. What time?

— One o'clock?

— Okay, one o'clock.

We wandered along the beach toward my room, tossing sticks into the lazy swell washing in to shore. Then as usual she had to be off somewhere meeting Cleo or Murray or her dad.

Everyone except the Sawmill and Shirley's dad was hanging around in the hall by the old icebox-style fridge when I got back to the rooming house: Jack and Cheyenne, Carla and Dwight's mom, Janey and Dwight. They wondered what happened to me, was I all right? Carla whispered in my ear she wanted to do a little something for Dwight and my room was the only one big enough. We dragged chairs in, Jack brought beer and Wiser's, Carla brought Southern Comfort and chips, I got ice from the fridge. We poured drinks into mugs or juice glasses. Dwight's mom offered a toast. Nobody said much for a bit. Janey tried on some of Carla's jewellery. Then Jack mentioned that he and Cheyenne were getting married and moving to a trailer in Surrey, which made me think of Joe and his new girlfriend running a sports store in Cultus Lake, and Lorna at the insurance company, who wanted to come with me to UBC, but she hadn't, she was marrying Steve and keeping the baby, living on welfare. You can't just march into people's lives and overnight make them equal, I thought sadly, you can't just fix their lives with ideas, if something in them made them think they couldn't do it. But you can't just be friends with people who are powerful and equal like Dagmar either, people who don't know how it is to grow up on the outside, like Lorna and Carla and Cheyenne.

Dwight's mom asked if Dwight had any pictures of Shirley and we laid these out on the table and passed them around: Shirley holding newborn Janey; Shirley with Janey's one-candle cake; Shirley sunbathing on a dock; Shirley caught in the shower, holding the curtain across her and laughing; Shirley taking her grade three class to the aquarium.

Dwight broke down again. Janey put the jewellery back in its box, she'd probably never seen her dad cry. She reached her arms around his frizzy head. Daddy's going to be all right, he said, don't worry. He gathered her into his arms and managed a crooked smile over her shoulder at the rest of us. We're all going to Gramma's tonight.

Soon, I thought, all of us would go somewhere different, we'd say goodbye to the landlady who'd watched over us, and go live in other places, we'd never see each other, yet something held us together, living here side by side, something like that we-ness I'd wanted to find with Nigel or Dagmar.

Hawks would not accept handwritten essays. Therefore I would have to type. I headed into the main library vestibule, past the lineup of rain-sodden students at the tiny circulation office, waiting for grey clerks in a sea of library carts to return with the book they were hoping would transform their term paper from a groping in the dark to a clean triangular A. I pressed through the three-pronged turnstile into the stacks, wondering as I always did whether it counted the number of students in and the number of students out, tallying them up at the end of the day to see if bodies remained fallen somewhere inside. Captured like lint in study carrels, dozing, or locked in a trance by the dance of words in their heads. As usual I wondered whether the library sent clerks scouring the stacks at closing time in order to flush them out. It seemed unlikely that these mechanical milking stools on their sides actually counted anything, and extremely likely that bodies stayed there overnight, even bringing blankets, pillows, and snacks. Maybe even camping there for weeks, evading scouring library clerks by hiding in heating ducts or library carts or on the topmost bookshelves.

I plunked myself in front of an Underwood, spread out my copy of *Orlando*, my overdue library copy of *Elizabeth and Essex: A Tragic History*, and my pile of expensive typing paper, and began clunking away from some scribbled and crossed-out notes. Obviously Woolf had transformed Essex into Orlando; she even has Orlando meet the Queen just as Strachey says Essex does at the beginning of his book. This took me about two pages with quotes. Then what? The books had nothing to do with each other.

I flipped through *Orlando*, looking for clues. That Orlando is transformed into a queen, that Orlando the queen was in love with a poet, who was really Essex, that Alexander Pope was like Essex, that this was the whole fantastic crystal of truth hidden in *Orlando*, this was what *Orlando* was really about, and I could prove it because Strachey said " " on page x (footnote with book title, city of publication, publisher, and date) and Woolf said " " on page y (footnote with book title, city of publication, publisher, and date).

An hour passed, half of page three flapping its tongue out of the typewriter. But *Orlando* was really about Vita Sackville West, Dagmar said, Virginia and Vita — me and Dagmar, but I wasn't cut that way, but shouldn't I have tried it just to see what it was like? Shouldn't I have kissed her, torn off her clothes, touched her in all those places men had touched me? I then truly equal to a man!

What made it love instead of sex? What made you think you wanted it with *that* person instead of *that* one; that with *that* one, you'd find the great love? Anyway, I still loved Dagmar, whatever *that* love was.

Not as a girlfriend you'd supposedly spend hours with, like the women at the insurance company, plucking and pencilling eyebrows, loading up eyelashes with mascara, hours reading magazines on how to do it, more hours painting nails, waiting for them to dry, talking about pageboys and perms, French rolls and beehives, who was going with who, how to lose weight with the celery diet. Not as a woman who collected a hope chest, and held pyjama parties and baby showers, those rainstorms of pink frills and bows on a china bride frozen in her china lace.

No. Dagmar was never that. Dagmar was someone I could build a cabin with in the woods, splitting shingles, and lugging in a pot-bellied stove and a writing table. Someone I could write a novel with, invent a play, build a Trojan horse out of a shopping cart, oil drum, and paint buckets. Someone I could invent a language with that only the two of us spoke.

Dagmar chose to be male, chose to be female, like Orlando, whenever she wanted. Not some magazine womanhood. She wasn't even a woman. She was a poet or a casino gambler or a sailor. She played roles in lots of plays. She wrote the parts, painted the sets, and directed the performances.

Society was nothing at all when you took it apart, *Orlando* said. Just like Christmas punch, delicious when you mixed it up, but boring ingredients by themselves. I flipped through the pages. I couldn't find the quote. Instead, I found, *One can only believe entirely, perhaps, in what one cannot see.* Strachey said Queen Elizabeth was full of *discordances* of *real* and *apparent*?

Real or apparent. A theme in Shakespeare. What was the difference anyway? Was university real and important, like Mom said; or was it just a *bourgeois universippy*, like Dad said?

I bashed away nailing Woolf to Strachey. Some complicated theory that Pope and Essex were both poets, so Orlando, the society lady, was in love with poets: Addison, Dryden, Steele (storybook heroes of a faraway land in English lit essays).

Strachey's Queen thinks she's *a sane woman in a universe of violent maniacs.* Woolf's Orlando finds herself battered by clashing social standards and hostile laws against women. Strachey's Queen melts with the flatteries of young men, then thinks, *She was a woman* but *she was something more ... what was it? Was she a man?* Therefore, according to Hawks's theory, Woolf made Orlando a man-woman. Strachey's Queen dominated England precisely because she *abandoned ... the last shreds ... of consistency ... in order to escape the appalling necessity of having, really and truly, to make up her mind.* Therefore Woolf made Orlando constantly change her mind: should she go to Lady so-and-so's tea party or Lady such-and-such's ball.

Suddenly the whole thing made me furious – Strachey accusing one of the greatest monarchs in English history of dithering – the kind of story men told all the time about women, that was just a story, just a way to belittle women, keep them less important than men, keep them believing they were essentially weak and inferior, so that even Woolf said Orlando the woman wavered and hesitated, whereas Orlando the man lunged and plunged and sliced his sword at his enemy. And now Hawks of course insisting I should show how Woolf got her story from a man, she'd never have made it up herself. Hawks insisting that I go on telling this same belittling story. Insisting that I read it his way, the way a man thinks who's never seen women as anything but scatterbrained ditherers with no real ideas of their own. Whereas Woolf had given us the man-woman, the creature we all needed to be and tell stories about.

But how could I ever write that for a prof like Hawks?

Around me thick walls of books bulged their metal shelves. Books, the sheer weight of them, boxing the typing area, floor to ceiling, rows and rows of stacks, stacks of floors of stacks, books I should have read, ideas I should know, words that should flow out of me in facts and foot-notes and bibliographies, so that Hawks would know I knew them. All the stories men had told for centuries, stories of the half human, the man-man. Stories that kept making everyone half human. And you could never be buddies with a man because men to be men had to dominate; for them your only purpose was sex, for them your only story was how you made them important.

I'll finish Hawks's stupid essay, I thought, get a B, then rip it up and forget about it. Then I thought, no, I'll write my own thesis, which is that his Strachey-Woolf thing is bullshit, not what *Orlando*'s about at all. I'll get a C or maybe a C-, who cares?

At least I'll be writing my own story.

Meeting the blank page of it. The novel I was writing all the time where I staged the plays and directed the actors – I was a cabinet of curiosities – a dollhouse or actually a rooming house. I passed through my characters to their doubles. J, C, and D meeting their reflections, the way trees in Dad's watercolour lake kissed trees in his watercolour sky. And I, Frances, stepped through my U Girl mirror to see the real from the back of the glass, another I, writing this.

ACKNOWLEDGMENTS

Special thanks go to the Vancouver Public Library and the Canada Council for supporting my residency at the VPL in 2012, and particularly Amber Ritchie, Catherine Evans, and Daphne Wood, who enthusiastically supported *U Girl*'s beginnings during that residency. Enormous thanks to Ann-Marie and Shazia at Talonbooks for their thoughtful help in putting the finishing touches on the novel. Kevin, Vicki, Ann-Marie, Shazia, Chloë, Jenn, Spencer, and Les – what a fantastic team to work with!

I would also like to thank the following friends who gave me advice on various matters concerning seventies Vancouver: Brian Dedora for his advice on sixties art and artists in Vancouver; Lorraine Weir for information on women's studies at UBC, including her materials and books from that era; Rachel Blau DuPlessis for providing me with a copy of *The Feminist Memoir Project: Voices from Women's Liberation*; George Stanley for giving me a virtual tour of seventies beer halls and drinking establishments; Sarah Kennedy for lending me Ellen Tallman's books on Gestalt therapy; Melanie Fahlman-Reid for her recollections of Cultus Lake and the Biltmore lounge, her memory of Richard Weaver, and connection of *U Girl* to the blue fairy; Peter Quartermain (former skipper of *Egret Plume II* and navigation instructor with the Fraser Power Squadron) for his advice on reading charts, plotting courses, navigating boats in coastal waters, and manoeuvering a boat at the dock; blue-water sailor Eve MacGregor for ensuring the accuracy of my sailing terminology and for helping me to clarify various sailing activities; and Daphne Marlatt for her memories of Wreck Beach and suggestions about lesbian jokes.

I'm also eternally grateful to Peter Quartermain, Aaron Peck, Melanie Fahlman-Reid, and Daphne Marlatt for their careful reading and suggestions on early drafts. I cannot thank you enough for your dedicated and thoughtful readings and rereadings and your suggestions on points of historical accuracy. May every writer have such welcoming readers.

PHOTO BY MARLIS FUNK

MEREDITH QUARTERMAIN is known across Canada for her depictions of places and their historical hauntings. *Vancouver Walking* won the 2006 Dorothy Livesay Poetry Prize. *Nightmarker* was a finalist for the 2009 Vancouver Book Award, and *Recipes from the Red Planet*, her book of flash fictions, was a finalist for the 2011 Ethel Wilson Fiction Prize. In her first novel, *Rupert's Land*, a town girl helps a residential-school runaway in Alberta in the 1930s. The stories in her 2015 collection *I, Bartleby*, returned to her long-time home of Vancouver, its landscapes and past. Although born in Toronto, she grew up in rural British Columbia and her writing often addresses rural vs. urban realities.

Quartermain was the 2012 writer-in-residence at the Vancouver Public Library, where she led workshops on songwriting and writing about neighbourhoods, and enjoyed doing manuscript consultations with many writers from the Greater Vancouver community. She's now continuing these activities as poetry mentor in the Writer's Studio Program at Simon Fraser University.

She has taught English at the University of British Columbia and former Capilano College and led workshops at the Naropa Summer Writing Program, the Kootenay School of Writing, and the Toronto New School of Writing. In 2002, she and husband Peter Quartermain founded Nomados Literary Publishers, through which they've published more than forty books of poetry, fiction, memoir, and drama.

Join young writer Frances Nelson as she creates
a world and then finds herself getting lost in it.

"Things like this would happen, and I would think,
did that happen to me or did that happen to U Girl?
I became another I in my novel, a glowing novel I in
a glowing novel country. I passed through a frontier.
I became not I – I and not I at the same time."

Here's what the characters in Frances's novel,
The Turquoise Room, had to say:

"U Girl is my favourite novel to be in.
A truly postmodern roman à clef."

—DAGMAR LINDEGAARD
author of *Landscapes and Saturnina Sailors*

"Miss Nelson has made a singular contribution to what
some may consider an oxymoron: Canadian literature."

—PROF. G. W. HAWKS
author of *The Modern Novel Between the Wars*

"It was a privilege to have Frances Nelson as my student
and an even greater privilege to read her breathtaking
novel U Girl, an original voice coming to us from
the dark outside our tiny cultural flashlights."

—NIGEL BLACKWOOD
author of *Constellations of Darkness in the Novels of D.H. Lawrence*